CIVIL BLOOD

CIVIL BLOOD

V. RENAE

New Traditions Publishing

Published by New Traditions Publishing

ISBN 978-0-9992410-9-7

Typesetting services by BOOKOW.COM

ACT I.

...Startle the jubilant lion in his rage,
   Or clench the headsman's hand within my hair,
   Or kindle fire to speed my pilgrimage,
   Chariot of fire and horses of sheer fire
   Whirling me home to heaven by one fierce stage?
   Thy Will I will, I Thy desire desire;
   Let not the waters close above my head,
   Uphold me that I sink not in this mire:
   For flesh and blood are frail and sore afraid;
   And young I am, unsatisfied and young,
   With memories, hopes, with cravings all unfed,
   My song half sung, its sweetest notes unsung,
   All plans cut short, all possibilities,
   Because my cord of life is soon unstrung.
   Christina Rossetti, "The Vigil of the Feast"

1. RIVER.

"And the dark woman of flames returned to the flames below. She is burnt with hunger, and devoured with burning heat, and with bitter destruction for eternity."

Papa never needed notes when he did a sermon. He knew it all by heart. I glanced up from my Bible and watched as my grandfather stared out at the people behind us. He held my stare briefly, our eyes a mirror of the other's.

"Let us pray to Saint Michael the Archangel." He gestured at the congregation. I bowed my head and closed my eyes, just as everyone else.

"Saint Michael the Archangel," he continued. "Defend us in battle; be our defense against the wickedness and snares of the Devil. May He rebuke Her, we do humbly pray, and do thou, o Prince of the heavenly host, by the power of Him, thrust into Hell the Devil and all other evil spirits who prowl about the world seeking the ruin of souls. Amen." I raised my head.

"I command my congregation to our Heavenly Father, and to live through Him and by Him in all acts. In the name of the Father -" I touched my forehead. "And of the Son -" I touched my chest. "And of the Holy Spirit." Left shoulder, right shoulder.

Hands together.

"Glory be."

Mom took my hand as we stood, merging into the sea of red - red shirts, red dresses. The color of sacrifice, the color of the blood. Her skin looked even whiter when it was against mine. Oreo cookies, she said, all three of us - dark like our dad had been, but her kids through and through. I craned my neck as we walked to the back of the sanctuary, but the Jacksons were nowhere to be found.

"Have you heard anything about Sparrow?" I asked Mom, my eyes searching every face for the face I knew best.

She smiled. "Sure did."

"Well?" I pressed.

"Well what?" She couldn't hide her grin.

"Is she any better?"

"Let's go see if we can't find out."

We crossed the threshold of Church and stepped into the lot. Even as the sun was setting, the humidity made my clothes stick to my skin. My curls were heavy and damp on my forehead. Every breath was wet and hot. I let out the top two buttons of my shirt. The congregation continued across the lot and into the trees, in the direction of the lake.

"Where is every -" I stopped in my tracks. "The lake. For Sparrow." Mom let go of my hand. "No way. No way," I repeated. The smile threatened to split my face in half.

Mom nodded. "Way."

I laughed and lifted her into a bear hug. She laughed, too. "This is awesome! Glory be. I can't believe -"

"Y'all!" I shaded my eyes with my hand. My sister Nova was waving from the edge of the trees. Her curls, outstretched all around her head, caught the sunlight. "Hurry up!"

I jogged the rest of the way through the lot until my feet hit dewy grass.

"Can you believe this?" I called as I ran. I put my arm around her shoulder and dragged her along to the lake.

"Stop bein' so rough!" She shrugged me off, a protective hand over her protruding belly.

"I barely touched you," I retorted.

"Manchild," she muttered. "And anyways, what'd you think was goin' on? She's been sick for days."

"I guess I didn't think she'd Change before me." A pang of jealousy made my mouth twitch.

"Nobody did."

Any other day, the heat of the sand would have had me running to the water. But I was frozen still at the sight of Sparrow.

She stood with her face to the setting sun, her red dress billowing behind her in the wind. I still did a double take at the new haircut, but I'd know Sparrow anywhere.

"Hey," I murmured.

She turned around and beamed at me, her doe eyes wrinkled into tiny slits from the force of her grin.

"Hey."

I closed the space between us and hugged her tight. Her cheek rested against my chest as her head disappeared underneath my arms.

"I hear your heartbeat," she told me. I looked down at her. "I hear everything," she whispered. Her eyes were wild now. "Everyone."

"Already?"

She nodded and grinned. I looked up as Papa parted the crowd on the shore, making his barefoot way over to us.

"Why didn't you tell me?" I whispered as we separated.

"I was busy dying."

Abel stepped between us and took his daughter's arm. Papa walked ahead of them, into the lake, until the water sloshed around his knees. He tied back his long, grey hair.

There were people already standing in the lake, waist-deep, shoulder to shoulder. A wall of red between us and the other side. Pant legs were rolled as far as they could go and skirts tied up as more people joined.

There was a special buzzing in the air today - another Elder had Awakened. Nova's had been just as exciting.

And if mine ever happened, I'm sure it would be, too.

I followed until I was ankle-deep. Mom took my left hand, Nova, my right. Folded into the congregation, like I'd always been.

Abel held his daughter as she floated on the surface of the lake. Papa stood beside them, his hands hovering above Sparrow.

"When Silas the First destroyed the dark women of roses and flames," he began, speaking to the clouds above us. "Our Heavenly Father bestowed upon his bloodline the power to protect and guide His people. They became the Chosen, the keepers of the Cross, bathed in the blood and the Word. They are our only hope in the Great Battle against evil. It is a blessing to our congregation when a Chosen Awakens. Sister Sparrow has joined the ranks. She is the second successor to the Elders, Chosen beyond measure."

Two of three. I would be three. I had to be three.

"Today is the first day of eternity for her," he continued. "Of eternity with this congregation. And with Him." He held his hands up to the sky. "For the trumpet shall sound, and the dead shall be raised incorruptible, and we shall be Changed."

He put his hand on Sparrow's forehead and she disappeared under the water.

"And there are three that bear witness in Earth," Papa said.

"The Spirit, and the water, and the blood," we answered.

"And these three agree in one," he replied.

"Glory Be." Dozens of voices as one.

He let Sparrow up. She gasped and stood, rocking back and forth. Papa caught her arms. She had blood running from her lip down her chin, her neck, blending with the red of her dress. Baptized in His waters, washed in the Blood.

Her face was contorted in agony. Ecstasy. Both.

7

CIVIL BLOOD

Like a wave of nausea, I was jealous.
"Welcome home, Sparrow," Papa said.
Unbelievably jealous.
The congregation erupted in cheers.

1. JOSEFINA.

The air was dead tonight. There wasn't a single breeze to stir the humidity. It made my baby hairs cling to the skin around my ears. I pushed myself off from the wall and let the hammock rock under my weight.

We hadn't been here for three months and I was already sick of sweating. I stretched my legs out to the edge of the hammock and watched the freak show across the lake.

"I do find it interesting," my sister Elydia said. I glanced over at her on the porch swing. She dipped the polish wand until it was coated in black polish and applied it to her toe as she spoke. "This gathering they do."

"What do you think it is?" Carmen asked us, a steaming mug in his hand. How he could drink hot coffee on the surface of the sun was beyond me.

"Like, Baptisms, I guess," I said as I itched my elbow absently. All the citronella in the world didn't stop mosquitoes from feasting on me when the air was like this.

"That's not how you get baptized," she chuckled.

"If you're not Catholic it is," I replied.

"How would you know, you heathen?" Dia fluttered her eyelashes at me. I grinned. "Besides, I'm not sure they'll get salvation from that water. An amoeba, maybe."

We laughed.

The porch door slammed beside me. Bernardo stood on the lip, his back pressed to the screen.

"What are you guys doing?" he asked.

"Watching the circus," Dia replied, gesturing at the lake.

"What are they doing?" Carmen asked Bernardo, stretching around Dia to look at him.

Bernardo rocked on his toes and fumbled with a cigarette.

"Awakening… chosen… ritual," he said through his teeth as he lit the cigarette, trying to discern their collective thoughts. He crossed the porch and sat on the first step from the porch to the dock. "They've got some kind of cloud on them. Hive mind."

"Ritual," Dia murmured, eyebrows raised. She capped the polish and set it on the window sill behind her.

"It has to be a baptism," I glanced above the thickets of forest, which guarded Barton Heights from prying eyes. The only thing visible above the tree line was a white cross. Not a steeple on a church, but a hulking overseer. Bernardo nodded in agreement.

"Chosen for a ritual. You said it yourself." Dia nodded slowly, squinting at the gathering.

"I just said what I heard," Bernardo replied. My brother picked at the dried grey paint on his jeans.

"I bet it is ritual sacrifice," Carmen interjected.

1. JOSEFINA.

"What, like, they're drowning someone?" I asked. Carmen shrugged. "Could they start with the girl who wrote 'whore' on my locker?" I popped my gum and shoved off the wall hard.

"No, I'm sure they're very proud of her," Bernardo sighed.

"Do they always wear red?" Carmen asked no one in particular.

I shook my head. "Wonder what's up with that."

"Hides the blood." Dia wiggled her fingers and her eyebrows.

The people across the lake started to cheer. It carried on the water until it was a distorted echo of excitement bouncing off the walls of our house.

"Whatever it was, it worked," Carmen said.

"I don't see a dead body," Bernardo added as he ashed the cigarette on the banister.

I fanned myself. "Maybe they don't have AC. I'd throw myself in the lake too." The thought had crossed my mind a few times.

"Good point," Bernardo let out a stream of smoke. "It's awful outside. Why are you guys out here?" He smacked at his arm, a mosquito carcass in the center of a small splotch of blood.

"Sunset, fresh air, ritual sacrifice." Dia gestured out to the lake. "It's all I've ever wanted in a home."

She was right about one thing. The sunsets here were almost worth it. Once the sun went from blinding to orange and giant in the middle of the horizon, the sky exploded in color. Yellows and oranges streaked the sky where the light still touched, and it melted into blue and purple. The clouds went from white to grey to black. But the best part was the pink.

The brightest pinks, neon and muted alike, mixed with blue and purple right before the sun disappeared, a sherbet swirl. It made the world feel off-kilter, surreal, but only by a few degrees. These didn't happen anywhere else I'd ever lived.

Tonight the oranges were almost red. It melted down the horizon and mixed with the red backs of the people across the lake as they went back to shore. The light was wavering, the eerie halo of dusky light casting everything in a foreign glow. A girl stayed in the lake alone, the water up to her waist. Her dress floated on the surface around her. Soaked through, it was darker than red.

Red streaked the sky, the girl, the water. A bloody scene.

I smirked.

A ritual sacrifice.

2. RIVER

I honked for the fourth time, long and loud.

The yellow door to the Jackson house swung open and Sparrow stomped out like I had a hook in her jaw. She slung her bag over her shoulder and walked around the front of the truck.

I beeped the horn and she jumped out of her skin. Sparrow slapped her hands on the hood and glared at me. I beckoned her into the car with a grin on my face.

She slammed the door of the cab behind her.

"Good morning, space cadet," I said.

She opened her backpack, ignoring me.

"You look tired."

"Why would you ever say that to a girl?" she demanded.

"You are tired," I amended as I took off.

She pulled out the lipstick.

"And nervous," I murmured.

"Who, me? Surely you joke."

I came to the gate out of Barton and made a right onto Shell Court. The dirt road was our only connection to the 33, the sole main road through Thistlewolf. Barton's gate backed up to the forest; most of this side of town was surrounded by forests or orange groves.

A red brick wall with a set of gold iron gates was the only thing on Shell Court besides trees and dirt. I stared at it as we passed - I always did. From this side, the house was barely visible, shielded by the wall and the trees. But I could see it from my house, across the lake. The Manor. The only historical landmark in Thistlewolf.

As kids we said the house was haunted by ghosts. We weren't supposed to give credence to ghosts. But the house sat vacant so long we thought that had to be the reason.

Until the owners moved back in. Then we wished we had been right.

"You're not." Her voice made me jump as I turned left onto Remington Road.

"I'm not what?" I asked.

"Nervous," Sparrow mumbled through her open lips as she applied the lipstick in the foggy rear view mirror. "The rambling River is still."

I smirked. "I'm not the one coming in a week late."

She winced. "Don't remind me."

"I hear public school doesn't really start until the second week anyway."

"Is that some of your newfound mainstream wisdom?" she asked.

I slammed on my brakes as we approached the light from Remington to the 33. Sparrow wiped the streak of purple off her face with the heel of her hand.

"Sorry,."

"Sorry you didn't drive us into a tree?" she demanded. "Me, too."

I sighed and made the right onto the 33. Two miles to go and twenty minutes to make it. I sped up.

"I guess we should leave a little earlier tomorrow. First period's far from the parking lot."

"We have to do this again tomorrow?"

"Yeah, five days a week."

"That wasn't in my contract," she said as she rubbed at the spot where her lipstick had been. "I swear this won't come off." She rubbed harder.

"Drop your mind."

"It's dropped," she snapped. I grabbed her hand and flattened it on her leg.

"You don't have anything on your face," I told her. I took a deep breath and squeezed her hand. She inhaled, too. "And out." We exhaled together.

"Are you worried about the hair?"

Or lack thereof, buzzed shorter than mine.

She shot daggers at me. "I wasn't. 'Til you said that."

"I told you, it looks good on you." It did. "You look beautiful." She did.

Her mouth twitched. "I know." I smiled and put both hands on the wheel.

We slowed as the traffic came to a halt near the turn into the parking lot of the high school. There were no other cars on on the road.

She was doing better than I thought, all things considered. Every year the older kids would try and prepare us, and every year, no one was ready for how different Thistlewolf High was from Barton Heights Academy. For starters, boys and girls had class together. And no one prayed before lessons. And it was members, not good grades, the Elders wanted us to bring home.

With eight minutes to spare we pulled into C42, my spot, and I put the truck in park. Sparrow was staring at herself in the mirror. She flicked her fingernails against one another.

"Exhale," I said as I checked my own hair in the side mirror. I tried to fluff it up, to keep the curls out of my face. It never worked.

"You can exhale. You got to mainstream with everyone else." She opened the door and got out. I followed her. "You shared the new kid thing with them," she continued as we met at the back of the truck. "I'm doing this alone." She started off ahead of me.

"You don't know where you're goin'," I chuckled. She turned and glared. "I'm gonna be with you."

"For two classes." She rolled her eyes.

"Actually…" I dug my hand in my pocket and pulled out the pink slip of paper and handed it to her. She unfolded it, her eyebrows furrowing as she read.

She looked at me, a smile playing on her lips. "You lied to me."

"Mom talked to Mrs. Gellar." Mrs. Gellar was Thistle-wolf's principal. To us, she was Miss Lindsey, the choir leader. "We now have four classes together, thank you very much." I took the paper back and stuck it in the pocket on my button-down. "Feel better now?"

"Better? No. Less suicidal? Maybe."

I sighed. It was all I could do when Sparrow was like this.

Even at quarter til eight in the morning, the air was hazy and hot. Sparrow kept close to me as we cut through rows across the parking lot. It was already deserted.

"Are we late?" she asked.

"We're not early."

She kicked a rock in her path. A cherry red convertible sped through the row in front of us. I threw my arm in front of Sparrow, who jumped back as gravel and dirt sprayed up from the ground.

"Nice," I muttered, wiping dirt from the front of my shorts.

"Cute car, though. Soft-top, too. It'll be easy to steal when I burn this place to the ground." Sparrow stared down the car like she was memorizing its every detail.

"Oh, please, I learned years ago to keep the matches away from you," I said.

"Double A battery and a foil gum wrapper. Takes seconds." Sparrow snapped her fingers once.

I looked at her as we entered the courtyard. "I don't know if I'm impressed or terrified."

"I like to think it's an equal mixture of both," she replied.

"More like 60-40."

"What's our first class?" She ignored my jab.

"History. Building Three." I pointed.

"How about instead, you slit my throat?"

I sighed, loud and long.

"You want me to save it for the drama club, don't you?" There was a smile in her voice.

"What are you, a mind reader?" I bumped her with my shoulder and Sparrow winked at me.

"I think I tortured you enough this morning."

"You've tortured me enough for eternity," I corrected. I grabbed her by the backpack when we reached Mrs. Palmetto's classroom.

She took a deep breath. "Let's get this over with." Then let it all out in a gust just before walking through the threshold.

We sat down at the last available table. Front row, far left. No-man's land. Sparrow pulled her notebook out. I put my textbook between us to share.

"Thanks," she whispered.

"For what?"

"For making the Elders let me come."

"No one makes the Elders to do anything," I chuckled.

She rolled her eyes. "I know I'm your project."

The bell rang, and Mrs. Palmetto slammed the door shut before the last tone was done. She was not one to allow sliding in at the last second. She wasn't one for teaching, either, as it seemed. A week in her class had shown me her favorite thing of all was silent torture.

There were only two other kids from Barton in this class - Autumn Sawyer and Ivy Adams, the most popular group of girls back at the Academy. Not hard to do in a class of seven. They had carried it with them to mainstream school, though; pom-poms and twin ponytails, one red, one brunette.

I picked the table furthest from them for Sparrow's sake.

We watched as Mrs. Palmetto leaned in to a boy in the second row. I cringed imagining what her breath was like so close to his face. He stood up and walked to the trash can and spat something out. Mrs. Palmetto put her hands on her hips and pointed to the door. The kid left with his head hanging, the class all following him without moving their heads.

I glanced at Sparrow, who watched it all with wide eyes.

I remembered the moment in second grade when everyone realized who I was. Miss Beth was our Sunday school teacher. Sparrow was throwing a fit over having to share her crayons.

"River, what do you think Elder Ephraim would say if he saw Sparrow being so foolish?" Miss Beth had asked me.

We might've both been his grandchildren, but Sparrow wasn't a Matthews. That's how I learned the weight my name held. Sparrow stopped crying long enough to look at me, her giant eyes wet with tears. The Jackson name just wasn't the same. Her bottom lip shook.

I stood up and pointed at her. "If you're disobedient the ravens will poke out your eyes. Papa says so."

I remembered how her jaw set, her little face violently, suddenly still.

Sparrow never cried in school again.

The Elders said I had a way with her, that her wild, troubled mind latched to me to keep her out of trouble. Sparrow said they must have bribed me to keep her from embarrassing our family. But I loved Sparrow Jackson the way I loved the smell of leather, the way I loved honey. Our moms had been twins, and we were, too, even if we looked nothing alike. I had never stopped doing penance for that day in second grade.

She'd always be my project, my special thing, my other half.

"Mister Matthews," Mrs. Palmetto said. I snapped back to the present.

"Yes, ma'am?"

"Would you like to rejoin us here in the real world?"

My cheeks grew warm. My shoulders touched my ears. "Sorry ma'am."

She turned her attention back to the class. "Your homework tonight is to read chapters two through four and answer the reviews at the end of each chapter." The energy in the room drooped, a collective sigh coming from the throats of everyone. Sparrow exhaled loudly.

Mrs. Palmetto's eyes narrowed at her. I braced myself for the wrath.

The bell rang, saving us.

Sparrow jumped out of her seat and rushed ahead of the rest of the students.

"Hey, hey, you okay?" I caught up with her in the hall. I put my hand on her shoulder and turned her to face me, her eyes darting around us, her lips pursed as if she were in pain. "What is it?"

"I don't know if I can do this," she gasped.

"I know she's tough, but it's only one class -"

She shook her head. "This." She spun her finger around. "It's all so… loud." She looked at me. "I can't explain it. But I can't shut them up."

I'd worried this would happen. Her gift was too new. "We're gonna figure out how to quiet them. At least here. But I need you to stick it out with me. Don't prove the Elders right."

She shook her head, and her purple lips pulled upward. "You know how to get me."

"It's gonna be fine if you stick with me. I can't do it without you." I put my arm around her shoulder and opened the front door.

"Well, well, well."

I stopped. That voice always stopped me in my tracks.

Cecelia Sloane Chase, thank you very much. Everyone looked at her the same way. Up, down, up. At the top; dirty blonde ponytail, hazel eyes, peach lipstick. Pale arms crossed across the chest of her uniform. Moving down; skirt too short for school, but ignored because it was school-issued. One mile-long leg bent, foot up on the brick wall she leaned against. White tennis shoes. Back to the legs as they started towards me. I ended back up at her eyes by the time she stopped walking.

"Hi, baby." I slid my arm off Sparrow and put it around Ceci. "Sorry I didn't see you this morning. We were almost late." I willed Sparrow along with my mind and kissed the top of Ceci's head.

She leaned around my arm and looked at Sparrow. "Your makeup looks so good."

Sparrow raised her eyebrow and nodded. "Thanks." Ceci smirked at me and I squeezed her.

"I know your schedule's all weird now," Ceci said to me, toying with the ends of her hair. "Do you still have Delgado next?"

"Yeah, I only switched lit and chem. The rest of my schedule is the same."

She frowned. "Lit? Guess you won't be helping me make copies anymore." Ceci was a teacher's aide for the English building, a free agent with keys to the copy room. I had gone to English once since I started this school.

"Oh, I'll find a way," I whispered in her ear, blood pouring into my cheeks at the thought. We came to Building Two. Ceci's class was the first door inside.

She smirked. "Better. Bye."

I wrapped a hand around her ponytail gently and let it run through my fingers as she left.

"Bye."

Sparrow and I continued down the hall as I reeled. The smell of her perfume always left me a little glazed over. I had learned after almost a year how to play it cool around her, but she still made me nervous. Too pretty for me, too popular. I was constantly confused about why she kept me around.

She would say we met by accident, but I called it divine intervention. I was flexing my new license, driving around the boys last summer, when I passed a broken-down white Mercedes with a teary-eyed angel leaning on its hood. By the time I put her donut on for her, she was punching my number into her phone. And I'd never gotten enough of her since.

She had the biggest house in Thistlewolf, set to inherit every orange grove in Dunnaway County. She was cheer captain. She was Ceci Chase, so I was Ceci Chase's boyfriend- the only thing I was known for. Big shoes to fill, but I didn't mind having a built-in reputation if it included those legs wrapped around me.

"Yikes," Sparrow hissed.

I followed her gaze to a glaring Aliya MacNeil, propped against her locker, her eyebrow cocked dangerously high.

"Is there a black kid quota here? One at a time?" Sparrow muttered.

I pursed my lips. "No, that's Aliya, that's Ceci's right hand. She's watchin' to see if she's gotta report back."

"What is this, Alabama?" Sparrow leaned around me and waved to Aliya. "We're cousins, honey!" she hollered, turning heads and getting one serious eye-roll from Aliya.

I elbowed Sparrow in the ribs as we turned the corner, ducking my head to hide my smile.

"You're gonna get me killed," I chuckled.

"I assume death by cheerleader is a dream come true for you."

I shrugged. "Definitely not a nightmare."

2. JOSEFINA.

I shut my locker and frowned at the red streaks that still lingered. Lipstick was almost worse than magic marker. Greasier, thicker, more personal.

I rubbed at it with my thumb. It did nothing.

A fist came down over my head and smashed into the locker. I jumped.

"Oh my God, Che!" I hissed.

He leaned his head against the cold metal and grinned. "Sorry."

I rolled my eyes. "You're so not."

We started off together towards the music building.

Che Madrigal was the only person I knew in Thistlewolf besides my family. We hired him to landscape over the summer and he'd stuck, a baby-faced fixture with eyes like mine and soft brown hands. He drooled over my sister and my mom in equal measure, and cut herbs in the dead heat of July with my brothers. He just belonged.

When school started, and the wrath came down, he became my bodyguard. This building had a first period full of Barton kids, but Che made sure I got to the music building with no worries, even if it made him late to Spanish.

He was my first real friend in a long time.

"What's your excuse for ditching me Friday?" he demanded as we came down the stairs.

"Friday?" I pulled my gum out of my backpack. "What, the game?"

"Duh," he mimicked.

I rolled my eyes. "Get serious! Did you see my locker? I'm not trying to stir the pot if I can help it."

"You were supposed to hang out with me," he retorted as he stuck his hand out so I could set a piece of gum in it. "Besides, you don't know who did it."

"Oh, yes I do," I chuckled. "It was the redhead."

"How do you know?" he asked. I popped my gum and the relief was instant. We stepped out under the already blistering sun. Che shielded his eyes with his hand and looked at me. "Huh?"

"I just do, okay?"

"Mhm," he chuckled.

Bernardo wouldn't read her for me, and I hadn't seen her do it, but I knew it was her. Out of all those Barton bitches she was the one to watch.

"It's disgusting out here," I muttered, the humidity forming a layer of sweat on my skin. "How is it so nasty so early?"

"How are you not used to this by now?"

"Do you ever get used to being suffocated by a wet wool blanket?" I scoffed, fanning my face.

"Listen, come with me this Friday. We'll do our class colors, get in the spirit, it'll be fun."

"Hella fun."

2. JOSEFINA.

He shot me a look as we reached the music building.

"Fina." He turned and put his hands on my shoulders and dipped his chin to meet my eyes.

"Che."

"Ofelia told me to make sure you get a real high school experience this time. And I can't let a good, fine woman like her down."

I rolled my eyes. "You're literally disgusting."

"So we're going to the game Friday," he continued, ignoring me. "We're doing class colors. Okay?"

I scratched under his sweaty chin. "Just for you."

He smiled his big, puppy-eyed smile and then winked at me.

He took off back the way he came, cutting across the grass towards the humanities building. I crossed my fingers for him and went inside.

Air conditioning blasted me as I opened the door, almost forcing a triumphant smile on my lips. Foreign as they were to me, school hallways - especially quiet ones like this - were clinically comforting. The walls, ceilings, and floors blended together in a white-but-not-clean-white hue. The cement walls were cool to the touch and the echo my boots made on the linoleum made me nostalgic for something I couldn't remember.

Mr. Hart's classroom was the last one on the left. Advanced Piano. I set my bag down and started to sit when the door to Hart's office opened. Mr. Hart was a year out of college and the best piano player I ever met. He never graded tests on time and often wore mismatched socks. He was my favorite.

He beckoned me up to the Bechstein and opened a file folder.

"This is from my own collection," he told me, pulling out a yellowing score. "I think it'll give you something to do." If I was honest, I was Hart's favorite, too. He said I was his first student who required thinking outside the box. He struggled to find music to challenge me. He thought I was a prodigy. And not that he would ever know, but I'd been playing longer than he'd been alive.

The new piece looked promising, though, with enough sixteenth notes to keep me busy and a time signature I had to really work for. It was riveting, really. Having a challenge.

I went back into the hall and found an empty practice room. I closed the door behind me and sat down at my favorite Yamaha. Only three of its keys were out of tune, which was as good as it got.

I sat the papers up on the rest and started to clunk through the piece. I missed the feel of the keys under my fingers. We didn't have a piano at this house, there wasn't much room for one. Ofelia had told me to get an electric one, but it wasn't the same. The rumbling acoustic of a hammer striking a string and reverberating inside a wooden frame was irreplaceable. Even out of tune notes on a real piano were better than synthetic, hollow tones from a machine. Being alone with a piano and a piece, I started to relax for the time being.

Plus, no one had spit at me yet today. So that was cool.

But Che was right. Ofelia was, too. I needed to get a real high school experience. At least finish high school, this time without damaging any property. Teenagers with too much time on their hands weren't going to run me out. The newness would die down, and they'd find another target.

I hoped.

The bell rang too soon, and I took my time packing up the music. The English building was halfway across campus - not that campus was big. I had been on much larger ones than this before.

I shuffled up the concrete stairs outside of the English building, my hair was sticking to the back of my neck. When I got to Mr. Alfred's class, he was sitting with his feet up on his desk, taking roll as people shuffled in.

There was a girl in my seat. I'd been sitting here, front row middle right, every day for two weeks.

I tossed my bag on the table beside her and sat.

"Hi," she said - whispered. I looked over at her. She beamed at me from between purple lips.

"Hi," I replied after a moment, hesitant of the pleasant smile.

"I'm Sparrow." I would have laughed if her name wasn't exactly perfect for her. She was a ribbon that got snagged on a fence - long, fluttering, wispy. She had a boy's haircut and a supermodel neck.

Those Barton kids would eat her alive.

"Fina. I like your makeup," I offered. She ran pointed silver nails over her head.

"It's so people remember my name. Sparrow, with eyeliner so winged she could fly away."

I chuckled. "I think they would remember you without it." Her smile faded as quickly as it came.

"Am I in your seat?" Her eyes widened. "Oh, no, I didn't know." She started to stand up.

"No, it's so fine, dude. I'm like, all set here."

"You sure?" she asked. I nodded. She sighed and sat back in her chair. Her fingernails clicked against each other. "My gills are showing now that I'm out of water."

"No, you blend, honest." She did everything but blend, and based off of the look in her eye, she knew it. She grinned. Her mouth was bigger than her whole face.

A grey backpack fell to the ground next to me and Bernardo slid into the chair.

What happened to our table? His voice echoed behind my ears.

"This is Sparrow. This is my brother, Bernardo." Bernardo leaned around me and nodded at Sparrow. She looked back and forth between us.

"You don't look like her brother," Sparrow said, tilting her head to the side. Bernardo spat out a short laugh.

We looked related enough, at least everyone else thought so. Ofelia called us the faces of Gemini, with our heavy eyebrows and long wavy hair. We had the same eyes - we all had the same eyes - but I didn't see much else alike about us.

"She's adopted," Bernardo murmured as he took out his notebook.

The bell rang. "Adopted?" Sparrow repeated. "I always wanted to be adopted."

I coughed to keep from laughing.

2. JOSEFINA.

Alfred got to his feet. I still wasn't sure if he was really our teacher or a foreign exchange student who got too carried away with a prank. It was the mop of fiery-red hair which cancelled out his stubble. He laughed at his own jokes but his accent was charming enough to where no one cared. He and Mr. Hart were birds of a feather.

Alfred leaned forward with his fists on his desk. "Alright, then. Hi, everyone. Now I put it off as long as I could but we do, in fact, have to begin our Shakespeare unit this week. I know, I know!" He put his hands up as most of the class groaned. "I'm an English teacher from England and even I don't want any part of this. However, Macbeth calls." He rapped his knuckles on the desk. "Now, if you'd all open your -"

The classroom door opened.

It probably wasn't in slow motion, even though it felt like it. Everything felt slow - my heartbeat, my jaw working my gum, my blinking. I didn't know if I even was blinking anymore. I certainly stopped breathing for a few seconds, because by the time the boy made his way across the floor to Alfred, my chest was heaving.

I'd seen him before - I'd seen everyone before in a school this small - but I hadn't looked at him twice. I would have remembered his jaw line. I popped my gum and watched him give Alfred a yellow slip of paper.

Alfred squinted at the page. "Wait, you were in my seventh period?" he asked. The boy nodded. Alfred looked up at him - Alfred had to look up at everyone. "I don't think I've ever seen you before." The boy shrugged. Alfred chuckled. "Alright, then. Have a seat."

The boy turned and glanced over the classroom for a moment. I tried not to stare but I couldn't make myself move. I was glued to the spot. His eyes caught the light and reflected like sea glass, too green to be grey. He sat in the empty chair beside Sparrow.

I got mad at her all over again for taking my seat.

Sparrow didn't look at him. How could she not? I wondered what I looked like from the outside, my unblinking stare on these two strangers, but I didn't care. He pushed his black curls away from his face. Veins ran raised along his dark arm like small, blue streams, disappearing under the strained sleeve of his t-shirt. My eyes went back to that jaw. My throat tight.

He nudged Sparrow with his shoulder, but she stared at her nails.

"Sparrow," he murmured. His voice broke the trance, making me catch my breath so violently I almost swallowed my gum. Danger bells started ringing in my head. High school boys shouldn't sound like that. They shouldn't have jawlines like that or soft sea glass eyes like that.

I turned back to the front and stared at the chalkboard.

"I'm mad at you," Sparrow said to him.

"At me?" he replied. She nodded. He put his hand over his heart. "Why?"

"Because you ditched me."

"I had some things to take care of," he chuckled.

She wrinkled her nose. "Yeah I know."

I glanced at them right as he winked at her. I bit the inside of my cheek. Danger bells.

Sparrow turned to me and I looked down at my note-book. Heat started to rise on the back of my neck. He was looking at me, too. I could feel it.

"Macbeth," Alfred said. He knocked on his desk. "Blood, prophecy, witches, kings, some more blood." The sound of a pencil tapping on a notebook echoed in my ears. I took a deep breath and tried to focus. Alfred started to pace the room. "I saw some of you theatre folks cringe a bit when I said the title. Most refer to it as The Scottish Play, because terrible things tend to happen to those who say the name Macbeth." He knocked on my table and continued his path. The pencil tapping got louder. "No wonder when you consider the dark forces at play throughout the story," Alfred continued behind me.

I looked around. That pencil was going through some-one's eye in three seconds.

Sparrow reached towards the boy. "River, stop. You're annoying people."

River.

The noise stopped. My head snapped over to her, then I looked up at River.

The corners of his mouth turned up. "Sorry."

"Whatever." My voice was foreign to me.

We stared at each other for thousands of years. He held my dazed eyes with his own until my hands started to shake. No danger bells this time, only the liquefying of my stomach. Actually, of my whole body.

"What, are you short-circuiting?" Sparrow asked him.

River and Sparrow. Bernardo raised his eyebrows as he took notes. Interesting names.

My stomach sank.

That's why I'd never looked at him. All the Barton kids had stupid names.

River rolled his eyes at Sparrow. "Shut up."

"This is Fina, I took her seat but she's still nice to me." She turned to me and smiled. I tried to smile back. They must not have realized I was… me.

"I'm River," he said to me.

I nodded. "Right, she said that."

He smiled. "Right."

I popped my gum. "Nice to meet you both." I looked ahead.

"So, for tonight's assignment," Alfred continued loudly, eyeing the three of us. I looked down at my notebook. More heat to my cheeks. I had hardly written anything. "Please read Act One, scenes one and two. We'll group read tomorrow but I want you all to have an understanding going in, of how dense Shakespeare's stuff is."

The bell rang.

I jumped up and grabbed my things. I was the first one out of the classroom. Bernardo caught up with me.

"Hey." He took my arm and pulled me out of the flow of foot traffic. "Hey," he said again.

"I have to get to class."

His grip on my arm loosened. "Oh, don't do this."

"Don't do what?" I demanded. "I don't know what's going on."

I really didn't. My hands were tingling. Something ancient in me was pulling at my blood. My veins were fit to burst.

"We don't belong here. We don't need to stir the pot any more than we already do."

"I'm not trying to. I wanted to be nice," I murmured. I couldn't even convince myself.

"They don't realize who you are yet. When they do, you're going to regret any inch you gave them. They're from Barton. Treat them like it."

I pulled away from him in time to see River and Sparrow coming out of the classroom. I barreled through a group of kids and all but ran to the doors.

The danger bells didn't lie.

3. RIVER.

The auditorium chair squeaked under me as I sat. The junior class had an assembly today, so all the Barton kids except Micah would be together. Sparrow shuffled in and sat to my left.

"This seems stupid," she said.

"At least it got us out of seventh early," I replied.

"What is this for again?" she asked me. I shrugged.

"Oh, fresh meat," Ceci sighed as she sat down. "It's not for anything. It's the most boring twenty minutes of your life." She grinned. "So I'm here to help pass the time."

"Don't you have teachers to aid?" I chuckled.

"Since someone switched classes I've been doing a lot of aiding." She crossed her legs. "And not a lot of seeing you."

"I'm sorry, baby. I've been loaded with homework. Plus I start tutoring today for Hart's class. I'm bombing."

"Three weeks," she hissed. "You've been here three weeks and you're failing?"

"I'll get it back. I'm just bad at music."

"This isn't the Academy anymore. You actually have to try," she told me.

"Yeah, Ceci, I understand," I sighed. The seat next to her came down and Autumn leaned around to wave at me. I smiled at her. "Hey, Autumn."

"Hi. Hi Sparrow." Sparrow looked up from her phone. It was a trap. Ivy was heading our way, shuffling through the aisle with Clay in tow. Autumn wanted to watch Sparrow see it. Sparrow looked back at her lap.

Ivy waved at me, and Clay nodded as they sat beside Autumn. I gave the smallest acknowledgment I could while still being polite.

I still blamed Clay, even if everyone else blamed Sparrow. We could have had a golden year in mainstream, but no. He went and burned bridges with every girl in Barton over the summer. Sparrow was just unlucky enough to get caught up in his web. She was unlucky enough to wear the shame on her head instead of in her heart. She said she forgave Clay. But I wouldn't. She said he hadn't meant to do it. But the smirk he gave me as he sat down said otherwise. I never liked him anyway. Sparrow put on a good face.

"Hey, where's Forrest?" I whispered. The video began to play.

A hand clapped me on the shoulder. "Miss me already?" Forrest chuckled in my ear. I reached behind me and pinched any skin of his I could reach. He popped me in the back of the head. Ceci grabbed my arm.

"If a teacher comes over here I'll get caught skipping," she hissed. Forrest stuck his head between mine and hers.

"I'm sorry, Ceci. It's my fault. If you woulda brought me somethin' to keep me busy, I wouldn't be buggin' y'all."

"What should I have brought you, Monopoly or some-thin'?" Ceci retorted.

"If that's what you call Aliya, then yeah." Forrest raised his eyebrows. I tried not to laugh.

Ceci rolled her eyes. "You guys are stupid." But a smile played on her face. No one could be around Forrest too long without smiling.

"I mean it," Forrest told her. "You get me her phone number, or I'm stealin' your boyfriend." He shook my shoulder again and sat back.

"Everyone wants to steal my boyfriend," Ceci mur-mured against my cheek. Her hand started on my knee and wandered as she continued. "I'm gonna have to watch my back now that you're here."

"Can I watch your front for you?" I breathed.

"You're pretty good at it," she replied.

"You know what else I'm good at?"

"Talking during an assembly?" A shadow fell over us from the aisle as Miss Beth - no, here she was Mrs. Mc-Namara - leaned over us. "Miss Chase, I think you're about a year too late to this one. Come with me, please."

Ceci rolled her eyes as she stood. "Meet me in our spot after tutoring." She whispered into my neck, kissed my cheek, and walked out with Mrs. McNamara.

"How do you have a spot when we've been in school three weeks?" Sparrow muttered as she flicked her nails. I slapped her hand down.

"Why do you care?"

"It's gross. I don't like hearing her thinking about what you guys do in the copy room." She made a face. "I don't need your sin up close and personal."

"Yeah, well, I've been hearing about your sin all summer, so."

Regret hit my chest and reverberated. If it made a sound it was a tin drum. I clenched my jaw. Sparrow laughed her hard, stilted laugh she usually reserved for Abel.

I sighed. "Sorry. But I already get it from Ceci because I spend so much time with you."

"I was here first." She shrugged.

"Don't be mad at me," I told her.

"It's my natural state."

The bell rang and the room exploded in noise and movement. I picked up Sparrow's bag and followed her to the auditorium door. She was always mad and never mad at the same time. True best friends hated one another as much as they loved one another.

Che slipped in next to me as we headed up the aisle.

"Hey," I said.

"Hey, man, I saw Ceci leave. You guys have a fight or somethin'? Because you know I'll be there for her if she needs a place to cry." I punched him in the arm. He held up his hands. "Jokes, man, jokes." He reached behind him.

Fina came up next to him and held his forearm. I felt a jolt to my stomach. We all became packed like sardines as the aisle narrowed to the doorway.

"Hi," I said to Fina. She raised her eyebrows and popped her gum. Why did she make gum chewing attractive? It was the ugliest, most unladylike thing on the planet but I could watch her do it all day.

"Hey," she said. Her voice made my stomach muscles clench. Sparrow waved to Fina. Fina gave her a small wave back.

"River says his girl has a crush on me," Che told her. I raised my eyebrows. It felt weird talking about Ceci in front of Fina.

"No one has a crush on you except Bernardo," Fina replied. I laughed.

"Hey!" Bernardo said from behind me.

We reached the door and it opened into the lobby of the building, the wide open space between the auditorium and the cafeteria.

Sparrow turned and took her bag from me. The five of us formed a line as we continued out to the parking lot. "Did you get all the notes in Alfred's class today?" she asked Fina. "I get distracted by his accent."

"Ooh, you have a class with that?" Autumn fluttered her hand at Fina as she came up beside me. Her red curls slapped my shoulder as she shook her head, her nose wrinkling like she smelled something bad. "I'm so sorry."

Fina chuckled. "Whatever." Che took her hand and pulled her a little farther ahead. Bernardo followed them.

"Whatever," Ivy repeated in a high, nasally voice.

"Where did you come from?" I asked her.

"I'm surprised y'all have gone this long without catching what she's passin' around," Ivy said to Sparrow.

"Ask the football team," Autumn chuckled.

"Ask your dad," Fina replied over her shoulder.

"Excuse me?" Autumn demanded. Fina stopped and spun around. Bernardo grabbed the back of her dress as she took a step towards Autumn. I thought I was in a fever dream. I couldn't understand what was happening.

"Let's go," Bernardo said to Fina. Che put his hand on her arm and turned her around.

"Oh bye, Fifi, I'll tell the boys you're on your way!" Ivy called.

"Hey," I hissed, grabbing her arm.

Che pulled Fina in front of him and they picked up the pace until I lost them in the crowd.

"What was that?" I demanded.

Autumn frowned. "What are you talking about?" she asked.

"That was awful unladylike," I retorted. "That's what I'm talking about." Ivy put her hand on Autumn's shoulder.

"He's not Changed," she said. They both looked at me with pity. "He doesn't realize," Ivy continued.

Autumn glared at Sparrow. "You gotta keep him out of trouble with them. Wake up and smell the roses."

"The roses?" I repeated.

Autumn gave me a look and patted my arm. "It's okay, River. You didn't know. They blend pretty well if you can't smell it. You'll know when you've Changed." My head was spinning, standing on the outside of a secret.

"No way, it'd be breaking Barton Law to even talk to her if she was one," I replied.

"Blue eyes and roses," Ivy said. "Camejos for sure."

"Her eyes are brown," I replied, and immediately regretted admitting I noticed that. But the girls rolled their eyes in unison.

"He doesn't pay attention to anything," Autumn chuckled.

"That's why I have tutoring right now." I put my hand on the back of Sparrow's neck. "Think Micah can squeeze one more in his car and take Sparrow home for me?"

"Oh, there's plenty of room," Ivy said. "I rode with Clay." She smiled at Sparrow.

Sparrow plastered an equally fake grin on her own face. "Thanks," she said.

"Sure thing," Ivy replied through her teeth.

Autumn looped her arm through Sparrow's. "We'll get her home. Bye, River."

"Bye, River," Sparrow muttered. I started across the courtyard to the music building. The school had emptied out within minutes. I didn't see another soul around. Being alone was something I rarely got to be, and something I craved in the deepest part of me.

Barton was a unit. Units didn't operate without all their pieces together, thinking together, being together. But ever since Nova Changed and became the first successor, I felt a spotlight turn on over my head. It grew brighter the closer I got to Changing age, and it had been on full blast since Sparrow's turn had come. Everyone was watching, waiting for me to Change.

Or not Change.

I felt like my tongue was in the back of my throat. I shook my head, trying to clear the thought from my mind. I will Change. I was Chosen. Ephraim's grandson would not be Unchosen. There had to be a male successor and the men in our line were few and far between. Mom said I wasn't done cooking. She said the best ones take a little longer in His oven.

But at this rate I had to be getting burnt.

Maybe it was better not to be alone. I didn't have time to think about these things until I was alone. And thinking was like rocking in a rocking chair, Papa said - it gave me something to do, but it didn't get me anywhere. I always thought too much.

Cold air blasted me as I opened the door to the music building. Clearly I thought too much about the wrong stuff or I wouldn't have to be here after school because of music theory.

I opened the door to Mr. Hart's classroom. A slight figure was bent over the long table on the far wall. I shut the door. They put a finger up in the air.

A finger connected to a bracelet-covered wrist. A finger I had spent hours watching twirl around her wavy brown hair.

Fina. Her name echoed through my head like a stuck record, over and over. I felt my heartbeat in my ears.

"Hey," I said after a moment. She sat up but didn't turn around. I cleared my throat. "I'm supposed to have tutoring with Hart. Am I in the wrong place?"

"Nope." She still didn't look at me.

"Are you failing, too?" I asked as I dropped my bag in the first chair of the front row.

"Tutoring," she replied. I grinned.

Alone with her. I never thought this would happen. I took a deep breath and tried to stop smiling like an idiot.

"Sorry I kept you waiting," I said. I tried to wander her way, make it seem casual.

She shrugged. "Whatever." I folded my arms and rested them on the table as I knelt beside it. She had a guitar in front of her. As she turned one of its knobs, loose strands fell from her bun and hung over her face.

Don't brush them away, creep. I balled my hand into a fist under my arm. Her boot made a loud, hollow noise as her foot tapped against the floor.

"What are you doing?"

She plucked one of the strings and it sang. "Tuning this."

Terror made my heart plummet into my feet. "Do I have to play it?" I asked.

She looked up at me from under her hair. My face was hot. I could not humiliate myself like that in front of her.

She smiled, a smile like a secret, and shook her head. I exhaled and put my hand over my heart.

"Cool, okay. Yikes," I chuckled. "So what am I doing, then?"

"You're pretending to care about rhythms so I can get my community service hours," she said. She stood up and I watched her for a second, all white lace and dark, bare legs as she walked to the piano. She turned around and I scrambled to my feet. Such a creep.

"There's gotta be an easier way to get hours," I said. She pulled a chair next to the piano for me and sat on the bench, crossing her legs under her.

"Closer," she told me, pulling unsuccessfully on the seat of the chair. I scooted until it bumped against her bench. "So you can actually, like, see the keys."

I nodded. "Right, I can."

She popped her gum. "'Kay."

"Do you play this thing?" I asked.

"Yeah, that's why I'm sitting in front of it."

"Play me something." She shot her eyebrow up at me. "Please," I amended.

"That's not what we're here for."

I smiled. "I bet you're really good." Taunting.

"Good enough to tutor you."

"I mean, I really don't think I can focus unless I hear you play. I gotta make sure my tutor is qualified." Was I flirting?

She looked up at me and I froze. Her face was un-readable. Angry. Amused. I couldn't tell. I swallowed hard.

She pressed her fingers against the keys and a long, rich sound rang through the room.

"A whole note," she said over the last echoes. "It's four beats, and it looks like an O." She moved her fingers up and down the keys three times. She didn't look down, but held my eyes with her own.

Autumn was an idiot. Those were the deepest, warmest brown eyes I'd ever seen.

She held each movement for four counts. "Whole note," she said, and nodded.

"Whole note," I repeated.

"Right. Looks like an O."

"Looks like an O," I echoed. She nodded again. I couldn't think. I could only parrot her.

She did this to me that first day - sucked all the air out of the room. Made all the blood in my body rush to my head, where it slowed and coagulated, thickening like pancake syrup. It clogged the gears in my brain, clogged all rational thought. I tried to think through it, through red lightning and a blue moon and cardiac arrest and this visceral, ancient reaction to her face.

Didn't work then, and it wasn't working now.

"Hello?"

I blinked and came back to Earth.

"Sorry."

"Were you even listening?" she asked.

I smiled and looked down. "Not really. I have a hard … time focusing." When you're staring at me like that, please never stop looking at me.

"Do you have like ADD or something?"

"ADD?" I repeated.

"A. D. D." She drew out each syllable.

I shook my head. "I don't know what that is."

She popped her gum. "'Kay." She played another group of notes. "Half note, since you didn't hear me earlier. Two beats. It looks like a lowercase D." She drew the shape in the air with her finger. "You know?" She held a note for two beats. "Half note." She nodded.

"Half note. Sorry, I'm listening."

She pulled the board down over the keys and it landed with a bang. "You're so not." She uncrossed her legs and started to get up. I stood, too.

"Fina." The taste of her name in my mouth surprised me. She turned back to me. "I know I'm distracted. It's because I wanted to… talk about about what Autumn and Ivy said."

Her face twisted. Her mouth puckered and her forehead wrinkled, her thick eyebrows knitting together. She tilted her head as she sat.

"You do?" she asked.

I nodded and sat down. "Yeah, I'm really sorry." Her head cocked in the other direction. Her face was still a map of confusion.

"You are?" She looked down and lifted the board. She clunked out a few notes.

"It was really messed up, I don't know why they were actin' that way."

"You don't?" she chuckled, partially amused, and partially disbelieving.

"No," I insisted. Look at me look at me look at me.

She did. She turned the full force of her eyes on me. Maybe it was a change in the light. Maybe I'd only been seeing what I wanted to see. But right then, half of her left eye glinted at me.

Ice blue.

I had never been in an elevator before but there was one in my stomach and it was crashing fifty stories.

"You're a bad liar." She turned back to the piano. I stared at the top of her head, paralyzed. My mouth was moving but no sound was coming out.

Of course.

Of course.

That's why she made my brain stop working. That's why her eyes and her lips and her hair could have made me jump off a cliff.

Blue eyes and roses. Grapes of poison. Seduce and destroy.

She was a witch.

I stood up. My knee banged against the side of the piano. She flinched.

"I have to go." I tried not to run but with my back to her, the fear grew hard and cold in my chest. I grabbed my bag.

The door slammed behind me, the muffled sounds of the piano coming to life fading behind me as I got further and further away.

I hated when Autumn was right.

3. JOSEFINA.

It was 9 steps around the coffee table. I made the journey for the thousandth time, dragging my feet across the knitted rug. I didn't have gum so my teeth worked my bottom lip until I tore a tiny piece of skin off.

Headlights flashed beneath the curtains of the front window. I froze.

Moments, hours, later, the front door opened.

Che came into the den first, followed by Bernardo. Che tossed me my keys.

"Don't be pissed," he said. I gripped my keys tight.

"Why?" He looked at me, my eyes narrowed. "What did you do?" Bernardo started to laugh. I crossed my arms. "Che, I swear to God if you hurt my baby I will have a cow."

"Anything but a cow," Bernardo chuckled.

"You shut up!" I picked up a throw pillow and chucked it at him. It missed. He laughed harder.

"Che!" I was almost hysterical. "What happened?"

Che was grinning now, too. "I hit something. Something tiny!" His hands went up in front of him as I felt my eyes attempting to pop out of my skull. "An animal, a bird, I swear!"

"A bird," Bernardo laughed as he sank into the leather couch. He pulled me down by the back of my shirt. "Who runs over a bird? They have wings."

Che wiped his eyes and howled.

"Ugh, you are never driving my car again," I told him. I put the keys on the coffee table. He threw himself into the back of the couch and curled up next to me, his legs tucked under his body.

"I'll wash the bird guts off the grill," he murmured.

"I thought you ran it over?" I demanded. "Now its guts are in the grill?"

Che shrugged. "The thing had a death wish. I swear it flew down into the car. We're lucky it didn't crack the windshield."

"You are lucky because I would have cracked your head," I replied. He nuzzled his head against my shoulder.

"My beautiful, perfect-shaped head?" He batted his eyelashes at me. I rolled my eyes but my lips were already turning up. He always got me with his puppy face.

A loud gagging noise reverberated off the walls of the den as Carmen came down the stairs.

"Give me a break," he muttered as he popped Che on the back of the head. "Do you come here for business or for drooling?"

Che smirked. "Depends on if your mom is here or not."

"Dude!" I slapped his chest. He grabbed my hands and I struggled against him.

"What, what did I say?!" he demanded. "She's a beautiful woman!"

"Cut it out!" Bernardo reached over me. It was his turn to slap Che.

"Y'all are gonna give me a concussion!" Che hollered as he jumped over me to get a swipe at Bernardo.

"Good!" I replied as their combined body weight folded me into the couch. "Carmen!" I screamed against the leather. I could see with one eye Carmen getting up. He stood in front of where I had been sitting before I was made into origami. He palmed Bernardo's face with his left hand, Che's with his right.

"Okay, okay, okay!" Che put his hands up and I could breathe again. I sat up and gasped. Bernardo shot me a look between Carmen's fingers.

"Calm down before you break something of mine," Carmen said. He raised his eyebrows at Che.

Che reached into his pocket as Carmen let go of the boys' faces.

"My bad," Che murmured. He pulled out an empty glass bottle and gave it to Carmen

"That should have lasted two weeks," Bernardo said under his breath. I glanced at his hand, watching as he peeled green paint off his shorts and crumbled it between his fingers.

"Are you overdosing?" Carmen demanded.

Che sighed and rolled his eyes. "It's giving me wild nightmares, so when I wake up I take a little more, okay?"

"You take more of the thing giving you nightmares," Carmen repeated. He shook his head. "That wasn't the deal," he said as he walked into the kitchen.

"Carmen!" Che got up but I grabbed his arm.

"Sit down," I told him. He listened. I put my hand on his. "This is not stuff you can play with." There were lots that Che had to learn still.

"No, I know, I -" I shook my head and he went quiet.

"You cannot," I said. "Promise me."

His face fell. "I swear."

"I can't deal with something happening to you."

He smirked. "What, do you like me or something?"

"As if," I muttered as I stood. "Come on." I went to the stairs. I could hear his heavy footsteps behind me as we walked up to my room.

"I have a couple bottles," I told him as I opened the door. "Just don't tell Carmen, okay? He'd freak."

I opened the drawer at the bottom of my nightstand. Bottles of every shape and size clinked against each other. A few taller ones rolled on their sides. I took a blue square bottle from the middle and pulled the cork. Peppermint and the acrid, almost rotten smell of crushed Belladonna leaves made my nose wrinkle.

"Ugh, that's it," I said through my teeth. "I'd rather never sleep again." I capped the bottle and handed it to Che.

"If this can stop my nightmares I'll chug a gallon a day." He slipped it in his pocket.

"Did you totally miss the point, dude? Three drops a night, max," I told him.

"No, I know. Exaggeration."

"Plus, it's definitely not going to stop them. Sleep aides make you have weird dreams," I added.

"How's getting my guts eaten by birds for weird?" he replied.

"Ew!"

"Yeah," he muttered. "I'm on some railroad tracks, my top half on one side, my bottom half on the other, right? I'm alive, awake. Everything. And then." He pointed up and made a circle with his fingers. "Vultures. Tons. Come down and pick my guts off the tracks." He put his hand on his stomach. "When I wake up, I can feel it." He chuckled, but his face was ashen. "So wild, huh?"

I put my arms around him and squeezed him tight. I wasn't sure what the hug was for. I felt bad about his fear. I was grateful for him, for what humanity he gave me by existing in the same moment in time as me.

But something else, something electric and ecstatic, was bubbling up to the top of my throat. I had to keep it in.

He's only a kid.

"I'm sorry," I said instead, pulling back and putting my hands on his shoulders. "It sounds scary."

He smiled and held my eyes for a beat too long.

Bernardo knocked on the door frame and I felt the air whoosh out from between my lips.

"Hey," he murmured. Che turned towards him. "Sorry to kick you out, but Elian says it's time." He glanced at me. I nodded.

The three of us made a single-file train down the wide staircase, Bernardo first, Che in the middle. I slipped my finger into Che's pocket and shoved the bottle down until it was out of sight.

He glanced over his shoulder at me. "Usually you buy someone dinner before you get in their pants."

I rolled my eyes. "Again, as if."

"A guy can dream," he replied.

"No, no more dreaming for you." The stairs ended right near the back door, and the clattering against its single glass pane signaled a nasty rain storm. Bernardo opened the door. Sideways sheets of rain pelted the porch so he slammed it shut.

I glanced at Che. "No way are you walking home in that," I told him.

He shrugged. "I'm a swimmer, remember? This is second nature."

"Nonsense." Elian's deep, loud voice bounced off the vaulted ceilings. He brought the sun with him wherever he went. If Santa Claus was 20 years younger and did a great job on Atkins, he'd be Elian.

"Can I run him home before we start?" Bernardo asked him. Elian frowned - his beard moved downward, at least - and glanced at his watch.

"It's nearly time," he murmured. I gestured to the door as the sprays of rain continued to hit its tiny window.

"He could like, hang out until then," I replied.

Elian raised his eyebrows, cautioning me.

I sighed. "Like in the den."

"Of course!" he chuckled. "Would you mind waiting in the den until we finish? It won't be too long, I hope." He looked at me. "Although your mother loves to wax poetic on Mabon."

"Yeah, sure, I'll hang for a second," Che said. "Better than swimming home."

"It's second nature," I mimicked.

"Whatever," he imitated in his highest, most nasally voice.

"I so do not talk like that!" I yelled as he hustled into the den. Bernardo and I followed Elian into the kitchen.

"Don't toy with the boy when it comes to brujeria," Elian murmured as he put his arm around my neck.

"He totally has the Marcan," I sighed for the thousandth time.

Elian nodded. "Yes, as you've said." He steered me to the laundry room.

"Plus." I glanced over Elian's shoulder at Bernardo. "I'm like, 99 percent sure he had a premonition."

Elian's face opened up in surprise, eyes and mouth making the same perfect O. "You are?" he asked.

"Yeah!" The three of us entered the altar room.

"Do tell," Elian said, gesturing to the rest of the family.

"Do tell what?" Ofelia kept her eyes on the herbs in her pestle as she ground them with the mortar.

"Fina says Che had a premonition," Elian told her, beaming.

"Of course she does," Carmen muttered as he sliced into a pomegranate. "If I did this with every boy I found cute, we'd be a coven of thousands."

"He has the Marcan!" I pointed at my left eye, half-brown and half-blue, just like every person in the room. The Mark of the Witch.

"He has heterochromia, idiot," Carmen retorted.

"Which is all the Marcan is, idiot," I replied. Carmen and I didn't talk much. It always ended in screaming matches, tears, or burnt property.

"You know more than Ofelia?" Carmen demanded. "You've been a bruja all of five minutes -"

"Um, seventeen years isn't five minutes!"

"It's the blink of an eye -"

"Could we not have the same argument again, and instead hear this premonition?" Dia asked. She corked the wine she had been pouring into six glasses.

"Thank you," I said. "So, Che's been having these nightmares about birds like, eating his guts, right?" Dia looked up long enough to roll her eyes. I put my hands up. "And then, tonight while he was driving my car. He hits a bird, and its guts are all over the front of the car!"

It was quiet for a long second.

Then Carmen started to laugh.

Heat built behind my eyes. I took a deep breath. "So, the guts. And the birds. Right? Does that not sound like the beginnings of a psychic? It's pretty premonition-ish to me."

"Ish being the operative part of the sentence," Dia murmured. "I see where you're going. But I think it's a stretch."

"A coincidence," Elian offered.

"Seriously?" I demanded. "More like stone-cold proof! Did any of you show signs before you turned?"

"None of us were being converted," Carmen interjected. "So we wouldn't know."

Ofelia looked up from the table. "It's time," she said. "Light the candles, Fina."

"We're doing Mabon indoors?" Bernardo asked.

"Have you seen the weather?" Ofelia replied.

Dia rolled her eyes. "Earth signs," she muttered. "We can bring in some mud if it'll make you feel better."

"If there was one holiday in history where you didn't start a Zodiac argument, I would eat mud," Bernardo told her.

"You don't disprove my argument by doing that," she replied with a grin.

Ofelia clapped her hands together. "Bernardo, the wine. Dia, the offering. Fina, the candles. By the Gods, you are all in rare form tonight."

I went and knelt by the altar table. One fat orange candle sat in a circle of smaller, black and white votives. Ofelia sat three silver bowls beside each other, one with a halved pomegranate inside, its seeds spilling. The other held a shiny apple, dripping from the wound where she had shoved another knife into it. The third was empty for now. Dia brought over a cutting board with slices of thick brown bread and hunks of pumpkin.

She knelt beside me and nodded at the candles. I gestured over the table and flames rose on every wick. Bernardo, Carmen, and Elian sat the glasses of wine down, and Bernardo knelt to my right.

I looked across at Ofelia. She peered at me over the flame of the orange candle and smiled.

When I was a little kid, I spent so much time imagining my mother's smile. My dad burned all her pictures after she died because it hurt him to look at her face. When

I thought about it now, it seemed like I'd always pictured Ofelia's smile. It tugged at the string in my center and I used it to tether me to earth when I thought I might fall off the edge.

Ofelia tucked her short brown hair behind her ears and opened the sancti verba, the book of the Covenant.

"I want you all to clear your minds of the outside world and join me in this celebration. I cast our circle in the name of Rhiannon, our Blessed Mother, the leader of the light. She bore us, the Covenant, in her death and Marked us by destiny for the left-hand path. Our creator and protector, who gave us the gifts to win any Great Battle. She cloaks us in the whitest light as we welcome the turning of the year. We say goodnight to the summer light." Carmen picked up the apple bowl and cut a chunk out with the knife.

"We bite into this last fruit of summer," Ofelia continued. "And we hold the warmth of it in our bellies." Carmen slipped the bite onto his tongue and passed the bowl to his left. "The time comes now for darkness to descend, and we offer ourselves to Hecate as beacons of light, as symbols in the crossroads." I popped a hunk of apple in my mouth and gave the bowl to Bernardo. Ofelia gestured to the bread. "We thank the Blessed Mother for our bountiful offering as she plunges the earth into desolation."

Dia took the pomegranate bowl and picked up a few of the seeds. They crunched between her teeth as she handed the bowl to Bernardo.

3. JOSEFINA.

"This winter fruit represents the gifts we can find in the darkness, the richness of the night. The bridge is stronger than ever here in the home of our Blessed Mother. Our wishes, our hopes, our gratitude - everything is amplified in this hallowed house. We offer our totems of protection to the healing light of the full moon, and the sacred dirt this home was built on. We ask for cleansing and charging of our most precious talismans."

We put our necklaces and bracelets in the empty bowl, which I put in my lap so I wouldn't forget to bury it. "We raise our glasses to those who watch over us." I picked up my wine glass. "We offer this feast to our Blessed Mother Rhiannon." The wine stung the back of my throat as I tossed it back. "May we do well, be well, and wish well to all we encounter."

Ofelia nodded to me and I exhaled through my lips. Every candle went out.

4. RIVER.

Thistlewolf was a strip of land between two lakes. Lake Orange, a huge circle butting up to the back of the football field at school, and Possum Lake, which was shaped like a pear and had Barton Heights on its stem.

There was only one house in Barton on the lake itself. Papa said before him, the Elders all lived there together. They held Gatherings there, and kept an eye on the dark women of the Manor. But now it was the Matthews house. A piece of shore had been carved from the forest long before I was born, and the blue house with red doors had no neighbors beside it.

Since I could stand I had been sloshing through the muddy reeds, narrowly avoiding snake bites. Then, the summer of my growth spurt, I was the only one brave enough to cut the glassy surface of Possum Lake to get to The Tree.

When I first went out there, I didn't know what to expect. It looked like a miracle: one oak tree, limbs twisting together toward the sky, in the middle of the lake. Did it float on water? Was it twenty feet tall, rooted in the grass far below my feet? My fingertips had touched rock about a foot from its trunk.

My Tree was my spot to this day. I called it My Tree only to myself. I was still the only one who would swim out there. I liked it that way. There weren't many places to be alone in Barton. Isolation led to sin. But sometimes the quiet loneliness of My Tree felt more comforting than the hum of dozens during Church.

But tonight the rain kept me on the shore. My jeans were rolled to my knees and my feet splashed in the shallows. I felt the minnows darting around my legs, anxious from the raging storm. The rain was too heavy, the water too murky. I could hardly see, but it played tricks on my eyes. I saw fish jumping where there were only ripples from the wind and shadows from the ricochet of the rain on the surface of the lake.

It looked like there was someone at My Tree.

I jumped to my feet and leaned forward; squinting hard against the sideways sheets that now came from either direction. A crack of lightning shot across the sky above me and I saw, like a spotlight from Heaven.

There was a person at My Tree.

I never stopped asking myself why. Not as I pulled off my shirt, not as I took off my necklace, nor as I ran out into the water made cold by the wind.

The Tree was mine. Everyone in Barton knew it was mine. The one spot where I could be alone and someone had taken it from me.

I pumped my arms and legs harder against the rushing water. The water was cold, despite the heat from earlier. My jeans caused too much catch, making my legs burn. The rain bounced from the lake into my face and splashed into my nose. I could barely keep my eyes open. My anger propelled me forward like a shark hunting its prey. By the time I touched the rock I was full-on fuming.

They were sitting on the other side of My Tree, their back to me. If I didn't know The Tree like the back of my hand, they could have easily been considered a bush.

"Hey!" I hollered over the downpour, shaking water from my face that had started running in my eyes and mouth. They flailed and leapt out of their skin, practically stumbling off the edge.

Island of one. No room for outsiders.

I rubbed at my arms to warm them up. "What do you —"

Lightning tore the sky in two, turning my words turned to vapor.

My pulse rang fast and true in my ears, a cold shock coursing through my veins.

It was Fina. Fina was at my Tree.

"Dude, you scared me," Her words was hardly audible over the pounding rain around us. That voice- that gave me goosebumps during the day- gave me chills.

Goosebumps and chills were not the same thing.

"You scared me. What are you doing out here?" I heard my tone soften, almost breathless.

"What are you doing out here?" she retorted.

"This is my tree."

"Wait, what?" She crossed her arms, her eyebrows furrowing.

"This is my tree," I repeated. "I saw someone at my tree so -"

65

"So what, you're colonizing this tree? Are you planting your flag?"

"What are you talking about? What does that mean?" I shook my head. "Why are you out here in a hurricane?"

"Why are you?" she echoed.

"Is this how you conversate with people, by asking them the same thing they just asked you?"

"Conversate?" There was a smile in her voice. "Do you mean converse?"

Lightning crashed above us, shining a spotlight on her for a split second so I could see the smirk tugging her blinding lips upward.

Could a person's mouth taste like honey?

Hers looked like it would.

"You looked stranded," I continued, wiping water from my eyes and trying to focus on breathing. "I was gonna help you back."

She nodded and pursed her lips. "Do they call you River because you're a good swimmer, or did you become good at swimming because your name is River?"

I wiped the water from my eyes. "You're funny."

"You're not laughing."

"Yeah because it's freezing out here."

"You're wearing more clothes than I am."

I didn't need lightning, or the moon - but I wouldn't have minded the light of Heaven itself as I looked her up and down. There were two patches of white and miles of dark, soaking wet skin in between.

"That's true." I sounded like I had no tongue. She started towards me and my limbs went stiff. Someone had the remote control to my brain and they switched to a static channel. She passed me and her arm brushed mine.

The bottom of my stomach turned molten.

"I'm pretty hot-blooded," she murmured, voice low and dripping. She walked off behind me. I was rooted to the spot, burning to the bone where her arm had touched mine.

There was a splash behind me, barely noticable against the storm, a clap of thunder following. Before I could think I jumped in after her, popping under the surface and back up just as quickly. If I thought I couldn't see before, this was much worse.

"Fina," I murmured. Her name was foreign to my tongue but not to my brain. I let it roll around. "Fina," I said again, a little louder.

"So," she said finally, close by. I exhaled. "Do you always rescue heathen whores or did you like, lose a bet?"

I cringed. "I'm sorry." I was thankful for the dark, so she couldn't see the shame flooding my face. It got hotter the longer the silence sat between us. The only noise was the rain on the surface of the lake.

"You can't help it. I should have known better." The disappointment in her voice cut deep.

"Better than what?"

"You're just like everyone else over there."

I clenched my jaw. "No I'm not."

I barely believed myself.

I heard the slosh of something solid moving through the water, away from me. I followed the sound, blindly fumbling my way to it.

"I came out here to save you, didn't I?" I shouted in her general direction. I could only tell where she was by the slapping on her arms as they cut through the water.

"You came out here to kick me off your secret spot," she gasped.

"If you keep swimming that hard you won't make it to shore."

The slapping continued.

"I would never say that kinda stuff about you. I am not like them." My voice bounced off of the water.

She didn't say anything.

"I know I don't act like it, but I think you're..." I shut my mouth. What was I supposed to say? The most gorgeous thing I'd ever seen? The person who made gum-chewing hot? The girl who made me feel like my brain was running out of my ears?

Ceci. I love Ceci. I can't have these thoughts.

The silhouette of her head moved across the surface, her movement drowned out by the downpour.

"Can you say something? Please?"

She took a deep, ragged breath. My heart stopped.

"Are you cryin'?"

"River." Her voice was tight. There was a splash to my left, harder than raindrops, and then another. I reached my hand towards where her voice came from.

"Where are you?" I groped the water, trying to keep my composure. I stretched my leg and touched my toes to the floor of the lake. If I stood on one foot I could keep the water below my chin.

"Talk to me, Fina, make noise, I can't see you."

"I can't touch." There was panic in her words, bubbled with water, a tremble under her smooth tone.

"It's okay, I can touch, I'll g -"

Thunder rolled across the sky and bolt after bolt of bright lightning shot through the clouds like a symphony of cymbals, giving me just enough light to spot her.

I could only see her slicked-back hair, and wide, bottomless eyes staring back at me. I leapt towards her and wrapped my hand around her wrist, the heat from it nearly knocking me away. But a calm swallowed me the second I had her. I pulled her in, the heat of her body slicing through the water, sending goosebumps up and down my body as I pulled her close to me. I put my arm around her waist and lifted her up to my chest, my hand hooking under one of her knees, my foot still planted on the bottom of the lake to hold me still. Her skin was so hot but her limbs were shivering.

"Hey, I've got you." I wrapped her arm around my neck. "You're fine. I can touch, you're fine," I repeated. "Told you not to swim so hard."

I looked down at her, where I knew her face was, where that mouth was. I took a deep breath to keep my mouth from salivating. She smelled like oranges. I could feel the pulse from her wrist on the back of my neck.

Seduce and destroy.

Ceci, I repeated in my head to hold my focus. Ceci, Ceci, Ceci.

I pushed us across the lake on one foot, until I could stand up straight without drowning her. She was silent, breathing hard. Still shaking.

"Are you okay?" I whispered, not really sure why. No one was out here but us. But the way our bodies were pressed to each other, the way I could already taste her. It warranted a whisper.

"Scared," she breathed. I squeezed her to me. In the dark, in the rain, in this strange fever dream where she would let me hold her this way, I was brave. I would probably never be so brave again.

"You're fine."

"I know." Her fingers brushed the nape of my neck. It was so soft it could have been an accident. My stomach was in knots. The tops of her legs began to peek out of the water.

I cleared my throat. "You can probably touch now." I didn't loosen my grip.

"Okay." She didn't move either.

So I kept walking, the floor of the lake getting steeper and more uphill as we neared the shore. I prayed for more lightning so I could watch as she rose above the surface, the rain bouncing off her soaking wet skin and turning to steam, because man her skin was hot.

Everything about her was hot.

I stopped and stared at the shoreline. I felt her eyes on my face and I knew if I looked down at her, it would be over. I would kiss her and I would never forgive myself.

We were not in some parallel universe where I could kiss her.

We weren't in one where she would want me to, either. And I had Ceci.

4. RIVER.

I set Fina down in the water as guilt rocketed through my chest.

I let her wade ahead, keeping an arm's length between me and her back. The lights from her house cast an eerie glow on us.

I was only knee-deep now, but the water was at her waist. She had a tattoo on her ribcage, of what I didn't know - lines and dots that made no sort of shape I could recognize.

I swallowed hard and looked up at the sky. The rain beat on but the moon cut through the clouds, red-rimmed and heavy with accusation. Like the Heavenly Father himself was watching me sin with one silver eye, bloodshot from weeping for my wretched soul.

I was weak. But I couldn't bring myself to care, not when the bottom of the lake was eggshells and the rain allowed me to tread them without tearing the fabric of the universe.

I didn't realize I was holding my breath until she turned around to face me, walking backwards up the slope of the shore.

I exhaled hard. My eyes found the moon again to avoid my own slope, downward right into Hell for the way I wanted to be looking at her.

Seduce and destroy.

"Are you okay?" There was a smile in her voice. I studied the halo around the waxing moon. I had never seen it on a cloudy night before.

"Yeah," I replied, too high and too tight.

"You're a bad liar."

"Hmm," I murmured. My ankles were above the surface. I took a couple steps quick to make it to shore around the same time she would. Her shorts were draped over the canoe which had been tied to the dock. She slipped them up over her legs legs legs oh look there's the moon again.

"I'm dressed," she chuckled. I glanced down, not sure if she was telling the truth.

She was. Mostly. She'd barely covered any more skin. She worked her thick hair into a bun and stared at me expectantly. "Well?"

"Huh?" A smirk curved over that dangerous mouth.

"You never listen."

It came out before I could think. "You're distracting." Stop flirting!

She wound a band around her dripping hair. "I must be, for you to strand yourself on the wrong side of the lake. Don't tell me you're going to swim back."

Right. Forbidden territory. I would get in worlds of trouble if any of them knew I was here.

I chuckled. "I'm good, but not that good. It's not far to walk."

She put her hands on her hips. "I'm obviously going to drive you back, doofus."

"I like the exercise."

She cocked an eyebrow and looked me up and down. "Clearly."

I grinned. "Don't flirt with me."

"I would never." She glanced down. "Can I…?"

My heart jumped into my throat. Her left hand took my right wrist and turned my palm up to the sky.

Oh.

"You have a high mount of Venus," she told me as she ran circles around the heel of my hand. Her fingers burned my skin. "Do you know what it means?"

I shook my head.

"It means you're soft-hearted." Her voice was so quiet. "Rich in sentiment. Prone to rescuing damsels in distress."

I put my hand on my chest. "It was my pleasure, princess."

She chuckled and looked up at me. The moon reflected in her irises, the blue prominent in the soft light. She had freckles on her nose - I didn't notice before. Our hands stayed extended in the dead air between us, barely touching. My ring finger brushed the middle of her palm.

I could hear my heartbeat in my ears. Do not kiss her. Do not kiss her.

Or kiss her. None of this is real, anyway.

A shadow fell over us. We both jumped. A man - a boy, tall, thin - stood on the porch, at the top of the steps.

He crossed his arms. My mind began to loop the hundreds of different stories, the rumors of what they could do. I was on their land now. I had no way to escape except to try and swim back.

The boy nodded at me. "Hey." A voice I recognized.

I exhaled. "Hey, Che." I tried to steady my tone as confusion set in. I took a big step back from Fina and started towards him. He turned around, and the glass panes of the door shook as he slammed it.

"Che," she called in the dark. Fina pushed past me and jogged up to the steps, kicking sand in my direction and leaving me to my own devices and soaking wet. I deserved it though, for the thoughts that I had. It was a sin.

I walked the length of the lake until I reached the hole in Barton's fence. None of that could have been real. I didn't break the rules. I also didn't deserve anything so incredible.

So I imagined it. Of course I did.

But my wrist tingled from where her fingers had been. And I would never be able to erase the tattoo on her ribs from the back of my eyelids.

It had been a once in a lifetime moment, a parallel universe fever dream I could carry in my pocket. Something I could keep to myself, like the Tree.

For now.

Matthew 10:26. There is nothing covered that shall not be revealed.

1. BERNARDO.

Che took the porch steps gingerly and then bound across the flooded yard. He opened the passenger side door and sat, kicking his shoes together outside before swinging his legs in.

"Let's go," he said to me. I backed out down the brick drive and turned around before passing through the open gates.

"No Fina?" I asked him. I didn't have to ask. Che was one of the few I listened to because he was one of the few who screamed. Most people let their thoughts run off the back of their brains in Technicolor. Not Che. He let every thought hit him between the eyes all at once, a loud cacophony of unintelligible emotion.

I knew why Fina wasn't there, but it was proper to ask.

"Nah, she was busy." Flicker after flicker popped up in my mind's eye, the way subliminal messages were sometimes hidden in frames of films. If I knew what to look for I could find it easily. But all I saw was Fina's face and white hot jealousy.

"What happened?" I asked.

Che scoffed. "I go outside to get her, right? She's the one who told me to wait for her so she could say good-bye. So I go outside and she's by the dock with River Matthews." He scoffed again. "They're practically holding hands, both wet; he doesn't even have a shirt on. Okay? So I'm over here like, what the hell?"

"What do you mean?" I replied slowly, trying to pick things out of his mind and listen at the same time. Dirt turned to asphalt as Shell Court became Remington Road.

Che rolled his eyes. "I mean I spend a lot of time at school sticking up for her against his little buddies, you know? So she's gonna be dumb and give them more ammo? He has a girlfriend, of a long time."

I whistled low. "Yeah, I know." If there was a textbook example of why I still bothered with high school, Cecelia Chase in a cheer skirt had to be it.

Che chuckled. "Don't wreck, man."

"You know you can't bring her up when I'm driving."

"I can't bring up the word 'girl' when you're driving," he laughed. "You're worse than me."

I laughed. "Okay, anyway. Back to your story."

He sighed. "Right. So she follows me inside and I'm like, what the hell?" I nodded. "Of course she's saying they weren't doing anything but, no one believes it if they see what I saw. I mean, I believe her, because I know her. But then she wonders why people say the stuff they say." I could hear his phone vibrating in his pocket. "So anyways, forget her."

"Are you going to get that?" I asked him.

He shook his head. "Nah, it's her."

We turned onto Third Street, which led into the main stretch of downtown.

"You're mad at her because she was with another guy?" I clarified.

Che exhaled hard through his nose and shrugged. "No. Maybe. I don't know, man."

"Yes you do." I could hear him screaming it.

"You say she doesn't date. Maybe she just doesn't date me." Che sounded defeated, slumping back into the seat and playing with his hands.

I clicked my tongue between my teeth. "I don't think so."

None of us dated - mortal/immortal relationships only ended one way - but we all played in the sandbox. Fina liked Che too much to toy with him.

"They were pretty friendly."

"Listen," I sighed, tired of hearing the words come out of my mouth again. "I've been trying to talk you off the ledge that is Fina all summer. I know my sister. You two have a really special friendship. Don't throw it away."

"I don't know why I ask you," he said. "You don't have this problem."

"I don't chase girls like Fina," I chuckled. "You figure out who's worth the effort. It comes with experience."

We pulled up in front of his apartment building, Che quiet for a few more minutes, stewing in his thoughts.

"Right, but how do you get experience if you can't get experience?" He raised his eyebrows and made a hand gesture even I could blush at.

"Stop chasing such a tough sell. There are at least three girls on the JV swim who would let you take them on a date."

He opened the door. "Where's the fun in an easy sell?" he asked as he got out.

I laughed. "Oh, there's plenty of fun in it, trust me."

"Animal." He chuckled and slammed the car door behind him.

4. JOSEFINA.

By the end of Hart's class on Monday, I had worked myself into a near hysteria at the thought of seeing River. Panic would coil in my stomach, overwhelming and unannounced. I'd see a Barton kid and my heart would skip.

Who did he tell?

Who saw us that night?

What had I done?

But the memory stayed pure. The feeling of rain dripping in the spaces where our bodies weren't touching, the only thing that could fit between us.

I popped my gum.

Stupid and foolish, Fina. But I just couldn't bring myself to regret it.

There were only a handful of kids in Alfred's classroom when I arrived. I sat down and took out my notebook and pen, tapping the end against the paper. I kept my eyes glued to the lines as the door opened and shut, over and over, student after student entering the room. My foot was bouncing.

Bernardo sat down next to me. I pulled out the strips of paper still hanging on to the spirals of my notebook, trying to put my mind at rest. I balled each one up and piled them in the corner of the table.

Have you taken a breath recently? His voice invaded my head.

I think I forgot how.

An electric current ripped through me as the door shut again. I didn't look up, because I didn't have to. River ran his index finger along the tabletop in front of me as he walked to his seat. I inhaled deeply through my nose because my chest was threatening to explode. My foot kept going on its own, shaking my entire leg. Had anyone else seen that?

The bell rang for class to begin.

"Can I get your keys before I forget?" Bernardo asked as he turned our textbook to Macbeth.

"What?" I glanced up at him, blinking away the rainy memory.

"Your keys. So I can go get food while you're tutoring."

My knee slammed into the tabletop.

People turned to look at me. I cringed and rubbed at it.

"I forgot," I whispered. I looked at River, half a second, a reflex.

His head was resting in his hand, his elbow on the table. He faced forward but his eyes were trained on me. He didn't look away when our eyes met. He didn't even flinch.

I had to stomp my feet on the ground to keep them from jiggling. My nerves were so wound up I thought

I could explode out of my chair and up into the atmosphere.

Alone with him. Completely alone again. I heard my own breathing through my nose, heavy and shallow. I exhaled through my mouth and rolled my shoulders back.

I did not get worked up, not anymore.

I had spent years cultivating a calm exterior, a method for controlling myself. The gum had been doing the trick. Maybe it was time to move on. No boy - not even a boy like River - was going to undo years of hard work. The rolling boil had to stay under the lid.

Besides. Che was right. He did have a girlfriend.

But a girlfriend hadn't stopped him the other night. He wasn't just saving me. He'd carried me for so much longer than he should have. He let me read his palm. If Che hadn't come outside...

Nothing, Fina. You do not kiss boys with girlfriends.

What was wrong with me?

Can I have your keys? Bernardo interrupted my thoughts.

I rolled my eyes, pulled them out of my bookbag and tossed them at him. He grabbed them right before they hit the ground.

"Thanks," he muttered.

I was the first one out of the classroom once the bell rang. Third period had ended just as fast as it began. I had to get out before River could catch up to me. Not that he would try in public, but I couldn't take the chance.

I ran down the stairs and took a sharp right into the girls' bathroom. The handicapped stall was empty. I slammed the door and locked it, turning on the faucet and bracing myself against the edges of the sink.

If I could slow the boil nothing would happen. I stared down at the water running into the drain. I could be smooth and flowing like the water. I let the heat in my fingertips retreat before I looked into the dingy, rusted mirror.

I blinked the smoke from my eyelashes.

You worked hard to be here, you do not let anyone take this from you. I nodded at myself. You are better than this. I swallowed hard and stuck my hands in the cold water. I splashed my face, the heat sizzling it away almost immediately. You're more than what you are. You're still who you are. I nodded and reached for the paper towel dispenser.

It was empty. I sighed and lifted the front of my dress. I dried my face as best as I could with lace and smoothed my hair back with my damp hands.

I shook my shoulders and took one more deep breath. The boil was a simmer now.

I opened the stall door as the bathroom door was closing behind two girls.

The Barton bitches. I clenched my fists and kept my pace, trying to keep my blood from boiling again. If I could hurry past them before they realized who I was, we might all make it out alive.

I brushed shoulders with Ivy, and she drove her bony elbow into my side. I went to chomp down on my gum and bit the inside my cheek instead. Fine. Something else to focus on. Stay at a simmer.

"Ooh, I'm sorry," she chuckled, pouting her lip. Autumn turned over her shoulder and looked at me as I opened the door.

"Fifi is having a rough day," she chuckled.

It was all I could do to ignore them, but I made it out of the bathroom without simmer.

I hurried over to Building One. The bell had to have rang by now.

"Fina!" I turned at the sound of my name.

Sparrow was standing halfway across the courtyard waving at me. I waved back without breaking stride.

"Where are you going?" she yelled.

"Study Hall!" I said a little too loud for the smaller space.

"Why?"

I chuckled. "Because it's my class."

"We have Algebra right now," she said as she hustled over to me. Her long legs got her to me in only a few strides.

"No, Sparrow, that's fifth period. I'm going to be late -"

"It is fifth period." She furrowed her eyebrows.

My stomach dropped. "What?" She nodded. I shook my head. "Shut up." She nodded again. "I'm... having a weird day."

"Yeah, I noticed." She grabbed the end of my book-bag strap and started pulling me towards Building Six. "How's your knee by the way?"

I cringed. "Fine, thanks."

"Rough weekend?" she asked.

"You don't know the half of it," I muttered.

She smiled. "Sure I do."

We started up the stairs.

"You do?" My heart sunk into the pit of my stomach, my mouth going dry.

She shrugged. "Not hard to figure out the way you were both acting. Something happened."

"Shh!" I pulled her to the side before the entrance to the building. "Nothing... happened, okay?" Not techni- cally. I had like, an 80 percent chance of passing a lie detector test.

Her smile grew wider. "It was close, wasn't it?" She nodded towards the doors. "We're gonna be late. Wasn't it?" she pressed again as we entered the hallway. I felt like all the eyes in the school were trained on me, but no one met my gaze as we sped down the hallway.

I popped my gum. "You can ask him."

She opened the classroom door. "I did."

My heart stopped. He'd told her. He'd told someone about what happened.

"What did he say?" My voice was not as steady as I'd hoped. I cleared my throat as we sat down. "Like, what does he think happened?"

"Oh, no," she chuckled. "Oh, no no no."

"What?" I hissed.

"Between Cecelia's pom-pom army and him being the Prophet's grandson, you're probably the bravest person I know." The bell rang.

Mrs. Martinez switched on the overhead projector, and the answer key to the weekend homework appeared on the wall.

"The Prophet of what?" I hissed. Sparrow and I switched papers.

"Prophet to the Heavenly Father, duh. Your handwriting looks typed," Sparrow told me.

"Thanks," I murmured. It had taken me years of writing high school essays to get it like that. Hers was scrawling, slanted, and barely legible. "Yours has character."

"If I'm anything, it's full of character. Now don't change the subject."

"You changed the subject," I whispered.

She considered what I said. "Probably."

"And anyways, I'm not trying to take anyone's boyfriend," I said, rolling my eyes. "I know you guys think it's like, my hobby or something, but it's not. He came out there after me."

"Came after you where?"

"The la -" I paused. "You said he told you."

"He did," she answered, too quickly.

"No he didn't!" I hissed. "He better not tell anybody."

Something I hadn't thought about reared its ugly head. The second anyone found out - Barton, cheerleader, or otherwise - the rumors about me would gain undeniable gravity. There would be an anecdote with weight. One I knew would be true. And I couldn't stand tall if I knew that.

"If it makes you feel better," she murmured as she turned her attention to my homework. "He really likes you."

My heart thudded so hard I thought it might break my sternum. It knocked the wind out of me. The danger bells went wild.

"It doesn't," I whispered, to her and myself, the pit in my stomach only growing deeper now.

By the end of seventh period, I had convinced myself. I would either make River afraid of me, to the point where he wouldn't tell a soul he had ever been alone with me; or I would make him so mad he would fall in line with everyone else from Barton Heights. Whatever I thought could happen was proving to be too dangerous even in theory. Why had I even let myself think it?

I got to Hart's classroom before his last class was done filing out. I sat at the upright Bechstein and pulled out the music he'd given me at the start of school. I was almost playing it by memory now. I spread it out and waited until the door shut before I began to play.

The song felt like I felt. It began with a lilting treble hand section that was either melancholy or medieval, depending on the speed. But there was a jump down the bass clef that became almost violent in its thunder. I felt it reverberating in my chest. The sound enveloped me. It reminded me of the cathartic rawness of sobbing.

The last notes drifted away from the piano and consumed the emptiness of the classroom.

"You're amazing."

I jumped, slamming my hands down onto a cringeworthy note. River was standing by the door, his arms crossed. His mouth was turned up, the way someone would watch a dog chase its tail. It infuriated me.

"What are you doing?" I demanded.

"Coming… to tutoring?" He dropped his bookbag in a chair and came towards the piano.

"How long have you been there?"

"Long enough." He smirked again. "I knew I'd get to hear you play."

"I wasn't playing for you. Are you making a habit of sneaking up on me or what?"

He chuckled. "How did I sneak up on you when we're supposed to meet in here?"

"Whatever," I sighed. He had my brain in knots. I picked up the sheet music and shoved it in the folder. He crossed his arms - wow he had nice arms - on the top of the piano.

"Are you mad at me?" he asked. I glanced up at him, ready to let him have it.

Big mistake. He was staring down at me through his thick lashes. It shouldn't have still affected me so much. He stared a lot in Alfred's class. But I still hadn't figured out how to prepare myself for the shifting of my atoms when his eyes met mine. I remembered somewhere in my brain about my plan to break this connection, about how it wasn't sustainable or safe. I tried to remember the danger bells.

I could hear myself breathing. He just kept staring. How could someone look at another person like that? It was obscene.

It took every ounce of my strength to drop my eyes to the keys.

"Ready for a pretest?" I asked him.

He cleared his throat. "Sure, I can take one."

I went over to the table and grabbed a worksheet from the stack. I handed it to him, my eyes on the floor behind him. I sat on the bench and waited for him to finish, trying to focus on the sound of his pencil scraping against the wood of the piano.

A knife wouldn't have made a dent in the tension - we needed a chainsaw.

"I don't want you to be mad," he murmured, his eyes glued to the worksheet like a disobedient child. I watched my fingers twisting and untwisting in my lap.

"Did you tell Sparrow what happened?"

"No," he replied without looking up.

"She asked me about it."

He sighed and set the pencil down. "No one has to tell Sparrow anything. She's… perceptive." He shrugged.

"Are you lying?" My heart beat hard in my chest, turning my blood to lava.

He looked down at me. "Does it look like I'm lying?" I didn't dare meet his eyes again. He picked up his pencil with a sigh and continued the pre-test. "Did you tell anybody?"

"There's enough stories about me in this place. I don't see a reason to add a true one."

"We didn't do anything wrong," he muttered. We didn't, but the way I felt about him was wrong.

"I bet your girlfriend would disagree."

I flinched when he slammed his pencil down and shoved his paper away. It floated down to me, like a butterfly in a storm. I held it against the wood and stared at it, unfocusing.

"I never lied to you about that," he said. His voice was tight. "Don't you think I feel bad? I didn't mean for this to happen."

Heat rose in my face. My fingers started to tingle. But I wouldn't look at him. Not now.

"For what to happen?" I demanded. I closed my eyes and took a deep breath.

"This," he whispered. I felt his eyes on me again. I willed mine to stay shut. Looking into them would not end well for me.

"This?" I repeated. "This is nothing."

"You're a bad liar," he replied softly. I knew it though, with every fiber of my being.

I opened my eyes. It was his turn to look away now, past me at the chalkboard.

"Seven out of ten right," I tossed the paper back at him.

"Great," he retorted.

"Guess you don't need any more tutoring."

"Guess not."

I picked up my bag and started towards the door.

"Hey, I promise, okay?" he called. My hand hesitated on the knob.

"Promise what?"

"Not to tell anybody," he said. I turned to look at him. "I don't want to make things harder for you."

I tried to keep my face smooth, unreadable. One way or the other, I had told myself. I had set out to cut the string.

"Then stay away from me," I told him quietly, keeping my eyes on the wall ahead of me.

"Alright." Sadness. No mistaking it. I left the room, slamming the door behind me before I could change my mind.

String, cut.

5. RIVER.

"Only Silas the Prophet had the power to keep the dark women at bay. One had blood of fire, and this was the Devil, Aradia. The other had blood of roses, and this was the Evil, Rhiannon." Clay wiped the sweat from his brow. "Pass."

Micah cleared his throat and continued reading. "When Silas the Prophet destroyed them, the blood of roses returned below rather than touch his lips, for he knew her grapes were grapes of poison. The Devil was banished back to Hell, where she waits to do works once more, pass!" By the end, he was barely mumbling.

"Our Heavenly Father bestowed upon Silas the Prophet's line the power to guide and protect his people," Forrest read. "They became the Chosen, keepers of the Cross, bathed in the blood and the Word." Forrest looked up at me with a smirk. "Pass."

I sighed. "They will be our only hope when the dark women return from below."

A shriek echoed across the lake. I snapped my Bible shut and stared at the cover. I tried not to look over there anymore. I didn't stare, either. Not when I could help it.

"Speak of the Devil," Forrest muttered.

"Man, you see them all the time, huh?" Micah scoffed.

"Unfortunately," I sighed.

Clay tilted his head. "Not so unfortunate." He pointed in their direction. I sighed and looked across the lake.

Two red and brown shapes were standing in a canoe. The sun bounced off the metal of the boat and I had to shield my eyes to get even a second's glance. But I knew one was her.

"Buncha creeps," Forrest murmured. He shook his head.

"That house has always been evil," Clay said. "Now we see who owns it. Shoulda burned it down years ago."

I nodded noncommittally. I could steel myself against the hideous comments, the hateful stares. At school I'd gotten good at playing along. But I couldn't add to it, not even after what she'd said, her final words stinging against my chest.

Two boys stood on the dock, watching the girls. Bernardo I recognized - it was the hair and the paint. He always had paint on his pants. But the other guy seemed to loom over the lake itself, wide and large with a deep-set frown. The canoe moved slightly and the glare vanished. My eyes zeroed in on Fina. She wore a blood-red one piece. I was grateful. It meant I'd stay the only one who had seen her the way I saw her that night at My Tree.

I had no right to be grateful.

Someone made a gagging noise. I turned to the boys and found six eyes staring at me. Watching me watch her. Forrest gagged again.

I rolled my eyes. "Y'all are dumb."

"That's why you're nice to her," Micah chuckled as he wiggled his eyebrows. "How is she?"

I lunged at Micah. He slid back right before my fist connected with his shoulder.

"I have a girlfriend," I retorted.

"So do I," Clay said. "But that girl's tempted me so bad I deserve sainthood."

"Who?" I asked. He nodded towards the canoe. I narrowed my eyes. "Fina?" I demanded. He nodded. "When?"

"I see her between sixth and seventh. And… let's just say sometimes I'm late to seventh." He smirked.

My jaw tightened. Forrest staggered around the porch dramatically, hanging his head over the railing. He made heaving noises and held his stomach.

"How late?" Micah demanded. He grabbed Clay's arm and shook it. "How late?!" he repeated.

Clay laughed. "Depends on how many clothes we're wearing. Or, were wearing."

Forrest stopped fake puking and came back over. He dropped down cross-legged. I tried to unclench my teeth.

"Are you serious?" Forrest asked in a whisper. Clay shrugged.

"He's lying," I interjected, the words pouring out before I could stop them. Clay's head snapped to me, eyebrows raised. I should have kept my mouth shut, but I couldn't.

"Oh yeah? How do you figure?"

The light bulb went off.

"Where's her tattoo?" I asked.

Forrest grinned. "What?"

"Wait, what?" Micah echoed.

"She's got a hidden tattoo, Clay. Where is it?"

"How do you know?" Clay demanded. "Huh?"

"This is the first time she hasn't worn a two-piece all summer." I nodded towards her. "I see it all the time."

Clay smiled. "Lower back."

"Awesome," Micah said as they high-fived.

"Wrong," I chuckled.

Clay narrowed his eyes at me. "Listen, I'd love to argue about a slut's tattoo but I have a football game to get to." He stood up. "I'll see y'all." He jogged down the porch steps and disappeared around the side of the house.

"Maybe he didn't care to check for the tattoo," Micah offered.

"Can't miss it," I sighed, my eyes drifting across the lake. The other girl was in a red one-piece, too. Her heavy dark hair was slicked back from her round face. Her lips matched her suit exactly.

"Maybe you couldn't. We know you're a sensitive little guy," Micah said.

"Who's been with twice as many girls as you," Forrest retorted.

"That's not cool, Forrest," I told him. "Two times zero is still zero."

"Yes!" Forrest high-fived me. Micah gave us a thumbs-up.

"Never gets old," he muttered.

"You're the one who got nailed down by a Barton girl," Forrest said, shrugging. He turned to me. "So where's the tattoo?"

"Oh, she doesn't have one," I told him.

"What?!" Micah demanded. He jumped to his feet.

I laughed. "Yeah, I lied."

Micah threw his hands up. "I'm leavin'. Y'all are a bunch of mean, hateful liars. I don't know who to trust anymore." He stomped down the steps.

I wiped the tears from my eyes and tried to catch my breath. Forrest was sprawled on his back, his legs kicking wildly as he howled.

"Man, Clay's gonna make your life fun now," he chuckled. "Woo!" He shook his head. "Them two let mainstreaming go right to their heads, man."

"Only two years left." There was a splash and another scream on the other side. We watched as the boys who had been on the dock swim to the canoe. Fina was gone.

"How many of them are there?" I wondered aloud.

"Too many," Forrest sighed.

"Way too many." I jumped and turned in the direction of the voice.

My little sister, Willow, stood in the frame behind the screen door, her arms crossed. Thirteen going on 47. She looked past us, across to the other shore. She shook her head, and her mane of tight brown curls spread across her shoulders.

"Y'all goin' to the game still?" she continued. "It's about six." Forrest stood and brushed his hands on his shorts. He held one out to me but I ignored it.

"Yes ma'am, Miss Matthews," he chuckled. "We're goin' right now."

She nodded. "I think you should." She opened the screen door and held it for us as we passed through.

"My keys are on the table," I told Forrest. "I'll be there in a sec." I looked down at Willow. "How long were you there?" I said through my teeth.

"Long enough to wanna puke," she replied.

"Bible studies are boys-only for a reason. Mom would freak if she knew you were bein' nosy."

"But you're not gonna tell her, are you? Just like I'm not gonna tell her what y'all were talkin' about out there."

"Go ahead," I chuckled. "You're only gonna get yourself in trouble for sticking your nose where it don't belong." I walked towards the kitchen. I heard the screen door snap closed.

"Like how you stuck your nose right up on their side of the lake the other night?"

My stomach fell into my toes, my body shocked in place. I turned on my heel, eyes wild. Willow stood in the middle of the living room, an evil smirk across her baby face.

"You don't know what you're talkin' about," I muttered.

Her smile widened. "I know enough to make the Elders come askin' questions," she replied.

I sighed. "What do you want?"

"You clean the bathrooms. For a month."

"A month? Get real."

"Suit yourself. Our bathroom will be a lot cleaner once you're an apostate, anyway."

"Fine," I muttered. "Okay? Now keep your mouth shut."

"Love you," she called after me as I stormed out the front door.

"What was the holdup?" Forrest asked out the passenger side window. I slammed the door of the cab behind me and reversed hard.

"Be glad you don't have sisters," I muttered as I gunned the engine. "She was spying on us for who knows how long."

"I didn't think it was a big deal," he replied. "Otherwise I would have said somethin'."

"What?" I demanded.

Forrest shrugged. "I heard her come home."

"You heard her come home?" I repeated. "And you let me run my mouth about witches and tattoos? Have you lost your mind?" My mind went straight back to Fina. I had told myself countless times that I did nothing wrong, but something in the pit of my stomach said the opposite.

"I didn't think it was a big deal!" he insisted.

"Of course it's a big deal, Forrest! She's gonna run her mouth to my mom, or, if I really piss her off, Papa, and he'll Barton Law me off the face of the planet."

"If your parents can't know about something you said, you shouldn't have said it," he murmured. We pulled onto the 33 and my tires squealed.

"Your parents are not Elders," I spat. "You don't get it. You'll never get it, okay?"

Forrest looked over at me. "You're actin' crazy, River."

I snapped my jaw shut. He was right, guilt was seeping from my every pore. Of course I was acting crazy. I had been acting crazy since the minute I met Fina. Witch madness. Grapes of poison. She was poisoning me, turning me insane. Why else would I still be obsessed with the thought of her?

I pulled into the parking lot.

"I'm sorry," Forrest said to me as he took his seatbelt off. "You're right. I don't get it."

"I shouldn't have freaked," I replied. "Let's drop it."

The parking lot butted up to the football field. We fell into the crowd funneling through the one gate. The stands were still pretty empty. This was only the third game of the season, thanks to the storms we'd been having. If I missed one more, Ceci was going to murder me. Forrest and I hustled past the rest of the students to get a seat close to the ground.

I whistled at Ceci as she and Autumn stretched on the track in front of us. Ceci's head shot up and she stuck her tongue at me. I winked. She looked even better in her cheer uniform. I had to bite my lip to stop the thoughts racing through my mind.

Micah slid down the bench until he was sitting next to me, with Clay following him.

"Hey, Clay, good to see ya, buddy!" Forrest called. I started to laugh. Clay shot us a look as he sat.

Ceci and Aliya MacNeil picked up the paper banner and ran to the goalpost. The marching band stood in their bleachers and began to play the fight song.

The speakers keened with feedback. "Please welcome your Thistlewolf Rottweilers!"

A couple dozen guys barreled through the red, white, and black banner to little applause. As the game started, it was clear to see why. No one was here to see them play. They were only here for the cheerleaders. What the team lacked in skill, strategy, and basic talent; the cheerleaders made up for in spades. It was laughable how hard the girls tried to rally the crowd any time the ball made the slightest movement in the right direction.

By halftime, I was ready to leave. There were only so many times I could watch even the hottest girl do cartwheels before it got boring.

"Micah!" A red ponytail bounded up to the gate. Micah leaned forward as Autumn stood on her tiptoes to reach over the fence. "Hold this for me." She pulled off her promise ring and handed it to him. She looked at me. "Ceci asked me to ask you to get her a Coke. She'll meet you at the concession stand."

I stood up and shuffled past the rest of the guys. The concession stand stood in the shadow of the home team stands, practically in a sinkhole. Mosquitoes darted around my ankles as I trudged through the soft, muddy ground. It reeked like rotten eggs. Anyone who wasn't in line for a four dollar soda was hanging out under the bleachers. I paid for Ceci's coke and went to wait for her.

I turned the corner of the concession stand and ran right into someone, dropping the Coke all over my shoes and the black boots in front of me.

"I'm so sor -" I froze mid-word and followed those black boots, right up the legs, to the face of their owner. I didn't have to look,but I needed to. I needed to take what I could get.

Fina stood inches from me, unmoving, unblinking. The cold, fizzy soda was spreading across my socks. Her eyes were glassy, her nose red.

"Are you okay?" It sounded like my voice but I didn't feel my mouth move. How did she do this to me?

She sniffed. "I was until I got Coke in my shoes."

"Is that why you're cryin'?" I asked in a softer voice.

"I'm not crying," she snapped, sniffling hard and turning her head.

I nodded. "Okay." My chest ached. All I could focus on was keeping my hands at my sides instead of touching her. She was going to have to be the one to turn away. My legs were paralyzed.

"Um, hi." Ceci's voice came from behind me. Like a videotape being fast-forwarded, my legs turned me in her direction, too fast. I stumbled a little.

"Hey!" I greeted, my voice too high. I motioned to the cup on the ground. "I got your drink but…"

"You got caught," someone else interjected. Che came stomping across the grass towards us. His face was ashen. The veins in his arms stuck out as his hands clenched into fists at his sides. "I should have known this was where you went," he said to Fina.

"What are you talking about?" I chuckled. "We literally bumped into each other." I gestured at my soaking wet shoes.

5. RIVER.

"Listen, Cecelia," Che said. "You are way too fine to be putting up with this." He pointed between Fina and me.

"Have you lost your mind?" I demanded.

"Excuse me?" Ceci said over me.

"Ignore him," Fina muttered. She stepped between Che and me and tried to move Che away, but he grabbed her arm, his eyes locked with mine.

"That's your thing, not his," he retorted.

"Hey!" I put my hand on Che's chest.

"Don't touch me," Fina spat, wrenching her arm away. Che looked between Fina and me, his mouth hanging open, his eyes wild. I had never seen him like this.

"You have to have everything, don't you?" he shook his head a little.

"What are you talking about?" I repeated.

He gripped my arms now, looking wildly around him. "The vultures," he muttered. I finally noticed the glaze over his eyes.

"What is wrong with you?" I demanded, shaking him off. He turned to Ceci. My entire body tensed. He had lost his mind. If he touched her, I'd go ballistic.

"Ask them about the lake," he told her. "And when you dump him, call me."

Che stormed off, past Ceci. The look on her face made me want to sink into the ground. Her bottom lip trembled.

"What about the lake?" she asked. I scoffed and turned to Fina, completely at a loss.

She was gone.

"She's not here," Ceci snapped. "What about the lake?" she repeated.

"I have no clue what he's talking about. I mean, she lives on the other side of the lake from me. I don't know what he's talking about."

"I know when you're fibbing."

"Ceci, he has a thing for you. He wants us to fight so he can hit you up." I closed the space between us. She crossed her arms as I reached for her hands.

"He's not the only person to say that about you and her," Ceci told me as her voice cracked.

I shrugged. "You know how people talk."

"Not about my boyfriend. Not without a reason."

"Gimme a break," I chuckled. "He's clearly not right in the head."

"Then tell me the truth. Or I'll go ask him. I saw how she looks at you."

I sighed. "They live across the lake from us, okay? She got caught in a storm so I swam out to help her. Che saw us and got mad. That's it."

"That's it," she echoed.

"Yes," I sighed and reached for her face, but she slapped my hand away.

"Then why did you say you didn't know what he was talking about, River?!" Her voice got louder until my name was practically a scream.

I put my hands up in front of me. "Because I didn't think it was a big deal!"

"Clearly you did because you lied!" I rubbed my face and exhaled hard through my mouth. "I know you think

I'm stupid, but could you pretend you don't for just a second?"

"Who thinks you're stupid?" I interjected. I was panicking. "When have I ever treated you like you were stupid?"

"Right now!"

"I told you the truth, Cecelia, I did not cheat!"

"Yet!"

I don't know why I started to laugh. My girlfriend was in tears. My worst fear had come true. And I was being accused of something I didn't do. I had finally snapped. I think I laughed because she was right.

It was less of a laugh and more of a stuttering of my lungs, like a lawnmower that wouldn't start. I put my hands on my head and laughed harder.

"Are you laughing at me?" she demanded.

I shook my head but I couldn't stop.

How many times had I talked myself out of kissing Fina? How many times had Ceci been the second or third reason for that, not the first? I stared down at her, at her beautiful furious face. She was right beyond measure. And she deserved better than me.

"You're a son of a bitch, River Matthews."

She left me standing in puddle of soda, laughing into the wind.

2. BERNARDO.

"Tonight, a community is mourning a suspicious freak accident involving a fifteen year old boy. We now go live to Michelle Mathers for the story. Michelle?"

I wiped my eyes with the back of my hand as I turned up the TV.

"Chester Madrigal was an honor roll student at Thistle-wolf High School. Tomorrow night would have been his debut as a starting member of the Varsity swim team. But Che, as his many friends called him, would never make it to the meet. Madrigal was killed Friday evening by the 10:21 train coming into West Orange Station. But what has investigators scratching their heads was the amount of damage to the young man's body."

"I never seen so much damage done," a man with mirrored sunglasses told the microphone. "He looked like he been dragged three, four miles, but the station was 'bout a mile from where he was hit. Makes no sense."

"Many students take shortcuts across the tracks to avoid the traffic on County Road 33, when leaving Thistle-wolf High School. But police and parents alike are urging kids to reconsider. The train conductor is not currently under investigation."

They cut back to the man with the sunglasses. "I mean, to tell you the truth, the way he ended up, he had to have thrown himself in front of the train. There's just no other explanation. If I had to give my opinion, knowin' what I know about these tracks. Suicide." I flinched at the word.

"Chester Madrigal's family could not be reached for comment."

Che only had his mother. And us. I shut off the TV and tossed the remote control onto the table. Dia and Carmen were in the kitchen when I entered. Both leaned against the counter, arms crossed, staring at nothing.

"Is mama back?" Dia asked me. I shook my head.

"Where's Fina?" Carmen's voice was soft. I pointed above us, to her room. "Still?" I nodded. "Have you checked on her?"

"I did, this morning," Dia told him. She glanced at me and shook her head.

The sliding glass door opened and Elian came inside, his face bright red, the sleeve of his shirt wet.

"Ofelia is at the funeral home with Betta," he said. Betta was Che's mother. "I'm meeting them there to help get Betta home. She's in no shape to make any arrangements at the moment. If you could all…" He put his hands out and pushed them towards the ground. "Keep an eye on Fi."

"Sure," Dia murmured. Elian took his keys from the top of the refrigerator and went out through the garage.

Carmen put water in the kettle and turned on the stove. The silence was deafening and unsteady, with a tremor right below the surface. It was as if we all stood in a balloon. A wrong move in any direction would implode the illusion of control.

We knew better than to become close to mortals. This was the only way it ever ended.

"I hate to see Elian that way," Carmen said. He took a mug out of the cupboard. "I know he feels responsible but there was no saving the boy."

Flicker after flicker passed through Carmen's mind. Pink and red and brown and white mashed and mixed together, not a human's body but a paint spill in a hardware store. I hated to look. I couldn't stop looking. Carmen and Ofelia and Elian going to identify the body - the silver, cold, steel, dark, so cold, a freezer for meat. We can't let his mother see him this way.

When I came back into my own mind, I thought only of vultures.

5. JOSEFINA.

I sat in the first pew, my chin in my hand and my elbows on my knees. I stared at the steps which led to the altar, where a wreath of white flowers and an 8x10 photo of a 15 year old boy were still resting.

There was no open-casket service for kids who got hit by trains. His right arm and most of his torso were still being scraped off the tracks.

Even to see him one more time, painted and folded with his eyes sewn shut, would have been better than his yearbook picture propped up on an easel.

We were the only two in the room now, he and I and the moon through the stained glass of the chapel. I grew up in churches like this but hadn't been inside in ages. I knew who ran things. I knew what the order of the universe was. It made the death of someone I loved so much harder because I knew his mother thought he was in heaven.

Everyone thought he went to heaven. I wished he could be, too.

I wished it because he was supposed to be floating in the leaves outside, howling against the windows like the wind. I should have felt him in my bones, and then I would remember that souls never die, but burst into millions of bits of cosmic energy and spread through the universe, to be found in places like a heads-up penny or a cardinal.

But he wasn't there.

And heaven wasn't real.

So where was he?

I couldn't cry. Crying would have meant a release, a purging of the grief and guilt in my chest but I didn't deserve to purge.

He was dead because of me.

"Fina?" The whisper echoed in the empty chapel. I knew the voice, but I didn't move. "Are you okay?" My eyes felt glued shut.

A hand touched my back. I flinched.

"Hey, Fina, it's River." I nodded. "The priest is leaving." I nodded. "We have to leave." I shook my head absently, "Fina, I know, but we have to go. You can't be here by yourself."

"I'm not," I whispered.

"Please come with me." He was suddenly in front of me on his knees, his hands gently placed on mine. I could only muster a nod, pulled from deep within me. I didn't want to get up, I wanted to stay here with Che. He pulled me to my feet. The world spun. He looked down at me with soft eyes. I stared at the picture of Che, with River blurring in front of him. A door behind the altar slammed and someone cleared their throat. River's hand fell between my shoulder blades, guiding me.

5. JOSEFINA.

"Let's go before the priest starts yelling." His voice was gentle.

He led me out of the church, away from the emptiness. We stepped into the humid night, draped in shadows from the streetlights. In the parking lot was only lonely white truck, which I realised River was guiding me towards.

"Let me take you home," he murmured. I shook my heavy, heavy head. I couldn't go home.

"I can't see people," I managed.

"Okay. No people, just you and me. Wherever you want."

I could not believe my heart, my broken betrayer heart, when it skipped a beat as he said the words. How could it still want these trivial, meaningless things with this trivial, meaningless person?

Everyone was trivial. Everyone would end someday, except for me.

"Why are you here?" I asked, my voice breathless.

He stared ahead as we walked, enough space between us for the wind to blow through.

"He was my friend, too." He shoved his hands in his pockets.

Duh, selfish. You're not the only one who lost someone.

"Why are you still here?" I amended.

He sighed. "I couldn't talk to you with everyone there, and I wanted… I don't know…"

I shook my head. "Please don't." I cleared my throat to stop my voice from shaking. "Please."

"Okay." We stopped in front of the truck. "I was waitin' for you to come out and you never did, so I went inside."

"I didn't want to leave him." I sounded pathetic. He closed his eyes as if my words were fists, hitting him in the stomach with as much force as they hit me. I didn't stop. "He was alone when he died, and he's in there alone, and I don't want him to be, like-"

"Alone," he murmured back. I could see it there, the pain of loss, fractured in the space between his eyebrows. "I get it."

"No, you don't." He couldn't, not the way I did. He couldn't feel this guilt, the way it tore me open and changed the perspective of myself. I was a mess, held together by the memories we had created together. There was grief, and then there was loss. Che was my loss.

River opened the passenger side door and ushered me in, keeping his gaze on the ground. Absently, I climbed into the truck. If only for the moment, I could pretend that everything was okay. When the door closed, a sense of safety enveloped me like nothing else before. The windows were tinted dark, making all the lights outside a hazy blues. The seats still smelled like leather. There was a rosary hanging from the rearview mirror and a tube of purple lipstick in the cup holder. Sparrow's color.

He got in and started the engine, knocking the truck in reverse and then shifting forward, his foot staying off both pedals. We crept along the parking lot, the silence broken a couple times by my sniffling.

"My dad died when I was six," River murmured. I looked over at him. He was looking straight ahead, his curls framing his face, his knuckles clenched against the steering wheel. "He drowned out at New Smyrna." The corners of his eyes crinkled. One death always triggered another, as if grief was electricity, illuminating all the demons that people carried.

"Harsh. I'm sorry."

He half-smiled. "I don't remember him. My family told me stories, that's all I really know about him." He cleared his throat. "Where do you want me to take you?"

"You can take me home." I played with my hands, my fingers lacing and unlacing, and sniffled once more.

"I said anywhere you want, is that where you want to go?"

"No," I sighed. I had no idea where I wanted to go. Anywhere and nowhere. River made a sharp right and turned into the parking lot of Junior's.

"Okay. You think about it," he said as he took off his seatbelt. He turned the air up a notch. I pulled my knees up in the seat and stared at the cross swinging between us. I could feel his eyes on me, waiting for me to admit something.

"He's dead because of me." It fell out of my mouth before I could close it.

"You pushed him on the tracks?"

I flinched at the sarcasm in his voice. "Maybe," I said.

"Nobody goes before their time. There's a reason for everything, even if we don't see it or like it." His voice was low and flat like he had been telling himself the same words, rehearsed a thousand times by his own voice. It reminded me of a father telling their child why they couldn't have a toy they wanted.

"He got fifteen years on the earth," I told him through my teeth. "Fifteen. It was not his time."

"I don't pretend to understand, but…" He shrugged.

"But what? Tough shit? He just dies and that's it?" I demanded, heat rising to my cheeks.

"I mean, that's not what I believe." He flicked the cross hanging between us.

"Believe," I spat. "Believing is not knowing."

"It's all I got." It was all he needed.

I looked at my feet and tried not to blink. If I blinked it would be over. I would rip in half and my insides would pour out.

I didn't know how it was possible to be too full and too empty all at once.

"It's not your fault," he said after a long moment.

My chin trembled and my nostrils flared, the familiar pressure beneath my eyes threatening its dangerous game. River's fingertips touched my arm so lightly I thought I imagined it. But then everything inside me roared up-wards, a tidal wave of grief. I put my face in my hands.

"I really hurt him," I whispered.

And then I was crying. I was not daintily crying, dab-bing my eyes with a handkerchief. I was choking on my own sobs, harsh and feral sounds ripping me open and echoing with each inhale and ragged exhale. The force of my heart breaking should have busted every window in the truck.

River put his arm around me and pulled me against his chest, and I let him. His other hand rested on the back of my head as he rocked us side to side. His own breath shuddered now and then, nothing like the heaviness of me trying not to drown, but enough to let me know.

He did get it.

He tilted his head down. "It'll be okay," he whispered in my ear. His fingers rubbed my scalp.

I shook my head. "No it won't."

He pulled back and looked down at me. The green of his irises were so beautiful against the bloodshot whites of his eyes. He even cried beautifully. I wasn't so lucky.

"I know," he whispered. His hand ran down my neck and up to my cheek. He brushed a tear away with his thumb. My breath caught in my throat. He smiled.

It hit me all at once what he was doing. What this was.

I yanked away from him. "Wow," I chuckled, quickly rubbing tears off of my cheeks. "Your dedication is impressive." I opened the passenger door and jumped out.

"Wait, where are you -"

I slammed the door shut and took off down Main Street with my heart trying to catch up. Sobbing hysterically took a toll on the body. I wiped my face with my hands, then crossed my arms over my chest.

I heard another door shut. "Fina!" I didn't look at him but could hear his feet slapping asphalt as he jogged after me. I got a jolt of adrenaline but kept my pace even. I would not give him the satisfaction of a chase.

Not when he would certainly win.

"What are you doing?" he panted, inches from my back. I didn't answer. He ran in front of me and turned, stopping me short.

"What happened?" he asked. Little drops of sweat formed across his forehead, his cheeks flushed. His shirt clung to him, drenched in my tears.

I had given him an inch.

Don't ever forget who they think you are, Fina.

"You must have thought you were all in just now," I chuckled, my thoughts going a mile a minute.

"All in?" he repeated, his eyebrows furrowing deeply.

"You play a good game, letting me cry on you and all that stuff. But my best friend just died, so I'm not actually in the mood to slut it up with you." I tried to walk around him but he stepped in front of me. I uncrossed my arms and clenched my fists by my sides. I had to control the boil, it was getting dangerously close to being out of my control. "Get out of the way," I hissed, I dug my nails into the palms of my hands.

"That is not what I was trying to do," he begged. I looked up into his red-rimmed eyes. They looked back at me, soft, almost believable.

"Get serious."

"I am serious." He reached out for my hand and I yanked it back.

"Why not?"

"What?"

"Why not?" I repeated. "That's what like, all your friends want to do. Why are you any different?"

"Because I am! I care about you."

I snorted. "As if."

"I do. I wanted to be here for you."

"In my time of need, right?"

He rolled his eyes. "Give me a little credit here. I already told you I didn't believe any of that stuff."

"The stuff your friends made up? Why wouldn't you?"

He smirked. "Well…"

"Well?" I demanded.

"I happen to know you have a tattoo. And anytime the boys have bragged about you, they couldn't tell me where it was."

"You don't have to get naked to be a whore," I retorted.

"You're right. And even if they were all telling the truth, I don't care. I'm here to make sure you're okay, and get you home safe. Can I please do that?"

Say no. You say no, and you walk home. I looked up at him. Big mistake. Those eyes were what got me into this in the first place.

River raised his eyebrows, waiting. Why did that make my hands shake?

I rolled my eyes. "Whatever, fine."

We headed back to the truck together in silence.

I came down little by little, back to crippling reality. I wrapped my fingers under the hem of my dress. Don't pretend this is real. What's real is Che is dead. What's real is who you two are in the daylight, in the hallways. Meaningless and trivial.

The back of my hand brushed River's, completely by accident. He glanced down at me and smiled. Back up I went. If it was meaningless then it was also harmless.

If it was trivial it could be temporary. Everything was temporary, remember? Che was gone, and Che was not coming back. But River was here. For this one night it was him and I. If I knew it was a game then it wouldn't hurt when it was over.

Reality could wait until tomorrow.

We got back into the truck. River started the engine and reached up to pull the gear shift into drive. I put my hand over his to stop him.

"I care about you, too," I said quietly, almost hoping he didn't hear me.

He looked at our hands. "I know."

"How?" I didn't move.

"Because of how you look at me." He held my stare and nodded slowly. "Yeah, like that." He took my hand and laced his fingers in mine, then rested them on the seat between us.

My heart was pounding in my ears. I looked out the windshield so I couldn't get lost in his eyes again.

"Why were you cryin' at the game?" he asked me.

Tears welled up again. I sighed. "Because Che was acting insane, and he kissed me and I yelled at him. And he yelled back." I sniffed and rubbed at my eyes.

"That's why you think it's your fault," he murmured. The pity in his voice almost crushed me. I could only nod. "It was a freak accident, Fina."

I just nodded again. He didn't know about the dreams.

"I don't think your girlfriend would appreciate this." I glanced down at our hands. I didn't pull away. I wasn't going to.

5. JOSEFINA.

"I don't have a girlfriend." His voice was as soft as his thumb, rubbing circles in the back of my hand. He stared at the steering wheel.

"What?"

"We broke up at the game."

"Why?" It rushed out before I could stop it. I knew. I needed to hear it. My chest hurt from the force of my own heart.

"You know why," he chuckled. I shook my head. He looked down at me. "Because of this." He squeezed my hand.

"What is this?" I swallowed hard. My stomach tightened as I remembered what I'd said to him the last time he asked me the same question. He smiled and looked out the windshield.

"This… connection. Or, reaction, I guess. Like you turned on all the lights." There was space that lingered at the end of his sentence.

I crossed my ankles tight because my legs were shaking, my knees bouncing so hard they threatened to smash into the glove box.

"Like brand new old friends," I said, almost in a whisper.

"You get it, of course you get it."

"I feel it, too." He looked at me, eyebrows raised. I nodded. "I don't cry on just anyone's shirt."

He chuckled. "You can cry on my shirt any day."

A stab of sweetness hit the back of my throat and was immediately coated by bitter truth.

"No I can't." I said it with a smile but there was no humor in my words. I squeezed his hand. "You could never hold my hand in front of your friends."

But the tiniest, pettiest part of me wanted him to. I wanted him to want me, so much he couldn't hide it. I wanted the bitter rivalry that had been written in the stars to be swept away by him and I.

I also kind of wanted a reason to kill Autumn and Ivy.

His eyelashes cast shadows on his cheeks as he looked down at his legs. His free hand picked at some loose bits of leather on the driver's side door.

"I wish I could. You deserve that, so much more than that. I wish I was braver. But I'm not." His eyebrows pitched together. "I have a lot to live up to in Barton. My family runs everything there and it's… my future. A girl like you would get in the way."

"A girl like me?"

"A girl with a voice that haunts my dreams." My insides went molten. "I haven't stopped thinking about you since the moment we met. You make me feel so…"

He gripped my hand and exhaled raggedly.

"So what?" I breathed. I couldn't push air out of my mouth or nose. Everything below my neck had seized up.

He shut his eyes. "Alive," he whispered.

I leaned over and kissed his cheek. The stubble on his face scraped my lips. He smelled like rosemary pulled right from the garden, wet dirt mixed with pine. It made me smile against his skin.

5. JOSEFINA.

I started to sit back when he turned to me. He took my face between his hands. I wanted to remind myself to breathe but it was too late. I looked at his mouth, trying to swallow the lump in my throat.

His eyes searched my face.

"Can I kiss you?" He was so close to me the words brushed my bottom lip. I was melting off my bones.

I closed the millimeter of space between us and pressed my lips to his.

ACT II.

...Longing and love, a disenkindled fire,
And memory a bottomless gulf of mire,
And love a fount of tears outrunning measure;
Oh vanity of vanities, desire!
Now from my heart, love's deathbed, trickles, trickles,
Drop by drop slowly, drop by drop of fire,
The dross of life, of love, of spent desire;
Alas, my rose of life gone all to prickles,–
Oh vanity of vanities, desire!
Oh vanity of vanities, desire;
Stunting my hope which might have strained up
higher,
Turning my garden plot to barren mire;
Oh death-struck love, oh disenkindled fire,
Oh vanity of vanities, desire!
Christina Rossetti, "Soeur Louise de la Misericorde"

6. RIVER

Three honey buns. A pack of sunflower seeds. A 64 ounce Cherry Coke. A scoop of hard-boiled peanuts from the crock-pot near the shriveled hot dogs. I got behind Sparrow in line with my bounty, my stomach yelling at me. She laughed too loud at Jared - he was never funny enough to warrant that kind of laugh. She leaned over the counter and pointed her long, silver nail behind him. He sighed and reached for the white box with the red lid.

"Can't keep doin' this, Jackson," he said with a smile as he scanned the cigarettes. "That daddy of yours is gonna wring my neck."

Sparrow toyed with the cross on her necklace. "What my daddy don't know won't hurt 'em," she murmured, batting her lashes. I sighed. She threw a couple bucks his way and shoved the cigarettes into her bag. I dropped my goods on the counter.

"You hear me try to tell her no, don'tcha, River?" He scanned the last honey bun and pulled out a plastic bag. "$7.02."

"Don't hear nothin'," I muttered. Small talk with Jared was enough to make me want to kill. Plus I was starving.

I snatched the bag from Jared and hustled Sparrow out the door. "I got tutoring, space cadet." I said as we approached the truck.

"You're the one who couldn't wait an hour to get a stupid honey bun," she replied. We got into the truck.

"I'm starving," I retorted as I ripped open one of the honey buns.

"Besides, you got yourself a honey bun waiting at the school, anyway," she chuckled. I took off. Wailer. Third Street. The 33.

I'd turned a corner from infatuated to obsessed. I would focus on one thing and then my head would go: Fina Fina Fina.

"Don't know what you're talkin' about." She rolled down the window and smacked the pack of cigarettes against her palm. She took one out and put it between her lips. "Better be quick. I'm not going down for you again." I took a gulp of cold, sweet, fizzy goodness.

"Yeah yeah," she muttered around the cigarette as she lit up. She took a long drag and then hung it out the window.

Remington. Shell Court. I hit my brakes as asphalt became dirt. Sparrow tossed her cigarette into the woods as we came up on the gate.

"You can drop me here." The gate opened for us. She looked at me as she undid her seatbelt. "Feel better, okay?"

I smiled. "I'm good."

She glanced at the desecrated wrappers on the seat beside me.

I reached across and shut the door.

I kept the window down as I drove back up to school so I could throw the peanut shells out. The wind sent chills through me. I'd been so cold this morning I'd even worn a jacket. It was a windbreaker on the outside, olive green and waterproof, and a grey sweatshirt material on the inside. I zipped it a little higher and took a drink of my soda. I never got sick. Good soldiers didn't get sick.

A pang of guilt caught me off-guard as I parked at the school.

Maybe I wasn't such a good soldier anymore.

I finished the last honey bun as I hurried across the courtyard. It was already 15 after.

I tossed the wrapper in the trash outside the music building and took another huge gulp of Cherry Coke. I tiptoed down the hall to Mr. Hart's room, hoping to catch Fina playing.

She wasn't. I opened the door.

She sat at the table, her back to me. Her hands were busy in front of her.

"You're late." Her voice was thick.

"Told you I would be," I replied. She nodded. "What's wrong?"

"Nothing." She sniffed. I pulled a chair up to the table and tossed my stuff on the floor.

"Liar." She stared at the tabletop. I unbuttoned my jacket. "Fina," I reached out and ran my finger along the thin sleeve of her shirt. She sighed. I pulled off my jacket and let it fall to the floor, too - she was warm enough for the both of us.

"It's Che," she said after a long moment. "But it's fine." She handed me a packet. "Hart wanted me to go over this with you before your placement test."

"It's not fine," I said as I dug a pencil out of my bookbag. "Talk to me."

"I…" She sighed again. "I guess I didn't realize how big a part of my life he was until he wasn't there anymore. Being back here without him doesn't feel right, you know?"

I nodded. The less I spoke, the more she would.

"And the way things ended up with me and him…" I gripped my pencil as her voice tightened. "Makes me feel like shit."

I reached for her hand.

Instead I knocked my drink over into her lap.

She jumped to her feet.

"Oh, no!" I stood up and looked around for something, anything. I found a roll of paper towels near the chalkboard and ran them to her. "I'm so sorry!" She took a handful and blotted at her silky white top. It clung to her stomach, a spreading brown stain attaching it to her skin. She dried her bare thighs. "I'm really sorry, I'm so so sorry." I picked up her bag and dumped it on the table, trying to salvage its contents from the puddle.

A few textbooks tumbled out, mostly unscathed. One of the three notebooks looked to be a lost cause. A handful of half-empty packs of gum seemed to have survived. A black leather wallet skidded across the tabletop.

I looked at her. She was standing over the trash can in only a tank top, wringing out her shirt. I watched as she rolled up the tank top, exposing her stomach. I could see the bottom of her tattoo.

She glanced at me and rolled her eyes.

I came back down. "Sorry, just... what is your tattoo?"

"The Aries constellation," she replied.

I blinked. "Was that English?"

She rolled her eyes again, but now she smiled. "Stars in the sky make a pattern sometimes. When I was born, this was the pattern in the sky." She let go of her shirt, a wrinkled, damp mess.

I picked up my jacket and went over to her. "Here, you can wear this. I'm so sorry," I said for the fifteenth time.

She slid my jacket on and zipped the inside, leaving the buttons undone. It hung down near her knees. The cuffs of the sleeves hid her hands, making her look like a child. I chuckled.

"Don't laugh at me." She whipped me with one of the humongous sleeves. "Get back to work." She flung the sleeve towards the table. "What's the damage?" she asked as we went back over.

"I think this notebook's seen its last days," I said as I handed it to her. She chucked it at the garbage can and it went straight in. "Very nice!"

"Thanks." She pulled a long ream of paper towels and shoved them into her bag, blotting the wet spots.

I straightened up the pile of her things. There was a clear insert in her wallet. As I shook the drops off, a tiny version of the girl in front of me stared out.

New York State. Driver License. Camejo, Josefina T.

She held her hand out. I gave her the wallet.

"It never occurred to me that Fina was short for something," I murmured. "What's the T for?"

"Teresita," she said.

"Josefina Teresita. Sounds like a princess or something."

"Hosefina," she corrected. "And thanks."

"Do you miss New York?" I asked her as I dried the residual streaks on the table.

"A little. I liked the snow. I never saw it growing up so, it was cool."

"I've never seen snow," Christmas here was muggy, dark, and almost always had rain. I'd seen store windows decorated with fake snow; Christmas specials with snowmen and reindeer. We didn't do Santa Claus. But snow was still a beautiful foreign thing to me, so other and unknown it captured my imagination.

Like the girl sitting next to me.

"It's peaceful," she replied. She tossed the paper towels in the trash.

"So, you're not from New York."

She shook her head. "California."

"For real?" She nodded. "That's awesome! Do you know how to surf?"

She rolled her eyes. "Do you?"

"No, but I didn't grow up at the beach," I said,

"Neither did I," she chuckled. "California's pretty big, you know. It's not all beaches. I went like, twice a year max."

"I love the beach," I sighed. "We never go, though. Makes us miss my dad too much, I think."

6. RIVER.

"I get that," she replied.

Memories, blurry and larger than life, filled my mind. Getting slammed by a wave and my dad's strong arms pulling me out as I coughed. The taste of saltwater, the burn of it in my nose. How happy my dad was when he carried me out past the crest. He'd throw me up in the air and I'd crash down into the water. He'd always catch me before my face went under. It was one of the few memories of him that I had.

I cleared my throat. "Where did you grow up?"

"Glendale, it's near L.A."

"L.A., huh? Is that why you talk like you talk?"

"How do I talk?" she demanded.

"In a cute way," I tried not to smile "Unexpected, but cute."

"Speak fer yerself," she drawled, over exaggerating her mouth movements.

"I do not talk like that." She shrugged. "Stop making fun of me and tell me about L.A."

"Noisy," she muttered. "Grody. Way too much traffic. Driving in L.A. is like wishing to have a heart attack or something. The freeways are total death traps."

"Whereas here you have no freeways."

She smiled. "Which isn't great, either. I'm like way too aggressive for these country back roads."

"In your little racecar," I chuckled.

She pushed me. "Listen, not all of us want them big ol' pickups with the hemi and the drop or whatever." She put it on even thicker this time. "I'm not haulin' pigs er nothin'."

"When have I ever had a pig in my truck?" I chuckled, raising an eyebrow at her.

"I haven't known you that long, maybe you've hauled pigs all your life."

I rolled my eyes. "Even if I did, you don't put them in the bed of the truck. You get a..." I trailed off as she howled with laughter. "Okay, you know what? I won't even finish that."

"No, please do!" she cackled. I pushed her over. She caught herself on the table edge and gasped for air, her whole body shaking.

"You are such a brat," I muttered.

"No," she sighed. "A princess, remember?" She wiped beneath her eyes as her laughter subsided.

"I take it back," I told her.

She gasped. "You take it back?" I nodded. "I liked it."

"Well when you act like a brat you get called a brat," I retorted, grinning.

She turned to me. "How can I ever make it up to you?" She ran the back of her fingers along my jawline.

"Don't flirt with me," I whispered. The pit of my stomach churned. and I bit down on my bottom lip to calm it.

"Me? Never," she murmured as she scratched my stubble. "I like this." I may as well have been kicking my hind leg like a dog.

I turned my head and pressed my lips to the inside of her wrist, inhaling her perfume. Her fingers grazed the hair behind my ear. I held her arm in place and kissed her wrist again, up to her palm. Her fingers knotted in my hair. I stopped breathing.

I met her eyes, half-lidded under heavy lashes. Her mouth - her blinding mouth - was open slightly. Her chest heaved.

My shaking hand cupped her chin. "Can I kiss you?" I asked, but I was already closing the space between us.

I'd hoped once the fire from the newness of the first time wore off, it would be easier to kiss Fina without thinking I might die. But it wasn't. From the pit of my stomach to the inside of my mouth, I was scorched. The red-hot center of her, always so warm, always untouchable - it was almost unbearable.

She did taste like honey, and I wanted to pour her down my throat.

Just like the night of the funeral, my atoms were pulled towards her. I was half-standing, half-leaning over her body. One hand on the table, the other on the back of her chair. I could taste her tongue sliding between her lips, not full-on, but enough to make me want to beg.

Her other hand gripped the front of my shirt.

I pulled her leg up around me. I tried to open my eyes, but I could only focus on the burning in my mouth.

I took my hand off the table and put it on her thigh. She broke away as I slid it up her leg.

"Wait," she gasped against my cheek. I took her hand off my chest and looped it around my neck.

"Okay," I murmured, willing her mouth back to mine by rubbing our noses together. I caught her lower lip and bit it gently. Chills ran through me. I did it again, a little harder. My hand met the bottom of her skirt.

"Wait, wait," she sighed. She pushed my hand down to her knee.

I nodded. "Okay," I said again. I kissed the nook between her neck and her shoulder. My brain was melting from the heat, running out of my ears. The anticipation, the slow-build, was better than anything I could have imagined. I thought I would implode.

She put her hands on my chest and pushed, hard. I sat back, my hands up by my ears.

"Okay, okay."

"Stop." She straightened her skirt and turned back to the table.

"Sorry, I didn't know you wanted me to… stop." I cleared my throat and wiped my mouth with the back of my hand

"What do you think wait means?"

"I was waiting," I chuckled. "I thought you meant slower, not… stop. I'm sorry." I ducked my head and caught her eyes. "Okay? I guess I'm just… confused."

"By the word no?" She put her things back in her bag, but not before she pulled a stick of gum from one of the packs.

I stared at the table. "I thought you liked me," I murmured.

"I do," she replied as she chewed. "But I don't do that."

"Do that?" I repeated. I furrowed my eyebrows. "Do what?"

I glanced up in time for her to roll her eyes at me. "That."

"You don't?" I chuckled.

"Your surprise isn't totally insulting, don't worry," she snapped.

"Hey, sorry," I said, putting my hands up again. "It's just funny. All the Barton girls saying that stuff about you when you're just like them."

"First of all, not a compliment," she muttered. I smiled. "Second of all, don't tell me Clay is really dating a girl who doesn't put out. He's a creep."

"Barton girls don't give it away 'til the wedding day. Can't face the Heavenly Father if you're not wearing white." With a pang, I thought of Sparrow. She'd never get away with white.

She raised her eyebrows. "Wait, so you can feel me up but God forbid a Barton girl get felt up?"

I sighed. "Listen, when you're a guy…"

"Stop whatever you're about to say because I'm sure it's totally archaic," she interjected.

"I don't know why you're getting mad, I think a girl waiting for marriage is awesome."

"But you don't have to wait. Seems like a double standard."

"I mean, I tried to tell you why but you called me archaic." I didn't know what that meant, but I knew it wasn't nice.

She crossed her arms. "Plus, I'm not waiting for anything. I just don't."

"Is it a witch thing?" It spilled out before I could stop it. I bit down on my bottom lip and waited for lightning to strike me dead.

She shook her head. "No, it's a Fina thing." She spun her bracelets around.

"What about…" I pointed at my eye. In this room I could always see it. It must've been how we stared at one another. That biting blue sliver shone up at me like a piece of broken glass.

"Yeah, it's a Marcan de bruja. A witch mark. If you're born with it, and you're touched by magic, then you become a witch."

Chosen. Like us.

"Will you tell me another witch thing?" I whispered.

She leaned closer to me. "We can walk on water."

I rolled my eyes. "Okay," I muttered.

"We just say gradior. And the water is like concrete under us."

"Whatever," I chuckled. "All the stuff you can probably tell me and you want to pull my leg? Brat." I nudged her with my shoulder.

"I'm not pulling your leg."

"Fina. I saved you from drowning. I know you're lying."

She smiled her Mona Lisa smile. "You saved me… because I wanted you to save me."

I looked down at her, my mouth falling open. "You didn't need my help at all." She shook her head. "Brat." I smacked the "t" sound.

"I'd say I'm more of a creative genius, honestly. Not like I was getting anywhere near you otherwise. I had to take the chances I got, you know?"

"Case and point." I gestured around us.

She looked around. "Wait a second." She pulled her phone from her pocket and gasped. "Dude it's seven!"

"Wait, what?" I demanded. I checked my own phone. "How did that happen?"

"I don't know," she chuckled. She picked up her bag and swung it over her shoulder. We left the classroom.

She locked up behind us as I checked to see if the coast was clear. I slipped my hand into hers as we started walking. It felt right, being among these hallways and lockers with her next to me. I glanced down at her as we headed to the parking lot.

"What are you looking at?" she asked.

"You said you liked me, y'know that?"

She shook her head. "I so did not."

"You so did," I replied. "I can't believe you have a crush on me, Fina, that's so cute."

"As if," she chuckled as we got to our cars. "You're the one that has a crush on me."

"As if," I mimicked.

She pushed me toward my truck and opened the passenger side of her little red convertible, throwing her disheveled bookbag inside.

"Look, let's just agree to disagree," I told her. "I won't tell anyone about your little crush, okay?"

She closed the space between us and threw light, slow punches at me. I flinched and grunted as if they were landing, backing up until I was against my truck.

"Say sorry!" she demanded. "Say sorry!"

I grabbed her wrists and pulled her tight against me. "Or what?" I murmured.

She narrowed her eyes at me, but that wicked little grin wouldn't budge.

She touched her lips to mine, so soft it hurt, and then walked away.

"Hey, where you goin' with my jacket?" I called.

"Looks better on me," she said without turning around.

"You're still a brat!" I hollered as she shut her door behind her. She blew me a kiss and took off.

I drove home slow, trying to come down from the high she'd given me. I couldn't stop smiling, even as the chills got my teeth chattering. My stomach was growling by the time I got through the Barton gates. But I wasn't sure what I wanted. I was craving a taste I couldn't place.

Mom and Papa were at Chapel when I got home. A pot of chicken and dumplings was still steaming on the stove. It was my favorite, but my stomach turned at the thought.

I hunted through the kitchen, leaving cabinets and drawers open as I searched for the thing I needed, feral, like an animal. My vision was blurring, I was so hungry. I thought I would faint.

I opened the fridge and my legs gave out. I knelt in the cold air and pulled a defrosted steak off the bloody plate on the bottom shelf.

I ripped off a hunk of raw meat with my teeth.

Then I blacked out.

6. JOSEFINA.

"I say he knocked it over on purpose." Dia shoved more rice and beans in her mouth. She pointed with her fork towards me, drips of juice falling onto the table. "Backhanded bullying," she said around a mouthful of food.

I pulled the jacket tighter around me, trying sneak a whiff of it in the process. "I don't think so." I thought for a moment, mulling the idea around in my head. "I don't know." I stabbed at a shrimp.

"Or he wanted you to take your shirt off." Dia took another forkful to her mouth.

I rolled my eyes, hoping my cheeks didn't turn red. "Maybe. He stares at me like, a lot."

"Well you're a big-eared alien freak," Carmen interjected as he stood up from the table. "I'd stare, too."

I nodded. "Thanks." Carmen carried his dishes into the kitchen.

"At any rate," Dia continued through a yawn. "The jacket's great. I might have to borrow it if it ever gets cold enough here to warrant a jacket."

"That's the other thing," Carmen called as he came back into the dining room. "Why was he wearing a jacket?"

"These locals wear jackets for anything," Dia replied. "You could sneeze and they'd pull out scarves because they felt a breeze."

Carmen considered. "The jacket is nice." He glanced down the table at two untouched plates - one in Ofelia's spot, one in Elian's spot. "Do you think I should give up?"

"I was going to head over in a minute." I stood. "I can bring it to them."

"Put it away," Dia muttered as she scraped the last of the rice from her plate. "I'm sure they're helping Betta eat all the casseroles she's been given. Such a bizarre ritual of grief, don't you think? Sorry about your dead son, here's a tuna casserole."

"Dude!" I gasped.

She frowned at me. "It's true."

I went into the kitchen and dropped my dishes in the sink. I gripped the sides of the porcelain and took a deep breath. There was a lump in my throat.

I hadn't heard anyone directly say Che was dead, they all kept saying gone. I knew where he had gone, but the word dead was like pouring concrete over his memory and letting it dry. There were no more memories to be made with a dead person.

I ran the water as cold as it could go and rinsed my hands. I dabbed my face and took another deep breath.

I did not lose my child. This was not about me.

I shut off the spigot and dried my hands on the towel hanging from the oven handle.

Dia came into the kitchen. "Sorry," she murmured. I nodded, staring out the kitchen window. "What are you looking at?" Dia's voice got closer. "Oh, absolutely not!" she exclaimed. She started flinging open cabinets. "Where's the bleach? I've had it with that stupid thing."

"What stupid thing?" I asked.

"That forsaken bird! It's been pecking at my bedroom window for the last three nights! I'm killing it!"

I looked again, but there was no bird. In fact, I hadn't seen it to begin with.

"Good luck," I said. "I'm off to Betta's."

"Good luck yourself," she muttered, her head deep in a drawer. I grabbed my keys off the refrigerator and picked up my bookbag from the foyer as I slipped on my sandals.

I put my hand on the doorknob as three soft knocks landed on the other side. I furrowed my eyebrows, opening the door a sliver.

A broad-shouldered silhouette was descending the stairs. I flipped on the porch light and it froze in place.

"River?" I squinted between the raindrops. He kept walking, faster than before. "Wait!"

I closed the door behind me and ran down the steps towards him. I slipped on the fourth stair and caught myself on the railing, crying out as my legs slid away from me. I gripped the banister harder, my nails digging into the wood until they bent back. The fifth stair scraped the back of my leg as I landed, hard.

"Might have hurt less to just fall."

I glared up at him. His hair was soaking wet, the curls heavy. His shirt stuck to his skin, shadows from the trees making black patches on his chest and stomach.

"Well if I didn't have to chase you this wouldn't have happened." I got to my feet carefully, rubbing the stinging spot below my skirt. "What are you doing here?"

"I need help." I couldn't see his face from the shadows.

"Come here, River."

"I need help," he repeated.

I came down the stairs. "What's wrong?" He took a few steps towards me, until the light from the porch swallowed us both.

The shadows on his shirt were stains. Deep, wet, stains. The collar of his shirt was brown and red, a waterfall from the bottom half of his face. Like he had bitten his tongue off. He rubbed his forehead with the heel of his hand. His nails were filthy, caked with mud and blood and something else I didn't want to think about. A fresh red streak ran across his eyebrow as he dropped his arm to his side.

It must have been raining blood. I held my hand out to catch some. It was the only way he could still be standing with so much blood on him.

My hands caught only water from the sky.

I looked him up and down as my brain short-circuited. He didn't speak. His hands were clenched in fists at his side.

"I need help," he said again, softly. I reached out my hand, and it hung in the air between us. I was terrified to touch him. If I touched him then I would feel the blood and it would all be real. For now it was only a mirage of nightmares.

"What happened?" I could barely hear myself.

6. JOSEFINA.

River dropped to his knees. He laced his fingers behind his neck, folded in on himself, and screamed into his legs.

Chills sprung up across my entire body. The terror in his voice made my eyes fill with tears. He started panting between hysterics, his back spasming with each shock of pain.

I threw my bag over the porch rail and knelt down in front of him. "Hey," I murmured. He leaned forward and gripped my hands, his nails digging into my skin. I flinched but he didn't let go.

"I don't know what I did," he wheezed. I tried to shake him off but he dug deeper. It was starting to sting.

"It's okay. Look at me." He shook his head. "You're hurting me." He sniffed and his body trembled. I yanked my arms back but he hung on. "River, let me go." My heart beat was growing faster out of desperation.

And then I was on the ground. My brain rattled around in my skull as my head smashed into the brick. Rain dripped into my nose as I gasped. I coughed and rolled onto my side, my head spinning as I sat up.

A clump of shadows moved fitfully on the far side of the yard. I stood and ran to them.

"We have to," a familiar voice said, wispy and raw.

"I can't," River sobbed.

"Sparrow?" I whispered.

One of the shadows rose up and became the outline of a girl. Her teeth reflected in the barely-there glint of a streetlight as she grinned.

"Hi," she said.

"What's going on?"

"What are you talking about?" Her voice was high, dismissive.

I glanced behind her at the writhing pile that was her best friend.

"What's wrong with him?"

"What do you mean?" Her voice stayed light, pleasant, never faltering.

"He's hurt." She turned her head to look at him and the light caught bright red streaks on her neck. The blood and rain mingled on her skin and ran down her grey shirt in rivulets, soaking into the fabric. It made it look like a monster had ripped into her with its claws.

"You too." I whispered, taking a faltering step back. "What's happening?"

"We're fine. It's time for us to go home."

River sprang to his feet, his hands out in front of him. "I can't go home." It was a hypnotic drone. "I can't go home."

"You're not supposed to leave home," Sparrow said through gritted teeth.

"I can't go back," he repeated.

"You're gonna get me in even more trouble River!" Her voice bounced off the walls and rattled the tree branches above us. I covered her mouth with my hand and pulled her away from the house.

"Shh!" I looked up at the windows. No curtains moved. I let go of Sparrow. "Let my mom help you -"

"We're fine," Sparrow interjected, her voice hard.

"Listen, just come inside -"

"No." Her tone cut me.

"Why?"

"Because if they come looking for us and find us here
-"

"They can deal with it. Now come on." I grabbed her hand and cringed as stickiness sloshed between our interlocked fingers. I started to the house and was yanked back when she didn't move.

"Sparrow," I hissed.

"River?" she whimpered. I looked down where he was sitting.

Where he had been sitting.

I scanned the yard. Up by the porch. Near the gates, the wall.

Nothing.

"Where -"

"River!" Sparrow took off towards the back of the property.

"Sparrow!" I called, running after her.

"River!" She sprinted over the garden beds and the gnarled tree roots, tearing up the plants in her path, her long legs carrying her entirely too fast. My feet sloshed awkwardly in the mud as I tried to keep up, the rain growing harder.

She stopped short a few yards ahead of me, right before the grass became dirt. Her head swiveled left and right.

There was a banging noise from near the shore. The sound of a cheap pot hitting a frying pan, steel on tin. Sparrow was gone again, running to the noise.

The boathouse.

River was beating against the door of the boathouse. Every fist he drove into it left a dent streaked with red. He gripped the latch and tore at it with his fingers. He screamed, low and guttural from his core like a wild animal.

Sparrow reached him as he busted through, one of the hinges going flying. She had a fistful of River's shirt in one hand when I got got close to her. She dug her heels into the ground and grabbed the doorframe with the other hand.

Over their heads I locked eyes with Bernardo, who stood frozen against the back wall.

I put my hand out. "Consido!"

River should have fallen to the ground, unable to stand. River should not have been lunging for my brother as I said it, over and over again, willing it to work.

"Consido!" My spell was not working.

I grabbed Sparrow's arm and tried to pull them out of the boathouse.

"Stop!" She twisted her hand in River's shirt, tightening her grip. "Let go!"

"Get him out of there!"

"Let me go!"

"Pull harder!"

Sparrow barreled into me and we fell to the ground. There was a sharp stabbing in my hand. She put her hands out to catch her fall and something dropped in my lap.

Shreds of white cotton.

6. JOSEFINA.

Invisible hands squeezed my throat, my chest. Terror seized my body and rooted me to the ground. I watched Sparrow get to her feet and sprint back to the boathouse.

Bernardo's in trouble he's in trouble get up get up now get up.

But the blood, the sound of River's fingernails on the door latch, the way he screamed.

The blood.

Get up Fina.

Get up now and help your brother.

My fingers stuck to the palm of my hand. I smelled pennies.

Get. Up.

My legs were static but they moved. I couldn't feel them beneath me but they moved on their own. I hobbled into the boathouse.

As I stepped through the doorframe River fell to the ground, clutching his face. Sparrow stood between him and Bernardo, her back arched like a feral cat. River scrambled backwards on his hands, his eyes glued to her and she stared down at him, her chest heaving.

River got to his feet and turned to me, his eyes glued to my hand. I glanced down; It was bleeding.

He'd barely flinched in my direction before I kicked him in the leg, his knees buckling underneath him. Sparrow moved fast, throwing her body weight on top of him. They struggled in the small space until he was face up and she was pinning his stomach to the ground with her knee. Her hands held onto his shoulder.

"River!"

River keened low in his throat and thrashed beneath her.

"River stop," Sparrow commanded.

"I can't." His voice sounded like it came through a radio tuned between two different stations. He rocked his entire body, his head bouncing against the concrete.

"What is he doing?" I leaned over to look at his face.

"Get away," Sparrow snapped. I jumped back. He thrashed harder; over and over his head slapped against the solid ground.

"Stop him," I whimpered, my heart going crazy against my ribs.

There was one final thud and then River stopped moving.

Sparrow slid off him and sat against the wall, clutching one arm against her chest. She closed her eyes and sighed. I knelt beside her and put my hand on her shoulder.

She shook her head. "I can't tell you."

"Sparrow. Yes you -"

"No I can't." Her voice was her own again, wispy, light, nothingness.

"Are you in trouble?" I looked at her neck, at the dried blood which flaked off now like dead skin.

"I will be," she sighed. "No one's ever gotten away."

"Gotten away?" Bernardo repeated. "From what?" She didn't answer. "You came here, you made it our business."

"I'm sorry -"

"Stop apologizing and tell me the truth! He tried to kill me!"

"I wouldn't have let him!" Sparrow retorted, as if that fact made it better.

"That's not the point!"

"If they find out I told you, I'm dead."

"As if we're running to tell them," I muttered, gesturing to River lying knocked out on the grass, the rain crashing around us.

"He changed. He got away from me. I need to get him back to Barton."

"He changed. That's your explanation. He just like, changed?" I demanded. "Clearly, he's changed. He tried to kill my brother; he ripped a door off its hinges!"

I went cold from my scalp through to my soul.

"That's not his blood," I whispered. "Is it?" I asked but I knew.

She shrugged. "Some of it might be. Some's mine. Smells like a cat's, maybe a rabbit."

"Smells like a cat's," I repeated. "What kind of cult ritual gone wrong is this?" I got to my feet. "You have got to be kid -"

LOOK.

I snapped my jaw shut and looked at Bernardo. He was seeing what I wasn't. Not the blood dripping from Sparrow's arm, or from my own had. Not the crime scene on River's clothes.

He was looking at River's face, at the two white pinpricks of teeth against his bottom lip.

I swayed with the room and pressed my hand to the wall to come back. All the blood in my body rushed to my toes.

"Vampires," Bernardo whispered.

I almost laughed.

They wore crosses.

But then I looked at River's mouth, at the teeth - fangs, actual fangs - and the laugh died in my throat.

"No," Sparrow replied.

"No," I sighed. Of course not.

"Changed. The dead shall be raised incorruptible, and we shall be Changed," she murmured - recited. Those words weren't hers.

"We." I heard my voice but didn't feel my mouth move. I glanced at my hand and wiped the blood on my skirt. Two perfect holes, side by side. "You're one, too."

"That was an accident." She didn't look at me.

"I had no clue," Bernardo whispered. He slid down the wall until he was sitting, shaking his head slowly. "No clue."

"You didn't want to know," Sparrow replied. "You could have, if you wanted to. You didn't."

"You drink blood," he said.

"We do."

"Everyone in Barton?" I asked.

"Everyone born Chosen."

"How do you know who's born Chosen?"

"You don't. Until…" She nudged River with her foot.

"Is he dead?" Bernardo asked. I couldn't breathe.

"Sorta."

My heart stopped. "What?"

"We all die. But we come back." She smiled, as if that made it okay. "Like Jesus or the cut-off head of a worm." She staggered to her feet.

"You're immortal," Bernardo breathed.

She shrugged. "Chosen."

My heart leapt to life, beating too fast. I knew we couldn't be the only ones in the whole universe. Hope, against all reason, started to drown my horror. We weren't alone.

She grabbed River's arms and dragged him out of the boathouse. I followed after her, stepping over the trail of blood in their wake.

"Wait!" I called. She continued pulling a man twice her weight as if he were an empty wheelbarrow. "Wait, how are you going to get home? You can't just like, pull an unconscious body down the road."

When she didn't answer, I picked up his feet. I could only barely keep them from dragging through the muddy yard. We rounded the corner of the house. I dropped River's legs and ran ahead to ensure no one had come outside.

The yard was empty, but a blue pickup truck was parked outside the gates.

Sparrow made a noise like she'd been punched in the stomach.

"What?" I hissed.

"My dad," she moaned. She hauled River along as she spoke. "My dad left Barton. Oh, I'm so dead."

"I'll help you get him in the -"

"Fina," she chuckled. "No you won't. You don't do anything. If River asks to see you, or throws rocks at your window, or whatever lame thing you guys do, you say no. Okay? Please."

I looked down at River. His head was slumped onto his chest, his eyes shut gently, and blood dribbled from his mouth onto his shirt. I shook the sleeve of his jacket up over my hand as it slipped. He looked peaceful, even with blood covering the bottom of his face.

Sparrow's smile was soft, sad, when she met my eyes. "It was fun being your friend."

"Thanks," I breathed, not really sure what to say, what to do.

"Bye." She dragged his body up the driveway. I cringed to think what his back would look like after being slid over the bricks.

And then I remembered Bernardo.

I ran back towards the boathouse and slipped in something wet on the grass, almost falling. I steadied myself and continued walking, but whatever I had stepped in remained between my toes.

I looked down and tears sprang to my eyes, my hand instinctively covering my mouth. There was a dead kitten beside my foot. I tiptoed around the carcass and took off to the boathouse once more, the image of blood coating River's front painted in my mind.

I paused in the open doorway. Bernardo had put his canvases and paints in a stack on the table. He poured vinegar from a vat onto the blood-streaked floor and used his t-shirt to scrub at the carnage.

My spell didn't work on them. I felt as if the air itself had been cursed. If we spoke about it aloud, it would stir up the evil in the world.

He stopped scrubbing. Let's hope we never have to use them again.

What do we tell everyone?

Nothing. He turned back to the floor. They will want to move. Do you want to move?

I froze. This was Rhiannon's house. We belonged here. I love this place.

So do I. So we don't tell. Not ever.

I grabbed a broom from the corner and swept the pink vinegar out into the flooded yard.

You spilled some paint.

He locked eyes with me and nodded.

I spilled some paint.

7. RIVER

"You did it!" Sparrow clapped and ran to me. I held the squirming squirrel in my hands. Its pulse thudded wildly against my scratched up fingers.

"I did? That was easier than I thought."

She grinned. "Of course it was. It's instinct." She put her hand over mine. "And then you-" She squeezed, the bones of the squirrel's neck snapped like toothpicks. I flinched. "It's easier at first if they're dead."

"And then-" I put my mouth on the roundest part of the squirrel's belly. My teeth slashed through fur, then skin, then muscle and bone and -

I closed my eyes. The warmth of Heaven filled my mouth and exploded against my tongue, like a jelly filled donut, and slid smoothly down my throat. I swallowed over and over like I'd been in the dessert for months. I'd had dreams like this, dreams of running and clawing and snatching and then angels singing and the blood of the lamb - a lamb - purifying me inside out. Communion, tenfold. Better than honey. How could anything be better than honey?

Sparrow was watching me through her face-splitting grin.

How funny it was that she was teaching me. Everyone thought it would be the opposite. Mom had made jokes about how Sparrow wouldn't eat people food, let alone hunt her own. I remembered how I clenched my jaw as she laughed with Abel. I'd sworn to them both she'd hunt because I'd teach her, and she'd be a wonderful hunter.

They'd believed me. And now they'd be pleasantly surprised.

"You got it, keep going," Sparrow urged as I squeezed the squirrel's body. A warm trickle went down my neck. She started laughing. "You're so messy! Typical boy."

Suddenly, like the bottom of a Cherry Coke from the gas station, I was coming up empty. I squeezed the body harder but nothing else came out.

I tossed the deflated squirrel on the ground.

My hands were red and sticky. There were a few drops of blood on my shirt. The inside of my mouth was buzzing. My tongue worked over my lips, trying to catch anything I'd missed. I'd been so hungry but now I was full to my gills.

I was Changed.

"This is the weirdest, most amazing thing I've ever done," I told her.

"It never gets old," she replied as she wandered. I stared down at the dead squirrel.

"Cat, rabbit, or squirrel?" she asked.

"What?"

"You've had cat, rabbit, and squirrel now. Which is best?" She kicked the body away from us, where it thudded somewhere in the distance.

"When did I have a cat?" I chuckled, deliberating.

"At the Manor."

The pit of my full stomach went cold.

How could we have been so careless? I was out of my mind. I didn't remember until I woke up yesterday what I had done. I was inches from Fina's throat. I was seconds from getting Bernardo - if it wasn't for Sparrow.

I would have killed Fina's brother.

What must they think of me?

"No one's mad."

I turned around. Sparrow was swinging from a low tree branch. "Fina almost cried when she found the kitten. I just think they're scared."

"What are you talking about?"

"You said, 'what must they think of you?' The same. But scared."

"They didn't know." The words bubbled from my lips.

She shook her head. "They knew we were weird. Didn't know why. Did you finally smell them?"

I inhaled deeply. Even a mile away I could get a hint of roses. But Fina still smelled like oranges to me.

I nodded. "I get it now. I get the whole thing. The names, the hate, all of it. If I had to smell that so close and not taste it, I'd be cursing them, too."

"Oh, you'll get to," she chuckled. "Once you're safe around others."

"I feel pretty safe," I murmured. "When do I get a Friend? Who's your Friend?"

She looked at her nails. "Forrest, usually. I always figured it would be you once you Changed so I took what I could get."

"I had a reserved seat?" I asked, holding my hand to my chest with exaggerated flattery.

"If you'd taken any longer I think they would have paired me with Ivy to keep her off of Clay."

I started to laugh. "That would have gone over well."

"She looks like she would taste like gasoline. Like if you bit into her, your teeth would crack and fall out." Sparrow's eyes went wild.

"Don't be ugly," I choked between gasps of laugher.

"Hey if you wanna sink your teeth into her, you have a great time. But I will pass."

"Who taught you how to hunt? Abel?" I asked her.

She snorted. "Abel, acting like my father? Don't be ridiculous."

"Hey, he saved your tail the night I became Changed. Both of ours," I muttered.

"Yeah, don't think I'm not still hearin' about it." She rolled her eyes. "You owe me forever for that little stunt." She nodded towards the road. We headed up to Church. "Nova taught me to hunt actually."

"And once you drank you could hear everything?" I asked.

"I woke up hearing everything."

I sighed. "That's what I was afraid of."

I didn't wake up with anything. No Elder gift to speak of. Not even a hint of one. There was, apparently, a loop-hole I hadn't thought of - I could be Chosen, and still not be a successor.

"I'm sure there's a reason," Sparrow said, answering the question in my head. "And I'm sure we'll hear all about it."

I shrugged. Bitter thoughts became unrighteous words.

"Okay, Abel," Sparrow chuckled as we crossed the lot in front of Church.

"Being nosy is not ladylike," I retorted.

She laughed harder. "Because I care." We crossed ourselves and I opened the door to the sanctuary.

Papa smiled at us from the pulpit. "Have a seat." He gestured to Nova, a basketball under her dress and a grin splitting her face. I sat beside her, with Sparrow to my left. Abel and Mom sat across the aisle in the Jackson's pew.

Papa folded his hands and leaned forward, a smile playing on his lips.

"Three generations of Elders in one room." His voice didn't echo through the sanctuary like it usually did. It was so quiet I had to lean in to hear him. "Glory be."

"Glory be," we replied. I was smiling, too. Papa met my eyes.

"How do you feel, son?" He glanced at my bloody shirt. "I see you're getting the hang of it."

"Not really, Sparrow just helped me get my first kill."

Papa raised his eyebrows. "She did?"

I looked at her and nodded. "She did a great job."

"Well, glory be!" Papa clapped his hands together. "It brings me great joy to see all of my Chosen finally together. Nova joined at long last by her Council. Sparrow moving in our Heavenly Father. Our new Prophet adjusting well."

"Prophet?" I repeated, in stereo with Nova. I pointed at myself. "Me?"

Fireworks went off behind my eyes. The word stuck like a skipping record to the front of my brain. Prophet Prophet Prophet.

"Him?" Nova whispered. I glanced at her face, reddening with every second. Her eyes were glassy. "I was first. I thought I…"

Papa nodded. "You thought, Nova Grace. It's an awful waste of energy to think about such things. They're decided for us before we even arrive on this earth. You're a woman, soon to be a mother. You're a Pike now, not a Matthews. How could you be Prophet?" He shook his head.

Clouds of guilt started to build over my haze of elation. I turned away from my sister as she nodded, a single tear running down her cheek. I swallowed the lump in my throat, feeling her shatter quietly next to me.

"Now that all three of you are Changed, it is more important than ever for each of you to exhibit Silas-like behaviors. No more backsliding. No more idle minds. If your road to salvation was lonely before…" He whistled low. Mom and Abel chuckled. "It does not get less lonely. But it is terribly rewarding to do His works and bring Him His glory."

"Glory be," Abel interjected.

"The responsibility is great, not only for yourselves but for your brothers and sisters. You are our eyes and ears in the mainstream. You have to be strong enough in your convictions to make difficult decisions without the council of the Elders. You have the power to invoke Barton Law outside the gates."

Sparrow gasped. "What?" she breathed. She grabbed my hand and squeezed. Papa met my eyes and raised his brow, only a little, only for me. She let go.

I had the power. That was my gift.

I took a deep breath as the room started to spin. "What does that mean?" I asked, my mouth full of cotton.

"Whatever it has to mean," Papa answered, his eyes stern. "If you're going to be Prophet one day, you'll have to exercise judgment as instructed by our Heavenly Father. What He says, you do. We don't let our minds get in the way of His plan."

But my mind was racing now. I'd only ever hoped to be Chosen. To be Prophet never occurred to me until the words left Papa's mouth. How could I deserve that? To have all of Barton at my feet? To have my name strike fear and awe into the hearts of the congregation?

But I didn't really deserve it. Nova did. She was always the leader. I looked to her for advice my entire life. If I had to choose a Prophet, it would have been her, not me.

I guess the point was it wasn't our choice.

"He has told me the great battle is coming," Papa continued. "Either make the tree good, and his fruit good; or else make the tree corrupt, and his fruit corrupt: for the tree is known by its fruit." He slammed his hand down on the pulpit. "Our tree is known by." Slam. "Its." Slam. "Fruit." Slam. "I need only the most loyal, devoted soldiers in my ranks. I need soldiers who can look the Devil in her face and smile knowing He is King."

"Glory be," Mom said.

"I need soldiers who can glorify Him with their temples and their gospel and build our ranks for this battle."

"Glory be!" Abel shouted.

"I need well-oiled cogs in the machine of salvation that is Barton Heights. I am counting on the three of you to bring me these many fruits. Can you do that?"

"Yes," I answered.

"I need you to prune any bad fruit before it infects our tree. Can you do that?"

"Yes," Nova and I hollered. Sparrow jumped.

"I need you to die for our Heavenly Father as easily as live for him, can you do that?"

"Yes!" The three of us yelled.

Papa smiled and nodded. "Pledge it to me, my Elder council."

We all stood, hands over hearts. "I pledge allegiance to the Gospel, His most holy word. I will make it a lamp unto my feet and a light unto my path. I pledge allegiance to my Prophet and to the Father for whose glory he stands. One kingdom, one enemy, one purpose."

"Glory be to the Father," Papa said.

"And glory be to Barton," we replied.

7. JOSEFINA.

Junior's Cantina was at the dead end of downtown, one alley away from the Third Street Apartments where Betta and Che lived.

Had lived.

Junior's was like if taco stands in L.A. also served biscuits and gravy for some weird reason. There were two restaurants in Thistlewolf, and Junior's didn't have as bad of a roach problem, making it the obvious choice.

I sat on the curb in the parking lot and powered through my elote, which I suspected was just corn covered in mayonnaise. My siblings had left me here so they could run to the bank. Plus, Carmen wouldn't let me bring my food in his car.

I stood up and threw my garbage in the dumpster. I brushed off the back of my shorts and started across the lot to cut through the alley where the bank was.

The back door slammed behind me, disrupting some feeling deep inside my chest. I turned around, nervous.

Head down, hands in his pockets, River was walking towards the parked cars.

"Hey." He glanced in my direction and walked faster. "Hey!" I turned on my heel and jogged to him. He stopped and faced me, his eyes on my shoes.

"Hey."

"You die in my boathouse and all you have to say is hey?" I crossed my arms.

"What are you supposed to say when you die in someone's boathouse?" His voice was flat, his shoulders rounded in on himself. I stepped towards him and he stepped back.

"How are you?" I could hardly hear myself over the a/c units running out back of the restaurant. I was afraid to be any louder - he looked like he might shatter.

"Great," he muttered. "I'll see you around." He started off again.

"I think you owe me like, an explanation or something," I replied.

He paused. "Probably."

"Why did you come to my house?"

He stared off behind me. "Because I still had the taste of a witch in my mouth."

I felt heat flood my face. My fingers tingled. I could still taste him, too.

"They weren't even going to let me go to school until I was Changed." He talked to the specter behind me, eyes focused on nothing. "But then they weren't sure I would, since I was so late." He met my eyes finally, and his own squared. His face became tight. He looked different now in a way that I could not pinpoint. "I don't think I can be around you anymore."

"It's a little late, isn't it?"

"If I hadn't met you this never woulda happened."

Ouch.

I swallowed the lump in my throat and nodded. "So now is when you become like the rest of them."

I never should have entertained it for a moment, the idea that he was different. None of them were their own person.

"Are you kidding me?" he hissed. He closed the space between us. "I tried to kill your brother, Fina. How can you even look at me?"

I realized that his fingers hovered near mine, almost touching. The relief which flooded me was so intense I felt my eyes prick with tears. I took a deep breath and shook my head.

"We would've killed you first," I replied, and I hated how true my words were.

His head cocked back. "Excuse me?"

"You know what we are. You couldn't have hurt us."

"Your hands tell a different story." I crossed my arms to hide the scratches.

"You were scared."

"I was hungry," he retorted.

I bit my lip. "You're not going to scare me now, so."

"Then you're not as smart as I thought." He rubbed at his forehead. "If Sparrow hadn't been there, it woulda been ugly. I would die if I hurt you, Fina, I really would, so -"

"Cute." I jumped at the sound of the new voice. River winced, dread flooding his face as he rolled his eyes closed.

"Whatcha doin', River?" Clay put his hands in his pockets as he made his way to us, a cocky smile pointed in my direction.

"Apologizing," River said. Clay raised his eyebrows.

"To that?" He stopped a few feet away and inclined his head at me.

"Yeah." River's tone was biting. He turned back to me. "This conversation's not over."

"Finish it," Autumn said, appearing from nowhere. I closed my eyes and exhaled hard through my nose. How long had they been listening?

Autumn crossed her arms. "Go 'head," she said.

"Do you have like, any other hobby besides bugging me?" I asked her, exasperated. "Just curious."

"Nothing personal, I just hate everything about you." She shrugged her shoulders.

"Whatever." I looked up at River, eyebrows raised. I knew there was no point, but the smallest part of me, the miniscule mortal coil left in me, wanted him to prove it.

Whatever it was.

I wanted him to want me enough. Even though I knew he couldn't. I had to be kept in shadows and secrets, in rainy lakes, not in the sun or the school hallways. I still hoped against hope.

"Let's go," River said to them.

"Can we give you a ride?" A man's voice asked. A car door slammed to my right.

My stomach fell into my toes as Ivy and Micah got out and started our way.

Four - five - on one.

They had been watching us. It was a set up.

River took a huge step back and the wind swept through the space between us. I was scared for the first time. I tried to meet his eyes, to beg him without words not to make me hurt them. He had to call off the wolves or the wolves would start a war.

He wouldn't look at me. His eyes darted between the duo on foot and the two who stood against the car, leaning, waiting.

"Don't get too close, River," Ivy called out. "You know their kind eats kids." She glared at me. "I bet her jaw opens like a snake."

"Are y'all followin' me?" River asked.

"It's a small town," Micah replied. "We were in the area."

"Great. See you at home." River glared at Micah without blinking.

"We're lookin' out for you," Ivy approached River, keeping her eyes trained on me. "Don't want you to catch anything."

"Then let's go home," River said, half firm, half pleading.

"No, y'all were having a pretty serious talk," Autumn retorted. "We can wait. Wrap it up."

"It's wrapped, now leave." I replied, still waiting for River's eyes. Autumn's face darkened.

"No one was talkin' to you, Fifi."

"You said y'all. Which means you all. Like, me and him included."

"Like, does it?" she mocked. "That's totally weird I had like, no idea."

Every part of me wanted to blow her away. I chuckled. "Whatever."

"Whatever," Ivy interjected in a high voice, mocking me like a child. "Everything is so whatever like I don't even know." She crossed her arms. "Do you think it's cute to sound so stupid?"

"River thinks it's cute."

"Fina," River warned. He was still wild-eyed, glancing all around us as if there were dozens of people rather than a handful.

Because they were closing in on us.

I noticed it now - the smooth, small, soundless steps weren't registering to me before. But the distance between me and the people who hated me most in the world was getting smaller.

I was a cornered stray and they all had nets.

"Go home," River whispered to me.

"Back to Hell where you came from," Clay interjected.

Fury flared through me, an explosion in my chest. I was angry.

So angry.

I did not deserve this. I hadn't done anything to these kids except exist. I was in their town, their school, because my family had lived here long before I was ever born. I didn't choose anything about myself, but every part of me made them hate me with a passion. The unfairness of it, the lack of reason, had me seething.

I'd always had a bad temper.

7. JOSEFINA.

"Seriously, what is your damage?" I demanded. I turned to Autumn and Clay.

Autumn stormed up to me. I braced myself for a slap, a punch - she was going to hit me. I needed her to. I needed a reason; the smallest reason would be enough. If she stepped on my shoe I would kill her.

River angled his body a little, trying to keep space between us.

"My damage?" Autumn asked over his shoulder. "You are my damage. Your nasty poison blood and your nasty slutty coven need to get out of my town."

"Get over it!"

"I'm not gonna let you get to River, you slimy whore."

"Hey!" River interjected. Autumn looked at him and her face crumpled. She shook her head. There was sadness in her eyes.

"Such a waste. Who's gonna lead us if your soul's already gone?"

"My soul is just fine. This isn't ladylike behavior," he said to her. Autumn crossed her arms, some unspoken words crossed between their silence.

"You wouldn't know it anymore, judgin' by who you've been slumming with." She cut her eyes at me.

"Are we done talking?" Ivy asked. I turned around. She was a few feet from me now, her hands on her hips.

Carmen's Denali pulled into the lot and rolled by slow. The kids from Barton flinched back, only a little, but enough to make me smile. I looked at Ivy, her upper lip curled in disgust.

"I sure hope so," I said.

The Denali parked in the way back, where the lot turned to dirt and trees. Dia, Carmen, and Bernardo got out.

"She had to call her muscle," Autumn chuckled. The boys were staring at Carmen, sizing him up. There was a lot to size.

"What's going on here?" Carmen asked.

"Nothing," River said.

"He wasn't talking to you," Dia snapped. She looked at me, asking without asking. I nodded.

"Can't even fight your own battles," Autumn spat. "Even if you were one of us you're still not woman enough for him."

My eyes bugged out of my head. I tried not to laugh but it came anyway.

"Oh, my God," I chuckled. I looked up at River, then back to Autumn. "You're jealous."

Autumn launched across River's body with her arms outstretched.

Sometimes I forgot how stupid I was, but when Autumn's fangs were inches from my face, gnashing like a rabid dog, I remembered.

River's shoulder slammed into my chest as she pushed through him. I fell to the ground as he caught her around the waist.

"Stop it!" he commanded.

Bernardo grabbed my arm and pulled me to my feet. River threw Autumn behind him and came towards me. Bernardo stepped between us.

"Back off," he threatened River, who put his hands up.

"Listen -"

"You listen," Carmen interjected as he came up beside me. "Pick on someone your own size." He put his hand on River's shoulder and pushed him back a little.

River lowered his hands. "When you find someone, let me know."

Carmen's shoulders went up to his ears. "I think I just did." I stepped in front of Carmen as he went towards River again. Carmen had at least five inches and 100 pounds on River. This wasn't going to be good. I wasn't tall enough to break the eye contact, the simmering rage that vibrated through both of them.

"Back up." River's words were so soft; I only knew he'd had spoken because of the rumble in his chest.

"Yeah Fina, back up." Carmen grabbed my elbow and pulled me out of the way. I dug my heels into the dirt but nothing slowed me.

"Guys, stop," I said.

"Listen to her," River told Carmen.

Carmen smirked. "Or what?" He pushed River again.

River shoved Carmen backwards into Bernardo. Bernardo caught him before they both spilled on the dirt.

"Hey!" I interjected, running into the small space which now stood between them.

"Get out of the way," Dia murmured. Carmen was bouncing on the balls of his feet now. He shoved past me, shaking off my hands as they gripped futilely at his arm.

"Carmen," I pleaded, but I no longer existed to him or River. They were trembling towers of rage.

Carmen's right arm reared back as his fist made its way to River's nose. I turned around. I couldn't stand to see it. Bernardo met my eyes.

You have to tell them our spells won't work, I told him. Don't kill anyone, he replied.

That was all it took. That half a second to warn me not to lose it. Half a second where he wasn't paying attention.

Clay tackled Bernardo and Bernardo's head slammed into the lip of the Denali. I bolted towards them. We're outnumbered. We can't cast and we're outnumbered.

"It doesn't work!" Dia called to me. She started running. "It doesn't work!"

Autumn grabbed a fistful of Dia's hair and yanked her back. Dia's words stopped abruptly.

I stopped dead. My entire body stopped cooperating. I didn't know what to do. If I moved I would kill them I didn't want to kill these kids -

There was more than one voice screaming behind me. My heart jumped into my throat and something turned my body back on. I was moving, without knowing how, I was turning around toward the sound of the screams.

River was on his knees with his face in his hands. Micah stood in front of him, hands in fists in front of his chest. Carmen was the one screaming, stumbling in my direction, his hands covering his mouth and nose.

I grabbed his forearm and started dragging him to the car when something warm ran down my outstretched hand. Carmen's blood was gushing, steady as a faucet, running from his mouth onto the ground, and now onto me. He must have knocked out some teeth.

I held back my gagging and shoved his head down.

We had to get out of here. Outnumbered, can't cast. We had to go.

We have to go. Tell Dia we have to go.

"Dia," Carmen mumbled under his hands. I turned to where I'd last seen her, but she was gone. I kept shoving him to safety. I spun around, trying to find Dia and Bernardo, but I didn't see them. "Dia!" Carmen repeated, louder. I followed his stare.

I saw her now. She was being straddled by Ivy, held down, while Autumn's foot connected with the side of her head in horrific slow motion.

I was fast, but Carmen was faster.

A pulsating wave barreled across us. The Barton kids fell to the ground. I looked up at Carmen, his poor, mangled mouth hung open wide, blood mixed with spit drooling from his lips onto his shirt. His visceral, keening sonic scream was only an echo in the back of my head, as if my ears were stuffed with cotton. He couldn't last long.

COME TO THE CAR.

I looked down and saw River crawling on his knees, holding his ears. I could see him screaming but I couldn't hear it. I was glad. Some screams needed to stay silent.

I ripped off my totem and leaned down to pull his hand from his face. He wrapped his arm around my head and cradled it to him so that my ears were covered. I peeled his hand away and shoved the totem into it.

COME TO THE CAR.

I stood up and looked into his eyes, too green to be grey. The veins underneath bulged black beneath the skin. I couldn't stand to look at his mouth.

I grabbed Carmen's arm and we ran to the car. Sounds came flooding back at lightning speed, assaulting my senses. The world went fuzzy. Bernardo threw a stumbling Dia into the backseat of the Denali and caught the keys Carmen threw to him. Carmen pushed me in behind Dia, but I fought back.

"Get in!" His mouth sounded full of broken glass.

"You're hurt!" I said. He shoved me between my shoulder blades and my foot slipped off the lip. My knee landed in the smear of Bernardo's blood. I climbed in and turned around to help Carmen up.

But he was gone.

"Stay with Dia," Bernardo ordered in a tight voice as he opened his door.

"No, you stay with Dia," I retorted.

I was done staying. I was done waiting and watching and not knowing what to do and being afraid.

It was against my nature.

The switch had flipped.

I threw open the door.

I could see them, just through the trees behind the car. Autumn, Clay, and the Adams kids formed a half moon around Carmen, who was backed against a tree. Even from here I could see how Carmen's legs shook. Rings of sound radiated from him, but they didn't go far enough from his mangled mouth anymore.

And there was a fresh wound on his neck, two perfect pinpricks streaming blood across his shoulder.

River was in the middle, distracting. Directing. Didn't matter. It was over.

I slipped through an opening in the brush and let the flames engulf me.

I built up the heat until I was an inferno, and made my way toward the group. Carmen was freed, and he stumbled my way, shielding his eyes from the light.

"Let's go," he muttered through his mangled mouth.

But I was beyond that.

"So, let's see," I said as I walked towards the group of vicious teenagers who were suddenly human again. Ivy took off through the trees. I let her. I had plans for that one.

Micah stood straight, arms crossed and fangs bared. But his eyes were squinted hard against the heat. Autumn stood mostly behind him. That made me smile.

"Let's see," I repeated. "Who dies today?" I tapped my fingers on my chin. "Who took a chunk out of my brother?"

Clay, his black eyes wide as he stared at me. Into me. I was only flames. Fina was gone. It felt so good to disappear into destruction. I missed this feeling of freedom, like it was natural.

That was why I wasn't supposed to. It was like giving an addict their drugs.

"Was it you?" I murmured gently, cocking my head at Clay. I took a step towards him.

"No," he replied, his voice shaking.

"Doesn't the bible say to tell the truth? Now some-one better start talking or," I pressed my foot into the ground and flames sprung up between Clay and I. "Ashes to ashes-"

"Fina," River's voice snapped my concentration just a flicker.

"You're already hurt, River," I replied, my eyes still trained on Clay's. Maybe I could fry his insides if I just stared long enough. "Don't be a hero."

"It was me."

8. RIVER.

Her head snapped in my direction and her eyes pierced through the flames. I wiped at my mouth.

"I didn't mean -"

"Stop talking," she said. The fire got smaller and smaller until only her hands were burning, her clothes and skin and hair in tact. But there was smoke on her eyelashes, curling above her head like a snuffed out candle. I had never been so afraid, yet so enthralled. I knew I was about to die but if she was killing me, it might be okay.

She turned on her heel and stormed back to the parking lot. I let out my breath and shook my hands, trying to gain back the feeling in my fingers.

I was alone in the woods now. I didn't know when my friends had left me, but I was glad they took the hint.

Once my knees stopped knocking together, I went back to my truck. I got a good look at myself in the rearview mirror and nearly recoiled. I looked like I'd been mugged. Blood dotted my entire front; shirt, skin, and all. I had a nice gash above my eyebrow and my nose, my godforsaken nose, stinging beyond belief. I touched my fingertip to it and my eyes welled with tears. I prayed no one would be home when I got there. I had to get rid of these clothes, shower, try to put my nose back in place. I cringed at the thought.

It wasn't until I was driving home that I realized how much of a chance I took. I'd had no choice. Fina wasn't letting anyone off easy. The only way she was letting them go was if I took the blame. I don't know why I thought I was exempt from her fury. But she could have killed me.

If I was in her shoes I would have killed me too.

Maybe she didn't want to hurt anyone, but I didn't fully believe that. Maybe she didn't want to hurt me because of what we had. That was a much nicer thought.

Had, being the operative word, because she now thought I took a chunk out of her brother.

I imagined our connection, the words said between us, the moments we had shared, all fluttering out my open window like scraps of paper.

My phone rang as I turned onto Shell Court.

"Hi," I said to Sparrow.

"Were you crying?" she asked. I sighed. Even that hurt.

"No. Long story, I -"

"I don't have time for it right now. Gathering got called."

"Why?" I reached the dead end to the Barton gate and waved to my sister's husband, Noah. He opened it for me.

"Ivy told your mom about Clay."

My stomach dropped into my toes. "Wait, what? Already? Are you there? Can you tell them to hold on, I just pulled in to Bar -" Another call beeped in. I glanced at the screen. "Mom's calling me."

"Bye."

I switched calls. "Hey, mom."

"Honey, are you crying?" I sighed again and hissed. Stupid idiot.

"No, I'm fine," I muttered.

"Gathering is being called for the breaking of an Expectation. Papa wants you there."

"As a successor?"

"As a witness," she replied.

"Right now?"

"Yes."

"I'm almost to Church."

"Okay." She hung up. I pulled into Church and flung off my seatbelt. My adrenaline was pumping again. I looked like a mess. Great.

When I entered the vestry, I saw the backs of the four offenders. Micah, Clay, Ivy, and Autumn were in a line of that order in front of the Elders table.

The table was as high as my chest, made of white marble, heavier than anything I'd ever seen. It was the place where I would hold court with my flock forever. Mom was at the right hand, Abel at the left. Papa in the center. Always.

My footsteps echoed on the tile. It was the only sound besides the crackling fire, always burning even in July, to remind us what awaited us if we strayed too far from the light.

I stood beside Micah, both of us stone-faced, as if we weren't covered in blood.

"Gathering is called," Papa announced. His voice rumbled in my chest. "Who gathers before us?"

"Autumn Joy Sawyer."

"Ivy Ruth Adams."

"Abraham Clay McNamara."

"Micah Joseph Adams."

"River Silas Matthews," I said.

Papa sat back in his chair, his fingers interlaced across his wide belly, a small smile playing on his face.

"I don't know that I've ever had to call a Gathering on an Adams," he chuckled, glancing quickly between Ivy and Micah. "And for Miss Ivy? I doubt this is your Gathering."

"No sir," Ivy said. "I'm confessing on behalf of someone in this room, someone I saw break an Expectation."

"Which Expectation?" Papa asked.

"Sullying the blood of the Chosen."

Papa's eyes fluttered in surprise. He nodded. "I see. Did they bite an Unchanged or a human?"

Ivy stuttered and glanced my way.

Papa turned his stare on me. "River."

"H-human," I murmured.

"Camejo," Autumn spat. Papa raised his eyebrows.

"That's not quite human, is it?" he asked me.

"No, sir."

"It's worse," Mom interjected. "At least for the one who did it."

"I swear I didn't drink, Sister Sarah," Clay exploded. "I don't even know how –"

"You may be quiet," Papa told him, his voice booming, Silencing Clay. His stare had me frozen stiff. He looked me up and down, taking in my ragged, bloody, appearance. I swallowed hard, my mouth dry. "Are you sure it wasn't you who bit a witch, son?" He gestured at my clothes. I shook my head. "Then explain."

I sighed. "There was… a brawl, I guess. Out at Junior's."

"You were fighting?" Mom demanded.

"We all were." I jutted my thumb at the rest of them.

"Each other?" Abel asked.

"Witches," Clay answered. Papa nodded slowly, waiting for more, his eyes pulled together suspiciously.

"You bit it in a fight," Abel murmured in understanding. He joined Papa in his nodding.

"But I didn't drink!" Clay insisted,

"And I made him throw up, just in case," Micah added.

Papa held up his hand. "You're a good friend, Micah. You and your sister, obedient soldiers. It takes courage to confess on behalf of another. Clay will be thankful when he is absolved. And still living." He put his elbows on the table and rested his chin on his hands. "But now I'm more curious about this fight." He raised an eyebrow. "Junior's is too public a place to be brandishing fangs and spilling blood, and y'all know that."

"It wasn't planned," I replied.

"Who started it?" Abel asked. I didn't respond. I felt eyes on me, the Elders, Micah, Autumn. The tapping of my foot on the tile sounded like gunshots.

"Honestly? Us," I answered.

"Oh, come on!" Autumn threw her arms up in the air and they slapped her sides as she dropped them. I stepped out of line to see her. "You're joking!"

"First of all, Autumn, you showed your fangs and got me into it with the big guy. Second of all, none of this would have happened if y'all weren't stalking me."

"None of this would have happened if you weren't talkin' to that witch!" she retorted.

The word bounced off the tiles and echoed in the high ceiling.

I stared at Autumn, unblinking, unmoving. She stared back, lips pursed and brow furrowed. She breathed heavy through her nose.

I turned back to the Elders. Papa was looking at me, lips in a thin line. A disapproving look he saved especially for me.

I looked up to him more than anyone else in the world. I saw in him what I was meant to be - a leader, a man who followed our Heavenly Father in every way, a man who upheld order. All I had ever wanted was to be like him. When he gave me that look I was eight years old again, caught laughing during his sermons or nodding off in Sunday school.

Not fit to be his successor.

I cleared my throat. "My Elders know I did somethin' really bad when I became Changed. And I had to apologize for that, even if it was to a witch. For my conscience."

"How did an apology become a fight?" Papa asked.

"Because people who so happened to be around at the same time started instigating." I cut my eyes in Autumn's direction. "And the girls got in each other's faces - I had to stick up for Autumn and he had to stick up for Fina. We got into it and then it exploded from there. It's really all a blur after I got a knee to the nose."

The Elders all stared at me, unblinking, deciding whether to believe me.

"Fina?" Papa said it like it was a four-letter word. My heart jumped into my throat. Use that big fat brain of yours, idiot. Speak. Speak now. The silence is damning you.

"Right, I saw her at Junior's and wanted to apologize for what I did -"

"There were other witches," Mom interjected.

"Not until later," Micah said. "The three older ones showed up after we did." I sighed in relief. I could have kissed him.

"Just in time to brawl," Abel murmured. "Sounds like a set-up to me."

Mom nodded. "She was bait."

"No, she was set up by all them so Autumn could get a good couple swings in."

"And yet you're the one covered in your own blood," Papa mused. "So were these witches that much better at combat than you or did you go easy on them because of Fina?"

"I thought we were here because Clay bit someone," I replied, trying to sort out my own thoughts on that same question.

"It's up to the Elders to decide why we've Gathered," Papa retorted, his voice even smoother than before. "An ambush by the witches warrants a bite. I only wonder why you weren't the one to do it."

"What do you mean?" I asked.

"You're the newest Changed. You look the worst off. Why didn't you bite the one who did this to you?" I bit my tongue. Papa raised his eyebrows at me. "You clearly don't care about breaking Expectations since you do not remember the enemy of the Cross. I'm surprised you haven't tried to persuade a taste from your friend Fina."

"Why would I do that?" I blurted. I clenched my jaw and willed myself not to give in.

"The closer you are to one the more you want it," Papa told me. He didn't shrug, but his voice sounded like one. "In fact, I would guess that's why you went to their home the night you Changed. The spirit is willing but clearly, the flesh is weak. We all fall prey to sin." Papa smiled at me. "As for Clay, your transgression is forgiven by this Gathering of your Elders."

"What?" I demanded, my back stiffened.

"Obey them that have the rule over you and submit yourselves, for they watch for your souls," Papa said. I bit down on my lower lip and the stretch underneath my nose made my eyes well up. "Clay is not much older than you and I cannot blame nor condone such a new Changed being in the path of a witch."

"We'll all be in the path of a witch when one gets home with a bite mark," I replied. Why couldn't I stop talking?

"Drop your mind," Mom cautioned.

"Are you scared, son?" Abel asked. "Because we can pull y'all out of mainstream if y'all are scared of some witches."

"We're not scared," Ivy replied quickly, shooting daggers with her eyes.

"I was asking River, since he seems to have the problem," Abel said.

"As the serpent beguiled Eve through his subtlety," Papa recited. "So your minds should be corrupted from the simplicity that is in Him."

I closed my eyes. "I am allegiant, and devoted, and focused. I see my brothers and sisters acting in ways that would disappoint you."

"Then why wouldn't you use Barton Law to stop that behavior?" Papa asked me. "Is it because your behaviors are the ones needing curbing?"

"I only think -"

"Exactly," Papa interjected, his voice softer than ever. "You think. You think you know what's best for you. You think because you've finally Changed that you've already taken your seat at this table, but this is not the case. The disappointment here is the one who's getting caught in public with Rhiannon's little whore. The one who's already backsliding so far from Prophethood, he can't even rein in a few teenagers."

Papa sat back in his chair, his hands resting on his stomach. His smile back where it had been before he eviscerated me.

"First Sparrow, now you. Clearly, my guiding hand was not strong enough. I'm sorry for that." I wanted to disappear into nothingness, sink into the floor below me. Anything to get away from the look in his eyes. It was worse than disapproval.

I had never disappointed him.

"I think restriction would give you something better to do with your idle mind, River. This Gathering is adjourned," he stood, his words piercing me. I stared at the floor as I rushed out of the vestry. I couldn't look at the rest of them. I could hear my heart in my ears.

First Sparrow, now me. I was ashamed of how deep that cut me. Two future Elders who were failing beyond measure before they'd even took a seat at the table. Of course we were disappointments. But Papa didn't use Barton Law on me. Why not?

I'd done the worst thing I could do, and I couldn't stop it on my own. I didn't want it to stop. Nothing could be wrong about the way her smile made my soul feel.

Her smile. I would never see her smile again after today. Her voice played over and over in my head: so now is when you become like the rest of them.

Chosen versus choice.

8. JOSEFINA.

I looked at the mirror in the visor above the driver's seat for the millionth time.

When I was mortal, my whole life was makeup, hair, the mall, the dance, the boys, the parties, the inconsequential things. To be coated in hairspray and caked in concealer again made my stomach hurt with sad, rose-tinted nostalgia.

I snapped the visor up. At least my eyebrows had recovered from those long-lost days of over-plucking.

Bernardo knocked on the window. I stepped out of the car.

"Ready?" he asked.

"Have you ever seen Carrie?" I replied.

He snorted, rolling his eyes. "At least try to have fun," he said as we started up to the gym. "We're playing pretend for the night. Young, dumb, normal high school kids."

"So you can scam on young, dumb, normal high school girls," I retorted.

"And you're going to be my wing woman." He put his arm around me and shook my shoulders. "It's going to be, how would you put it? Totally gnarly?"

"Gnarly is right," I muttered.

A white banner hung from the entrance to the building with huge red letters outlined in black:

THISTLEWOLF HIGH SCHOOL HOMECOMING - UNDER THE SEA.

"Under the Sea," I chuckled. "I'm like, 80 percent sure we did that theme when I was a freshman. There are no new ideas anymore, are there?"

"You know, I used to think the same thing. But then the string bikini was invented. Now I never say never."

I rolled my eyes. Cold air and muffled music blasted us as we entered the hallway. All the multipurpose rooms were in this one building: the cafeteria to the left, the auditorium to the right, and the gym at the far other end, all emptying to the row of doors behind us. A fire hazard to end all fire hazards.

I never thought about things like that when I was mortal.

"Hey, I'll catch up with you." I nodded towards the bathrooms.

"I'll wait," Bernardo offered.

"Don't let me delay the hunt. Go find your next victim so I can lure them in."

"Always the drama with you, Fi." He disappeared down the hall as I went into the bathroom.

I locked the stall behind me and sat, careful not to get my dress wet. The bathroom floors in this place were always wet. I balled up my long skirt and put it in my lap.

How many times are you going to do this, Fina? There is nothing to get worked up over. This is all pretend.

We're only playing teenager, like Bernardo said. Plus, those Barton girls are petrified of you since your little stunt. All of them are. You're a force of nature and don't you ever forget it.

I straightened my shoulders and opened the stall door. I looked in the mirror as I left, my head held high. A force of nature stared back at me.

The hallway had emptied when I came out of the bathroom. The click of my heels on the linoleum echoed all around me.

I felt a hand closed around my wrist and then I was being yanked into the deserted cafeteria. I opened my mouth to scream and a hand covered it. I shoved my elbows backwards but missed. My back hit the concrete wall.

"Please don't scream," River whispered. His hand left my face.

Heat surged through me, almost breaking the surface. I clenched my hands into fists and willed it back.

"Or do the fire thing," he added as I hissed, "Get off me." He did.

"Hi... wow." He looked me up, down, up. His eyes burned where my skin was exposed. "Just... wow."

"Good talk." I shoved off the wall and tried to push past him, but River's shoulder stopped me.

"Fina, you gotta talk to me -"

"No, I don't," I snapped.

"You know I didn't do it, right?" He blurted, stopping my struggle.

I thought my eyes would pop out of my head.. "Don't insult me, River. It was literally all over your face."

"That was my own blood. From when he kneed me in the nose?" He crossed his arms. "You think the first thing I do after groveling for almost biting your brother, is biting your brother?"

All the heat rushed away. Fire fully snuffed. He was right, as much as I didn't want him to be. River glanced behind me and inclined his head towards the kitchen.

"Come talk to me," he whispered. I stood with my arms crossed staring at the space he had been for several seconds.

Then I followed him past the stacks of chairs, the cash registers, the vending machines. I had eaten lunch in here twice. On the first day, when no one knew us. The day after that, Ivy dumped chocolate milk on my tray. Now I ate in the music building.

We stopped in front of the kitchen, hidden from the doorway by the shadows and the serving carts.

"You look so beautiful."

Danger bells, loud as sirens. Beautiful boys didn't call me beautiful, not without wanting something out of it. He was staring at me like we hadn't just tried to kill each other's friends.

"Why did you lie to me?" I asked, breaking eye contact. If I got lost in the grey-green sea, it was game over.

"I didn't know what you were gonna do when you…" He motioned outwards with his hands. "I had to protect them."

I pursed my lips. "From me."

"From the giant fireball that took your place," he replied.

My chest got tight. "That is me. Underneath. All the time."

He nodded. "We both got stuff underneath."

"You had to rescue your friends from me," I chuckled as the weight of his words hit me. This whole thing was so twisted.

"You rescued your brother from me. I call it square."

"Not square," I corrected. "Autumn kicked my sister in the head. So she still has to die."

"Can I help?" he muttered.

I looked up at him. "Don't ever lie to me again. I'm not friends with liars."

"Friends," he murmured, grinning. "I don't usually wanna kiss my friends so bad."

I smirked. "You only want to kiss them a little?"

"I wanna kiss you a little." His eyes raked over me.

I crossed my arms to hide the way it made me shiver. "And I'm not friends with creeps, either."

"We're not even friends, y'know. I usually know more about my friends than just their names."

"You know plenty about me," I replied. Enough. More than enough.

He shook his head. "I don't agree."

"Maybe you were distracted when I was telling you." I raised my eyebrows. He took in my outfit again.

"That's possible." I snapped my fingers in front of his face. He met my eyes. "Sorry, I just… wow."

"You said that already," I laughed, turning my head to hide my blush. Why did he have to affect me so much?

"It's not fair," he whispered, closing the space between us. "Every time I look at you my brain turns into syrup."

"Is that right?" I put my hands against his chest, as if I wanted to keep distance between us. But I just wanted to touch his chest.

"You get to be all funny and smart and I just stand here with drool comin' outta my mouth most of the time." He shook his head. "You are very distracting, y'know that?"

I stared up at him. "You told me once or twice. Try closing your eyes, maybe?"

He did. He closed his eyes, took my hand, and brought it up to his lips, gently kissing the back of it.

"I don't want to be friends," he whispered. "I want you. All of you. Your underneath stuff, too."

My lungs stretched at my tight chest, trying to get a breath to reply. "It's pretty dark subject matter for a dance."

"Screw the dance," he chuckled, opening his eyes. It was my turn to give him the once-over. The sleeves of his dark grey dress shirt were rolled up, and they showed off perfectly the veins along his forearms. His tie was the perfect length, a silver tie bar holding it in place just above his ribs.

"But you got all dressed up," I said. He stuck his hands in his pockets and shrugged. "Give me one dance. Then we can leave, and I'll tell you everything."

His Adam's apple bobbed as he gulped. "A dance? In there?" I nodded. He looked down at our feet. "You know I can't."

"If you want me to trust you with my secrets, you have to show me you're worth it."

His head shot up, his eyes squaring in on mine. "You know what?" I heard the sharp intake of my own breath. "You're right."

The balloons I called my lungs deflated. "I am?"

He nodded and grinned. "Yeah. Screw it." He shrugged. "Let's go dance." He held out his hand, a smile tugging at the corners of his lips. I took it.

We walked out into the hall and he didn't let go. I couldn't stop smiling, even as the danger bells rang louder than ever. Above us, crepe paper with the silhouettes of turtles covered the fluorescent lights. Everything was hazy in blue. We followed the pounding bass to the open gym doors.

An arch of blue balloons led us into the dance. Straight ahead, the Rottweiler mural was covered with nets, life rafts, and cut-out paper fish. An octopus pool floatie hung from either basketball goal. Green streamers came down from the ceiling, interspersed with papier-mâché jellyfish. Huge towers of white and clear balloons were anchored to the floors near the walls to give the illusion of bubbles. If it weren't for the sweaty shoe smell, it could have been charming.

"Darker than I thought," he murmured as he walked me over to the side. "Not that it makes a difference with the Changed but, I won't have a conniption, at least. It feels safer." He rambled, his eyes searching the crowd.

"You okay?" I chuckled.

"I mean yeah I mean I'm good it's just I'm kinda worried I don't want there to be a thing at the dance, you know?" His head was on a swivel, his eyes rolling around in his head.

"River." I put my finger under his chin and turned his face towards mine. "You owe me a dance." He bit his lip. I took his hands and put them on my waist. "Do you know how to dance?" I asked him. He shook his head. I smiled. "We'll take this middle school slow, then." I put my hands on his shoulders, keeping a good amount of space between us. No distractions. If he wanted to know the dirty, ugly truth, he could.

Even if it meant he'd never talk to me again. He deserved the truth.

We swayed back and forth to the mid-tempo song being played way too loud for the size of the gym, the bass pelting my chest and the lights assaulting my eyes.

"You've ever been to one of these before?" He squinted, wonderment passing over his eyes.

"A few," I murmured as I let my eyes wander. Couples were intertwined around us, a mess of arms and skirts. All in their own little world and not paying attention to us. "Back in California." They were all the same, really. Teenagers looking over their shoulders to see what teacher was watching before they got grabby, and that awkward tight circle at the center where no one dared enter that still had their virtue. "You?"

"California, New York, here. How many high schools have you gone to?"

"A few." They all blended together. "I haven't had a good track record with school."

"You're smart, though. You do good in Lit."

"Well in Lit." I winked as River made a face. "And thanks. It wasn't for grades."

"What did you do, burn down a gym?" he chuckled. I didn't answer, his face dropping. "You burned down a gym."

I focused on his tie bar. "And a library. And a couple of cars. A gas station near one of the schools." The fiery images of each incident playing in my mind as I recounted. I mustered every ounce of courage I could find and looked up at him. His eyebrows were raised. An amused smile played on his lips. "Not for the hell of it," I muttered. "They were accidents. I only recently figured out how to keep it… underneath the surface. I'm pretty sure this is like, my last chance before my parents homeschool me."

"Hey it's already November and no one's dead. You're doing pretty good." He pulled me a little closer. His hands closed behind my back.

"The night's still young." I let my arms wrap around his neck, squeezing it gently.

He chuckled. "You're such a creep."

"The song changed." I hadn't even been paying attention to it.

"It did?" he murmured. He pulled me tight against him. "One more secret," he said against my hair.

I racked my brain for a dance-friendly secret. My secrets would send a normal person running and screaming in the opposite direction. But then again, River wasn't normal.

"Can I ask you about a secret?" he asked when I didn't answer.

No no no no -

"Totally."

One of his arms dropped to his side. He put his hand in his pocket and pulled something out.

"Why did this make the piercing stop?" He opened his fist and my necklace stared back at me.

I sighed in relief. "It's called a totem. They protect us from each other's powers, spells, all of that. It made it so you couldn't hear Carmen's scream."

His eyes softened, green glass melting behind black lashes. "And you gave it to me?"

"I know it hurt. And you were already pretty hurt." My fingers brushed the nape of his hair. "Keep it. I have another."

"That's the nicest thing anyone has ever done for me," he murmured, his broad shoulders drooping ever so slightly.

How sad must his life be if that were true.

The song changed again, a thrashing house track that practically pushed our bodies apart as its bass reverberated in my chest.

"Let's split while we can." I could barely hear my own voice, but River nodded and pulled me through the crowd.

We headed for the door through throngs of hair-swinging, arm-pumping teenagers. One second River was in front of me, and the next he was gone. I kept shoving my way through people, hoping he was outside already.

Up ahead I saw the back of his head, but not before I saw Autumn and Micah. Her nails were dug into River's forearm. I couldn't hear her, but her face said it all. I made my way towards them, against my rational mind. The boil was starting.

"Can you leave me alone?" River yanked his arm away.

"You're embarrassing your family," Micah spat.

"Y'all are embarrassing me. My family isn't here. And no one's gonna run their big fat mouth to my family, either." He stuck his finger in Micah's chest. "Barton Law. Keep your mouth shut. You too, Autumn."

Autumn shook her head in disgust and led Micah away.

River turned around, his eyes hard. "Sorry, let's go."

"What was that?" I asked. He took my hand and pulled me to the door.

"What it always is. It's gettin' real old."

"No, I mean what you said. You said Barton Law." Back through the balloon arch we went, barreling down the hazy hall. I was surprised there were no teachers around. In any other school I went to there were adults littered all over, looking for students trying to sneak away into a quiet corner. This really was a small town. "What's Barton Law?"

"Let's just say I pulled rank."

I struggled to keep up in my heels. "Slow down," I muttered as I picked up my dress. "Where are we going?"

He stopped dead. I almost ran into his back. "I don't know," he said. "Do you have your car?" I nodded. "If anyone saw my truck gone it would be a disaster," he murmured to himself.

"What about Barton Law?" I muttered.

"Can we go somewhere in your car and we can come back so I can get Sparrow?"

"Can't Sparrow come pick you up?" I asked.

"Sparrow can't drive. Let's figure it out on the way."

We hurried out to the parking lot. The air was heavy and wet, the grass shining in the streetlights. We were both grinning as we cut through the rows, dodging students as we made it to my car. I slammed my door shut and started up the engine.

Young, dumb, normal teenagers. Just for tonight.

3. BERNARDO

I leaned back on the picnic table and took a drag from my cigarette, the familiar pull into my lungs easing the tension in my nerves. I brushed the ash off the knee of my dress pants as I let it all out of my lungs, a cloud of gray hazing my vision.

It wasn't like me to bat zero with these girls. Fina disappearing didn't help. I'd seen her car turn the corner to First Street. She was always a good buffer, but now I was alone with everyone else's nasty thoughts.

I exhaled and watched the smoke spin up into the humid air. I never did well on my own.

The door behind me slammed. I heard her before I even turned around. Sparrow was the only person in this town who screamed at me the moment she entered the room. Her thoughts raced like her namesake, all piercing the walls of my brain with ease.

Che had been a whisper, a soft knock against the wall. Sparrow blew through said wall with a sledgehammer.

The clicking of her heels on the concrete grew louder as she approached me. I took another drag.

"You wanna save my life?" she asked. I looked up at her. Way up. Then down. Then up again. Between her massive, strappy heels and microscopic lace dress were miles upon miles of legs. I hadn't seen past the bottom of Sparrow's knee before.

The game began once more.

"I can't believe your father let you out wearing that." I raised my eyebrows, pulling in a drag.

"My father didn't let me out," she chuckled and sat on the end of the table, turning just enough to not flash me. "So, do you wanna save my life or what?"

"By giving you a cigarette?" I replied. "I don't know if you're aware, but these actually take time off of your life. So if I were to truly save you, I'd deny you a cigarette."

"But if you want anyone's lips to be on your lips tonight, you'll help me out."

I pulled the pack from my pocket. "I'm listening," I opened the lid and held the carton out to her. She took one and picked up my lighter from the table, the familiar flicker cutting the momentary silence, followed with her face of relief.

"I'm considering letting you make out with me," she mumbled around the filter.

"You and I?" I repeated, chuckling. "Why would we do that?"

She shrugged. "You're cute. I'm cuter. Seems like a decent way to pass the time."

"Do you know another way we could pass the time? By dancing. I heard it's quite popular in there." I inclined my head towards the gym.

Sparrow leaned forward and looked up at the sky. "Nope, still intact. I thought the day you showed a sense of humor the sky would start fallin'."

I smirked. "Hilarious, truly."

"I'm not going back in there. My head's going to explode."

"Doesn't it make you dizzy?" I crushed the embers on the seat.

"I don't know what to do."

"Can't you shut them out? Stop listening?"

"Can I?" She screwed her eyes shut and her whole face twisted, as if she had a lemon in her mouth. Rays of green light streaked across my brain. I smiled. "I hear everyone. I always heard things. I thought I was crazy. Maybe I'm that, too, but now I know."

"I don't think you're crazy."

"Sure you do." I didn't answer. "Not so fun when it's reversed, huh? I see right through you. You and I, we have a common inherited trait." Tremors of anxiety rocked me, one quick horrifying shiver, and then they were over.

"You learn things about people you don't want to know. Be careful."

"Like how you heard how easy I was from the Barton boys?"

I swallowed hard. I geared up, ready with excuses to the hilt. One look at her and I knew it was a waste of breath.

"Exactly."

It was as if she took my brain into her hands, the way she pulled me into her memory.

Walking out of the gray doors of the gray building to meet River from the boys' side; the boys and girls were separate in the Academy.

Clay and Forrest and Micah and River and she gets to them and they break up all laughing all smiling but River looks heartbroken and she knows, Clay told.

She hadn't meant to do it. He was all soft hands and sweet brown eyes and he said he loved her. He said he would marry her one day. Why couldn't they if he knew he'd marry her anyway? So she let him, in his truck, behind Church, and then he never talked to her again.

Abel knew by the time she made it home. He was waiting in the kitchen with the clippers. He took her hair like Delilah took Samson's hair, to weaken her. To shame her. Too bad for them, it made her prettier and angrier than ever.

And then the eyeliner, the lipstick, the nails. She's a lost cause. Let River deal with her. Good.

"They write you off," I said.

She nodded. "Just the way I like it. Invisible." Free. I heard the shaky word in her mind like it was an answered prayer.

"Tonight's outfit doesn't exactly scream, don't look at me," I replied, gesturing to the lacey get-up.

"Not to the right people."

My throat tightened. I was the right people.

"You're full of yourself, y'know?" she chuckled.

"What is dying like?" I hadn't meant to ask it.

She sighed. "Nothing."

"Nothing?"

"I loved nothing. It's beautiful. You never feel nothing until you feel nothing, you think you do, but you have no idea."

"And then you came back."

"Emptier. Happier."

"And the blood? You like it?"

She started laughing. "Well, yeah, now."

She saw herself so I saw her too, mouth full of sweet iron, dripping down her chest and arms, fingernails caked and flaking. The moon staring down at her, and her eyes on it like a moth to a flame. Everything and nothing. The wind and the leaves it carried.

Her purple lips formed a perfect O as she blew rings of smoke. I watched them until they evaporated.

"Red," she replied.

"I hadn't even formed the thought yet."

"You're red light. To me, at least."

"I doubt I'll meet many other mind readers," I chuckled.

"How many have you met?"

"One," I said.

"In a hundred years?"

I started. "One hundred ten, since you're so smart."

"What's it gonna be like? Being immortal?" she asked.

"It will be different for you."

"What's it like for you?

I looked down at my knees. "Terribly lonely."

She reached over and put her hand on mine.

9. RIVER.

I had a vague memory of the brick driveway Fina's little red car was flying down; a stinging on my back when I woke up, Changed. I knew I'd been here before.

I decided to play dumb.

"This place is beautiful," I murmured as she parked in front of the garage.

She smiled. "Yeah," she sighed and turned to me. "Okay, we're going around back because the stairs to my room are by the back door. So follow close and like, be super quiet, okay?"

"You are such a bad girl, sneaking a boy up to your room," I waggled my eyebrows.

She rolled her eyes. "Whatever." She closed the door softly and led me around the side of the house. The porch light glinted off the dented metal of the boathouse door.

My hand ached. If she noticed me noticing, she didn't say a word.

Possum Lake came into view, and with it, the porch light of my own house twinkled through the tree branches. We took the steps two at a time to the back door. She put her hand on the knob.

"Okay," she whispered. "Everyone should be asleep. I'll open the door, just take a right and go upstairs. I'll be right behind you."

"Oh sure, make me go first."

"Ready?" I nodded. "Set, go." She turned the knob slowly, making every effort not to let it click.

She eased the door open and motioned for me to come inside.

I shifted my weight on either foot. "You have to invite me in," I whispered.

She looked up at me. "What?" she demanded. I put my finger to my lips. "What?" she hissed.

I shrugged. "I can't go in unless you invite me. Manners."

"Vampire manners," she muttered.

"Do not call me that!" I whisper-shouted. She put both of her hands up.

"Why not?" she whisper-shouted back. "Is it politically incorrect or something?"

"Yeah, actually, it is!"

"Well is this really the time to worry about being PC? I mean I'm trying to sneak you into my bedroom here."

I considered. "Fair point."

She gestured to the open doorway. "Won't you come in, Mister Matthews?" she murmured in a low, dramatic voice.

I stepped into the dark, silent Camejo Manor.

The smell almost brought me to my knees. Every breath was ecstasy. I wiped my now-sweating hands on my pants. I took deep gulps to the point of hyper-ventilation. Angels were singing in my ears. The warm sweetness was overwhelming.

I was half aware of Fina shoving me to the pitch-black stairs. I tried to refocus on the fact that the girl of my dreams was pushing me into her bedroom.

Seduce and destroy. One way or the other. But I was past the point of caring.

She opened the door.

The room was lit only by string lights around the ceil-ing, corner to corner.

"You seem like a snooper," she said, grinning.

I leaned against her oak dresser. "I prefer observant."

Across from me was the bed, no frame, low to the ground, with a flag reading "California Republic" hang-ing above it. There was a throw across the mattress, with mismatched pillows peeking out from underneath. The blue walls were mostly bare.

Behind me on the dresser top was a massive mirror and a little TV. Three trinket boxes, all different, all over-flowing with bracelets and earrings. The bedroom door opened right into a desk and a hutch with three shelves.

The bottom one was full of books with titles like "Mis-ery" and "Lord of the Flies"; books I'd never heard of and would never have been allowed to read.

The top shelves held little pieces of her. Chunks of gemstone and stacks of cassette tapes and a crown of real, dying flowers. A shadow box of seashells sat next to a bottle of purple nail polish and a fuzzy, beaked and bug-eyed toy. A ceramic elephant kept a cup of pink, fuzzy pens company.

Across from me was a bay window cloaked in hunter green curtains. One nightstand had a lamp with a base made to look like an elephant, a striped mug, and a few brown glass bottles. The other had a dilapidated folder with sheet music spilling out and an open book bound in red leather, beneath a red candle.

I walked over and glanced at the book, drenched in scribbly cursive. I ran my finger down the crease and was met with a searing pain. I about jumped out of my skin.

"What?" she asked.

"Something… stung me."

"What?" I pointed at the book. "Oh."

"I guess I pinched my finger."

"Shouldn't be so nosy."

"Is it your diary?"

"Hmm," she murmured.

"It is!" I leaned over it and my joy disappeared. "And it's in Spanish."

"It's in Latin."

"You speak Latin?" I touched it and it bit me again. "Are you doin' that?"

"No."

"Did you enchant your diary?"

"Do I seem like a diary type?" She stood up and came beside me.

"Is that a trick question?"

She shoulder-checked me. "This is my grimoire." She took the candle off and picked it up. "I always wondered what would happen if a non bruja touched it." She lifted one side so the pages fluttered in front of me, all ink-soaked and smacking of roses.

"Well now you know. What is a grimoire?"

"My spell book." She wiggled her eyebrows.

"Spooky. Will you do a spell for me?"

"For you or on you?"

I froze. "You can't do spells on us."

She chuckled. "It's a joke, River."

"Yeah, I knew that." I stared down at the book, my heart slowing down. "What does this page say?"

"Oh." She slammed the book shut. "Amine Alba. It means Pure Spirit." She sat in the desk chair and put her ankle on her knee. "These things are brutal." She started to undo the strap on her pale pink high heel. Her shiny waves covered her face as she leaned over.

"What's Amine Alba mean?" I asked.

"Pure Spirit," she chuckled. "I literally just told you."

"Is it a spell?"

"It's a legend. Part of one." She tossed one shoe to the fuzzy white rug. "The legend of the Covenant."

"Which is?" I asked.

"Witches," she chuckled. "We are the Covenant." The other shoe dropped. "It predicts every one of us. Amine Alba is the last witch." She looked up at me.

"You?" I guessed. She nodded. "What does it say?"

She stood and went to the mirror. I watched her reflection as it pulled her hair over the shoulder and undid her necklace. I didn't realize she was wearing one - the plunging cut of her dress forced me to keep my eyes above the neck. I kicked myself now for not appreciating how the necklace must have sat.

"Can you see yourself in the mirror?" she asked.

"Why wouldn't I?" I replied.

She smirked. "Just wondering."

"Stop changing the subject," I chuckled.

Her eyes dropped to the dresser. "The Amine Alba will be born of smoke and sacrifice. She will be unmarred by flames or fangs and bring victory at the time of the Great Battle." She met my eyes in the reflection.

It should have terrified me, to know she was some sort of key in the Great Battle I'd spend my whole life preparing for. But if I had to guess, she was on my side. How, I didn't know. I had all the evidence in the world for the opposite conclusion. But I believed it with my whole heart.

"Believe it or not, this makes me feel closer to you," I said.

She turned around. "It does?"

I nodded. "I have a lot on my shoulders, too. Things I can't even begin to understand. It's nice to know someone could be in the same boat."

I watched her Mona Lisa smile spread until her teeth shone from between her red painted lips.

"I've never been in a girl's room," I murmured. "I mean, besides my sisters."

"You have sisters?"

"Two. Big and little."

"Harsh, middle child," she chuckled.

"And only boy." I ran the toe of my shoe along the edge of the rug. "You ever had a boy up here?"

"Che. Once, for like two seconds." She watched my foot make the trip around the rug. "I have dreams about him sometimes. I think he was a bruja."

"Wouldn't you… know?" I asked. "The eye and everything?"

"He had it. He had dreams about birds eating his guts …" She shook her head. "And then they did."

"Fina," I whispered. I went to her and hugged her head to my ribs. I kissed the top of her hair.

"Do you think it hurt or do you think it was like, instant?" I didn't answer because I didn't want to lie. "Did it hurt when you died?"

I shook my head. "It was like falling asleep."

She pulled away. I sat down in the desk chair as she fell cross-legged into the pit she called a bed. She put a black throw pillow in her lap.

"It hurt when I died." Fina pulled at the tassels absently.

The bottom of my stomach turned to ice. "You died?" I tried to breathe. She was right here. She was sitting in front of me, alive, she was fine. Breathe.

She nodded, her eyes on the pillow. "My dad is a lawyer. Was a lawyer? He might be dead. Not Elian. My real dad. And we had like, a lot of money. He was super powerful and… kind of evil? I don't know. He had tons of enemies. He drove a red Corvette and I drove a red Miata. I guess someone cut my brakes instead of his.

I ran off the side of a cliff. I hit my head, which hurt a lot, but then nothing."

"Oh, Fina," I whispered. "I'm so sorry."

"Don't be!" she chuckled. She looked up at me and smiled. "Oh my God, it was the best thing that ever happened! I didn't know what life really was before they brought me back."

"They brought you back?"

"Elian did. He can raise the dead."

It was quiet for a minute. Deuteronomy played on a loop in my head. A charmer, a consulter, a wizard, a necromancer - for all that do these things are an abomination unto Him.

"Well that's... something," I managed.

"I grew up with the same book you did," she murmured and glanced down at my neck. I touched my cross. "I've learned a lot since then."

I took a spin in the chair. "So, I hate to ask this. But if he can bring back the dead, why were we just at a funeral?"

She sighed. "Magic has restrictions. Especially resurgence. You can't have rotted. Your heart still has to be ... inside of your body. And if you're not a bruja, it's a one-time deal." I kicked off the desk and spun.

"So Che wasn't found in time?" I asked.

"Che... wasn't all there."

I stopped the chair with my foot.

"My parents and Carmen went to identify him," she continued. "His mom couldn't handle it. And Elian said ... " She took a deep breath. "He said there was no heart. No heart, no hope."

I rubbed my face with my hands. "Wow. Wow. I…
." I got up and perched on the edge of her bed. I put
my hand over hers. "Probably inappropriate, but I'm glad
that wasn't you."

She raised her eyebrow. "Jesus, River," she chuckled
and shook her head. "No, it should have been. When
Ofelia and Elian found me, I was in-between. Too dead
to heal, but too alive to bring back. So Dia did old magic
on me, like, blood-sharing stuff? I don't know. But only
me and her actually share blood. But I don't get hypno-
tism - that's her power - and she doesn't get fire. Which
sucks. But the three of them brought me back. And here
I am." I'd never heard her talk so much. It flew out with
no hesitation.

She trusted me.

"'So you woke up from your accident with a bunch of
strangers, totally unhurt?" I asked.

She nodded. "Still pretty, too," she continued. "Not
like halfway to 40. Lucky you."

I smiled, too. "Lucky me," I echoed. Then I registered
what she said. "Wait, halfway to 40?"

Her smile widened. "Yep. I'm permanently 17. At least
here." She gestured to her body and I said a silent, thankful prayer.

I furrowed my eyebrows. "But you should be… halfway to 40?"

She gave me that Mona Lisa smile. "1995 plus 17 is …
34?" I nodded, unable to speak. "Yeah, 34."

"You're literally twice my age," I told her.

"Literally, huh? You're starting to sound like me." She stuck her tongue out at me. My heart was soaring. She was teasing me. She was talking to me like we were friends.

"Hang on, back up here," I said. "Dia can hypnotize people?"

She nodded. "Yeah, it's way cooler than -" She snapped her fingers and a spark flew off, onto the pillow. She smashed it with her hand.

"I mean…. You'll never get cold, right?"

She laughed. "Does anyone get cold here? Except you I guess. Your jacket got a lot of compliments." She reached behind a pile of pillows and pulled my jacket onto her lap. "I think this is my biggest secret." She lifted it to her face and took a deep breath.

My chest ached. She looked up at me, her face still half-buried in my jacket. I pulled it down.

Her tongue darted across her bottom lip.

"Do you have more secrets?" I whispered as I slid my hand under her heavy hair. She leaned forward and rested her body weight on her hands, which she set on my thighs. Every muscle in my body flexed and tightened.

She doesn't do that! SHE! DOESN'T! DO! THAT!

"You know how I… don't do that?" she whispered against my ear. I took a deep breath and shuddered, trying to play it off as a nod. "It's not because I don't want to," she continued, lacing her fingers through the hair at the nape of my neck.

I didn't speak, didn't move. How could I break this moment?

"I just don't want to, like, set you on fire," she chuckled.

"I mean, I can sign something if you want…" I whispered. Her forehead fell against my shoulder as she laughed. "Saying I fully acknowledge the risk, y'know?"

She sat up so I could see her roll her eyes. "You're cute. But I can't take that chance on someone I like so much."

The fairy lights caught that sliver of blue and it flashed, and her teeth flashed when she smiled. Red lightning, exploding in front of my eyes, striking me somewhere between my ribs and my belly button. It sent shivers all over me. I bit down on my lip to keep from screaming to the heavens.

I loved her.

I knew it, in that second, like I knew the sun would set.

"I think that's enough secrets for one night." My voice sounded like it came from the bottom of a well. "I should go get Sparrow." I stood on my jelly legs.

"Why did you want to know all this?" she asked.

Because I love you.

"We're all scared of stuff we don't understand," I murmured with no idea of what I meant. "I wanted to understand you." That part was true.

"So you're not scared of me anymore?" She grinned.

I came back down to earth, if only for that smile. "No, you still terrify me."

"Good." She winked, a mischievous smile playing at her lips.

Back down the pitch-black stairs we went, our hands entangled. It was freeing to hold her hand without having a heart attack about who might see it.

But I still didn't dare breathe until the door closed behind us.

We got into her little red car. I wondered if it was the same kind of car she died in. I wondered what she must have been like. Would I have loved human Fina, if I knew her? I had hundreds of questions about the layers of Fina I had yet to unpeel.

I didn't ask them. I sat beside her in the car, silent. I thought about every possible way she would end me. And I thought how dangerous it was that this singular moment, in this car with this girl, her hand in mine, made it all worth it.

9. JOSEFINA.

I was the size of a leaf and running for my life. I heard the screech of my murderer close behind, yet far above. I had to get back to the burrow but it was so far. My legs were getting tired, my body drenched in sweat. The adrenaline was failing me.

The ground fell from under me as the talons closed around me, crushing my body. We went higher, and the world grew darker-

I shot up in bed, my head swimming with terror.

I shoved the blanket away and ran for the bathroom, but I covered my rug with vomit. My legs were shaking as I stumbled to the door.

Just a dream, Fina. I took a deep, putrid breath.

I stumbled bleary-eyed down the stairs into the kitchen. There was a pitcher of stomach relief brew in the fridge - I could smell the ginger from here. I stopped to take a deep breath to steady myself, the floor wobbling beneath me.

The light in the kitchen was already on.

Dia was hanging over the island, her head on her fore-arms. I went around her to the cupboard and got each of us a cup. The oven clock read 3:33am. I slammed the cupboard and she groaned.

"Drink the brew," I muttered, holding back a wave of nausea.

She shook her head. "I have to get out," She whispered into her arms.

"Get out?" I repeated, opening the fridge. "Get out to where?"

"Out," she said behind me, more urgent. "Out of the raven." I heard dishes clattering together from the wink.

I grabbed the pitcher and fought a yawn. "What are you talking about?"

"The raven, never flitting, still is sitting, still is sitting." It was hardly a whisper.

"Are you drunk?" I demanded as I poured. Behind me, I heard her slice into something thick. "You're totally going to slice your finger off, let me help you," I chuckled, turning around to see what she was struggling with.

Dia slid down the dishwasher, bent at the middle and clutching herself, groaning. Sweat poured down her ashen face.

"Dia, drink this -"

I dropped the cup.

A puddle spread from a black handle, buried to the hilt in Dia's chest.

I watched from above like a specter as I went in Elian and Ofelia's room. I shook Ofelia awake and said, "Something's wrong with Dia" in a voice that wasn't mine. Ofelia looked at me through puffy eyelids as she struggled to sit up.

"What do you mean?" she rubbed groggily at her eyes.

I heard myself say it again. "Something's wrong with Dia."

Then the screaming started.

My parents bolted out of bed, the three of us running into the kitchen.

The knife was out of Dia's chest and in between her hands. She rammed it into her side and howled.

Elian put his hands on my shoulders and squeezed. Ofelia wouldn't stop screaming, not even as she went to Dia and worked the knife slowly from her flesh. She healed Dia's wounds with her other hand.

Dia leapt at her and reached for the knife again.

"Please!" she howled. "Please, get me out!" she sobbed.

"Elydia," Ofelia murmured. How could she talk and scream? "Dia, listen to me."

Elian kissed the side of my head. "Hush, Fina, hush. It's okay. You're okay." It was me who was screaming. I shut my mouth and pulled away from him.

Elian rushed Dia and pushed her shoulders against the dishwasher. "Dia," he said gruffly. Ofelia dropped to her knees and held Dia's spasming legs. They both knelt in puddles of her blood. One of Dia's hands thrashed in her gore.

"The raven!" The sound came from the bottom of her stomach. She smashed her head into the dishwasher.

"Fina," Ofelia murmured. She met my eyes and nodded at the windowsill. There was a brown glass bottle sitting there. I watched my body pick up the bottle and remove the cork, my hands shaking.

Elian was sitting on top of Dia now, physically re-straining her. The knife was in the sink, her blood bead-ing off of it. The sounds of struggling made my hair stand on end. Elian grabbed Dia's face and pulled her jaw open. He was covered in her blood, soaking his pants. It was ev-erywhere. Dia's eyes were wide open, searching for some-thing, her mouth held open like a trapped animal.

"Fina!" Elian spoke through clenched teeth, bringing my attention back. I poured half the bottle into her gap-ing mouth.

Elian shut Dia's jaw and waited until she swallowed. My legs gave up and I sat behind my parents. I couldn't look away from Dia. She struggled, still, against Elian, trying to thrash her head and arms about, until her eyelids became heavy and her movements exaggerated, until they closed completely and Dia had gone still.

Elian sat back and wiped his bloody hand on his pa-jama pants. He grabbed the towel from the oven handle and cleaned off Ofelia's hands, his mouth a tight line.

Ofelia looked over at me, her eyes glassy. "What hap-pened?"

My eyes went back to my sister. "I had a nightmare. I threw up. I came down for some…" I found the cup, the pool of cloudy yellow tea it swam in. "She was in here, wanting out."

"Wanting out?" Ofelia repeated. "What do you mean?"

I shook my head. "Something about a raven. I'm the raven, out of the raven."

"The raven?" Elian asked. I nodded. "A nightmare, perhaps?"

"A nightmare that drove her to suicide," Ofelia replied. She got to her feet and lifted Dia's chin so she could look at her face. "My poor child," she sighed.

I heard a sharp intake of breath behind me. I turned around.

Bernardo was standing in the doorframe, his hands over his mouth. Carmen's silhouette was right behind him.

"What was she spelling?" Carmen asked.

Ofelia looked green. "What?"

Carmen nodded at Dia. "In the blood."

I looked at the puddle near Elian. A V with a line in the middle. A K, upside down with a lowercase D going through it. Elian turned his head.

"A...R..." he murmured. "You can't hear her, can you?" Elian asked Bernardo. Bernardo shook his head. "AR, AR, AR."

"Tony!" Carmen shouted as he snapped his fingers. I jumped and covered my face with my hands.

"Oh, my God," I moaned. The floor seemed to fly up towards my face.

When I opened my eyes I was propped up against the washer. The back of my neck was cold. I sat up and a bag of frozen vegetables slid to the floor.

Bernardo peeked around the corner. "Hey," he murmured.

"What happened?"

"You fainted," he replied.

"How cliché of me. Where's Dia?" I started to get up, my head a whirlpool.

Bernardo grabbed my arm. "Hey, take it easy." He lifted me to my feet.

"I'm fine," I lied, shaking him off. "Where is my sister?"

"In the altar room."

A pile of crystals and candles sat on the floor beside the altar table. In their place was Dia. She lay lifeless in the place where we celebrated life. Every other member of my family was leaning on the walls, sprawled on the floor, all buried in grimoires.

I approached Dia the way I would approach a sleeping baby. Her stillness was horrific. I knew she couldn't be dead, not with Elian feet away. But the solidness in my chest where my heart should have been was only growing.

I wanted to touch her but I was too afraid.

"Fina," Ofelia said. I flinched. "Are you alright?"

I nodded and looked at the grimoire she had in her hand, outstretched towards me.

"What's going on?" I asked.

"Antonio Reyes," Carmen told me. "AR. She was trying to talk to him."

"To Tony?" I said. Tony was Dia's husband. He died before I was ever thought of.

"To Tony," Carmen repeated, nodding. "She overdosed on some potion, is my guess. She wanted to see him again."

I shook my head. "No, Dia would never do that. She's better with potions than you are, she would never mess up like that."

"I don't think it was an accident," Carmen murmured.

"She was babbling about ravens -"

"The point is, she took something," Ofelia interjected. She picked up my grimoire from the table and held it out to me. "Look for ingredients in potion recipes that could have caused this behavior, so we can brew an antidote."

The sancti verba, which Bernardo currently had in his hands, had belonged to Rhiannon. It would turn to the page a bruja needed, as long as they knew what they needed. Pages we had never seen before would present themselves in just the right moment. It was as if Rhiannon spoke to us through the sancti verba from beyond.

But the other grimoires were not so enchanted. The only sounds in the altar room were the sound of aged pages being turned.

Crush Noche Buena leaves with blade. Six drops of Albus Rosemary. Two drops bruja blood. Six drops bruja blood. Hot water. Cold water. Dittany root. Tea leaves. Coltsroot flowers.

"I don't even know what causes astral projection," I whispered to myself.

"Acacia flowers are an ingredient in the sore throat brew," Bernardo said to no one in particular. "They can be hallucinogens."

"Dia's the one who knows all about potions. She would never take too much of something," Carmen murmured.

"Brugmansia," Elian murmured. "Out in the yard. Perhaps she wanted to communicate with someone beyond."

"By eating Angel's Trumpets?" Ofelia demanded. "She would never be so impulsive."

"We are talking about Elydia, right?" Carmen muttered.

"Then what do you think it is, Carmen?" Elian retorted. "If you are so sure."

"I'm not," Carmen murmured as he turned back to the grimoire. The tension in the room was palpable. "I think she was trying to tell us something. But I don't know for sure."

"Rosemary is also in that sore throat brew," Ofelia murmured. "AR. Perhaps she was warning us?"

"She was giving us a message," Bernardo said. I looked over at him. I could only see the top of his head. He was bent over the sancti verba. "Trying to, at any rate. But I don't know what it means."

"What does it say?" Elian asked.

"Aradia?" Bernardo replied. She looked up at me, and then at Carmen. Carmen shrugged.

"What is Aradia?" I asked him.

"Aradia of sulfur and flames," Bernardo recited. "As Rhiannon brought life and light, so Aradia brings destruction and darkness. She is the mother of demons, and master of belladonna -"

Elian stormed to him and snatched up the sancti verba. Bernardo jumped back and stared at Elian, eyes wide, the way all of us were staring.

"That's absurd," he chuckled, thumbing through the sancti verba, much too fast. The pages fluttered in the opposite direction. He shut the book and then opened it again. His eyebrows furrowed. "Absurd," he repeated quietly. He opened the book backwards, but the pages turned on their own, to the dead center.

Elian dropped the book.

"Aradia," he whispered.

"It's not possible, Elian," Ofelia told him. "Absolutely not possible."

"What is not possible?" I demanded.

Someone started to laugh.

The table leg shook against my spine. I sat up and then stood. Everyone's eyes were on me.

No, looking behind me. I turned around.

Dia's eyes were still shut but her mouth was wide open. Her teeth were shining in the dull light near the laundry room. She was shaking head to foot, laughing.

"Dia?" I whispered.

Someone grabbed my shoulders and pulled me away.

Ofelia went to one side of Dia, Elian to the other. She kept laughing.

"Dia!" Elian hollered. The laughing grew louder. "Dia!"

"Aradia," Ofelia whispered.

The laughing stopped but the smile remained.

Dia opened her eyes, rolled back so far that only the whites were showing.

"Ghastly grim and ancient raven wandering from the nightly shore," she murmured. She sounded like she was talking into an electric fan.

"What do you want?" Ofelia asked.

"'Tis some visitor entreating entrance at my chamber door," Dia replied.

"What do you want?" Ofelia repeated through clenched teeth. Bernardo slammed the sancti verba shut once more.

"Quoth the raven, nevermore," Dia chuckled.

Elian put his hand on Dia's chest. "Debe -"

"No!" Ofelia shrieked. She grabbed Elian's arm. Elian jerked away. Ofelia glanced at the totem on Dia's chest. "Tell me why you dare show your face in this sacred place."

Dia's head turned towards us. Her chin dipped down to her shoulder, her eyes lolling lifelessly. She still smiled.

She reached her hand out and wiggled her fingers at me. "Pretty little dragon girl," she chuckled. "Come here to me."

"Don't move," Ofelia commanded.

I couldn't even if I wanted to. I couldn't breathe.

"Aradia says…" Dia took a deep, human breath. "Come … home."

Her hand went limp as her eyes closed once more.

Ofelia snatched Dia's totem off her neck and put her other hand on Dia's chest. "Debellavi," she said.

Dia seized. She coughed, dry at first, and then something started to rise in her throat.

She gagged and exhaled a swarm of flies.

ACT III.

You linger, yet the time is short:
 Flee for your life, gird up your strength
 To flee; the shadows stretched at length
 Show that day wanes, that night draws nigh;
 Flee to the mountain, tarry not.
 Is this a time for smile and sigh,
 For songs among the secret trees
 Where sudden blue birds nest and sport?
 The time is short and yet you stay:
 To-day, while it is called to-day,
 Kneel, wrestle, knock, do violence, pray;
 To-day is short, to-morrow nigh:
 Why will you die? why will you die?
 Christina Rossetti, "The Convent Threshold"

10. RIVER.

"The valiant never taste of death but once," Alfred continued. "Of all the wonders that I yet have heard, it seems to me most strange that men should fear. Seeing that death, a necessary end, will come when it will come." He set the book down and looked out at us. "To live in fear of death, in Caesar's opinion, is worse than death itself. Certain events are beyond human control, and understanding of this allows for the dichotomy between fate and free will."

I glanced over at the empty seat for the hundredth time this period. Almost a solar eclipse. The sun wasn't where it was supposed to be.

Bernardo was here, if only physically. He looked pale, exhausted. I glanced at my phone but my text still went unanswered.

"Turn your vibrate off," Sparrow whispered, her eyes on her book. "It's drivin' me nuts."

"Must be someone else's, she's not answering," I replied.

"Something's weird," she said. "Don't know what."

"With Fina?" My hand worked on its own, tracing tiny triangles in the margins of my notebook.

"With the whole family." I could hear how annoyed she was with me.

A switch had flipped in my soul. From the second the Heavenly Father told me I was in love with Fina, she had become the sun, the center of the universe, the new Church. I never stopped thinking about her. I worshipped at her feet now. I was fully ensnared in the one trap I'd been warned about since I was born. I understood better than ever the danger in her, in all them, because I was in the thick of it. I had been prepared for this my entire life and I was still too weak to dig myself out.

Because I didn't want to.

The bell rang. Sparrow and I both had classes in the music building next. We caught up with Micah, Forrest, and Autumn between Three and Four.

"Peasants!" Forrest called to us. "Where is your respect for Thistlewolf's newly crowned royalty?" he demanded in a haughty voice. He flourished his hands and bowed towards Autumn. She spun and curtsied. Micah saluted.

Forrest threw up his hands. "Kings don't salute!" he told Micah.

"Kings do whatever they want," Micah chuckled.

"Forrest is more of a jester," I replied.

"He's not the one who's a joke," Micah retorted under his breath. I ignored him.

Forrest didn't. "Uh oh, you makin' these two fight for your affections again?" he asked Autumn. She rolled her eyes. "It stopped being funny in seventh grade."

Autumn shoved Forrest. "I wouldn't touch River with a ten-foot pole these days," she muttered.

"Yikes, you get one homecoming crown and you're too good for the little people," Forrest said. "You won't forget me, right Autumn?"

"I wish I could," she sighed, but there was a smile there.

"Me too," Micah chimed in, also grinning.

"I'll see y'all at home," I called as I turned the corner to Hart's room, glad to be getting away.

Thank the Heavenly Father for Forrest. I was safe for now, but I knew it would come out in the wash. Sooner or later, everything does. But time would heal all.

Lots and lots of time.

I sent Fina two more text messages throughout the rest of the school day. We were supposed to have our last tutoring session today. She never responded. The amount of disappointment I felt was ridiculous. I didn't even know if Fina felt the same way about me as I did about her. If someone followed me like a sick dog and worshipped the ground I walked on, I'd entertain them, too.

I had to stop by Hart's room after last bell, just in case.

An angel in white sat at the piano bench. My smile threatened to break my face in half. Had she always been so flawless? How did I ever miss those little freckles on her nose? They were the best part of her face.

The tiny voice of reason still pulled at me, still tried to get me out of the pit.

She looked up at me and the voice was silenced.

"Hi," she said, her voice almost hoarse. She cleared her throat.

"I missed you today." I sat beside her on the bench. She stared at her hands, twisting and untwisting in her lap. I picked up the one closest to me and laced my fingers between hers.

This was the thing I had been missing my entire life.

"I overslept," she rasped.

"I texted you when you didn't show up to Alfred's."

She nodded. "I saw. Sorry."

"What's going on?" I closed her hand between both of mine. She shook her head. "You can tell me, Fina. I wanna help." I ducked my head to catch her eyes.

They were red-rimmed, bloodshot. The circles underneath were a deep purple not even her eyelashes could disguise.

"Do you think I could be evil?" she asked.

"Of course not." Not anymore.

"Something bad happened and I think it was my fault." She cleared her throat again.

"You wanna tell me?" I pressed in a whisper, squeezing her hand.

"My sister was possessed, the night of the dance. She stabbed herself. And then she coughed up a swarm of flies."

"Possessed?" I echoed, not really sure what to do with the information. "Possessed by the Devil?" I gripped the cross on my necklace, like a reflex, like breathing.

"By something called Aradia," she looked at me with hoping eyes. I nodded. "You know who Aradia is?"

"The Devil." Who didn't know the Devil?

"I didn't, but I do now. I don't think I'll ever close my eyes again without thinking she's there. Our parents didn't think she'd have the nerve to come after our family."

"What did she want?"

"She told the little dragon girl to come home," Fina whispered, her head dipped low to her chest. My stomach coiled into a steel knot.

"Oh, Fina." She pulled away from me and put her head in her hands. "What are you gonna do?"

"What is there to do?" She looked up at me through red-rimmed eyes. "Why is this happening now? Three months ago I thought we were all alone in the universe, and then you, and then this. Why now? What am I supposed to do? Why does she want me?" Her voice cracked.

"Listen," I whispered. "My whole life I've been preparing to destroy the enemies of the Heavenly Father. They said I would know it in my blood, when the heirs of the dark women came for the descendants of Silas. And that's not you."

Her face changed. "You're a descendant of Silas?"

"Yeah, all the Chosen are. That's why we're Chosen," I chuckled.

"Chosen," she nodded, pulling back. "For murdering my ancestor."

"She's obviously still alive and kickin', since she just got your sister."

There was a long, long, long pause.

"I was talking about Rhiannon. Who were you talking about?"

I stammered. "I mean… there were women of roses and women of flame, Fina. What am I supposed to think you are?"

"So you do think I'm evil," she chuckled. "Your ancestor murdered mine, but I'm the evil one. 'Kay." Fina turned to face me.

"Silas had to destroy those women before they could destroy the world," I told her. It was like knowing my name, knowing that Silas destroyed the dark women for the Father, and the Father rewarded him by making us Chosen.

"Silas was conniving and cruel," she spat. "He killed Rhiannon because he was afraid of her."

I clenched my jaw. "Silas locked those heathens up to protect the mortals and they never stopped trying to get revenge."

"Revenge?" Fina repeated. "You have no idea what you're talking about."

"You didn't even know who Aradia was! Your parents probably didn't want you to know what you are!"

Fina closed her mouth. The tin echo of regret was instant, earth-shattering.

"I knew it." Her voice shook. She picked up her bag.

"Fina, look, I'm really sorry. I really didn't -"

"Save it," she interjected.

"Fina, please -"

"You know what? Maybe I'm evil. Maybe I'm not. But whatever I am, at least I belong to myself. You're a brainwashed pawn in a false prophet's cult, and I feel bad for all of you."

"What did you just say?" My teeth were clenched so hard, the idea of them breaking played somewhere in the back of my mind. "What did you say?" I demanded. I tried to stay where I was but I was heading towards her. I was looking through a red-tinted haze of fury.

I was thrown back in the same second by a rush of unbearable heat. I caught myself on the piano just before my head hit the keys.

The heat closed in on me. I shielded my eyes.

"You heard me," she said with that terrifying tightness. My hand was on fire. I bit down on the inside of my cheeks so I wouldn't scream. "Don't you ever come at me again." Her breath was against my ear. Even in hell, the voice gave me chills.

I nodded.

I inhaled cold, re-circulated air as the heat left me. I looked down at my hand. It was bright red.

The classroom door slammed shut and Fina was gone.

Once I could catch my breath again, I got to my feet and left, too.

It was nice while it lasted.

I took my time getting home. I was supposed to go hunting tonight but my fasting stomach was suddenly too knotted to be filled.

I was well acquainted with guilt. Nova liked to say guilty was my resting state, even before she inherited mom's feelers. I would confess to breaking lamps I'd never touched. I was convinced Mom had eyes on every side of her head, the way she could catch me before I caught myself. Now I knew it was the guilt I radiated at every turn.

But this was a new guilt. This was the remorse of hurting someone with the truth. I usually took every opportunity to display the truth of the Heavenly Father, the path of the Chosen was not meant to be easy. I never felt bad for speaking about the enemies of the Father.

The acidic doubt in the back of my throat was something completely new.

Mom was in the kitchen when I got home. Only one person in the house ate anymore, but it still seemed like she was cooking the same amount. I kissed her on the cheek as I passed through.

"Hey, where you been at?" she asked me.

"Had tutoring at the school."

"You were supposed to go to confessions with Papa." She didn't look at me, but kept chopping away at the veggies on the cutting board.

I sighed. "I completely forgot. I'm really sorry."

"He said you can do it next week but I think you're gon' have to be real nice to him when he gets home." She raised her eyebrows. "Can't let the mainstream come before the Works."

"Yes, ma'am. I'm sorry."

"I know it's a big transition. And I know you been distracted." Her tone turned. I squirmed under her accusatory stare. "But you can't take succeeding the Prophet lightly. There's no problem with pullin' you back if mainstreaming is distracting."

My stomach sunk and then leapt into my throat. Even seeing Fina from the corner of my eye between classes, even with her hating me; it would be better than not seeing her at all.

"If I can't be a guiding hand to a couple people in the mainstream how can I Shepherd the congregation?"

"I'll leave it all up to Papa," she murmured. "Anyways, Sparrow's waitin' for you in your room." She nodded towards my bedroom door.

"Really? She seemed ticked off at me today."

"Said she needed some biology help." Mom rolled her eyes.

"Biology?" I repeated to myself as I crossed the living room. Sparrow was good at science.

And we took chemistry.

I laughed to myself. Mom didn't know the difference between a proton and a neutron. Moms didn't have to. Moms knew everything else about the entire world. I opened my bedroom door.

I took each microscopic bit of information in one at a time.

My ceiling fan, swinging hard in a rapid circle. The belt tied to one of the blades. My desk chair, still turning in the middle of the room. The bare feet beside the chair wheels.

The smell of blood.

10. JOSEFINA.

I made myself sit in the tub until the water stopped boiling. My fingers were shriveled. I wasn't sure if I'd ever come back down. The bathroom was still a little smoky.

Revenge? He thought Rhiannon wanted revenge?

If Rhiannon had wanted vengeance there would be nothing left of Barton but bones. She was the center of the universe. She was bigger than emotions like revenge, she always had been.

I was not so gracious.

I had no one to blame but myself. I'd told myself over and over how foolish it was to pretend I could be normal.

Or happy.

Pathetic.

I looked in the mirror as I ran a comb through my hair.

Aradia didn't have to bother possessing me. There were already two different people in my body, each trying to be Fina. One was a human being. One was a structure fire.

I split my hair in the middle, the ends dripping on my collarbones. I gave myself two braids. A good one and an evil one.

Stupid joke.

I wished, like always, that Che were here. He brought me back down to earth without even trying. His humanity gave me humanity.

I heard voices downstairs on my way back to my room. I leaned over the banister and tried to peek around the corner into the den. River. I could pick his voice from a crowd.

"I'm sorry." Heat surged from my core. All my hard work and he undid it with two words.

"Brave," I muttered as I stormed down the stairs. "And stupid."

There was some clattering, clinking of glass on glass. A catch of breath and then sniffing.

"I'm begging you." His voice cracked on the last word. My heart dropped into my stomach. I turned the corner.

River was on my couch, elbows on his knees, his head in his hands. Ofelia and Bernardo stood around him. Bernardo had a bag slung over his shoulder. Ofelia had the sancti verba under her arm.

River stilled and looked up at me. His eyes were so beautiful, the green glowing against the redness. He stood and wiped his eyes with his shirt.

"What's the deal?" I crossed my arms over my chest and stood firm.

"We're going to Barton," Bernardo said as he passed. Ofelia followed close behind.

"Wait, what?" They both continued into the garage. I looked at River. "What is going on?"

"Aradia." River cleared his throat and took a shaky breath. "She got Sparrow." His bottom lip trembled. I crossed the room and put my hands on his shoulders, the hate that I felt just seconds ago evaporating. I watched the top of his head as his body started to shake.

"Hey, no." I slid my hands off of his shoulders, looking him square in the eyes. "Can't do this right now, okay? It's time to focus." I grabbed his chin and tilted it so he faced me head-on. "Let's go." I took his hand and led him to the garage. River and I got into the back of Bernardo's car.

"'Kay. Plan?" I clicked my seatbelt in place. Ofelia sat the sancti verba on her lap in the passenger seat, and opened it. My palms started to itch.

"We're going to hope we don't get killed on sight," Bernardo said as we barreled down the brick drive. "And then we vanquish it."

"Spells aren't going to -"

"I'm going to venture she's not exactly the same species she used to be." Bernardo's tone was hard, clipped. "Our spells work on demons, according to recent history."

"Do they know we are coming?" Ofelia asked River.

"We have a better chance if we surprise them," he responded, a shade over his eyes.

"A better chance of being totally murdered." I threw my hands in the air and let out a huff of air. "Why can't you bring her here?"

"They won't leave her side. She's at my house, I found her trying…" He took a deep, shaky breath. "There was a belt around the ceiling fan. I guess she fell trying to …" River shook his head, the pain evident in the way his shoulders sat.

"She's going to be fine," I told him. He met my eyes for the first time.

"Y'all gotta help her," he begged in a whisper.

"We will." Bernardo pulled up to a chain-link gate on wheels, topped with barbed wire. River's window came down.

A red-haired man stepped down from a shack. He leaned over and peered in the open window.

"You gotta be kiddin' me River," he chuckled, shoving his hands in his pockets. "You're tryna get me killed, man."

"Let us in, Noah." River's voice was steadier than before.

Noah shook his head. "Nah, you're gonna have to Barton Law me. I'm not goin' down for this."

"Fine. Barton Law. Open the gate," River commanded.

Noah nodded and reached into the shack. The gate rolled away.

Bernardo stepped on the gas. River ran his hands over his hair and exhaled through his nose.

"Just keep goin' straight," he told Bernardo. "Last house on the left, with the red door." I kept my eyes on the seat in front of me.

We stopped after a few seconds and River catapulted out of the car. We followed after him as best we could.

A woman stood on the porch, all swollen belly and huge curls. She paced a few steps in either direction across the length of the door.

"Nova!" River called. She stopped in her tracks. River jogged up to her. She looked at him, then at us, and her face exploded in fear. She grabbed his forearms.

"Have you lost your mind?" she hissed.

"Listen, they're gonna have -"

"They are gonna murder you!" She looked behind him again and our eyes met. Those same eyes, too green to be grey, under thick lashes.

River shook her. "Nova, come on, please, she's my best friend." His voice broke. Nova's eyes welled up in the same moment.

"Don't do that," she muttered.

"I need you to -" She reached over and opened the door. He kissed her cheek and ran into the house. We followed him, Ofelia, Bernardo, and me.

Nova grabbed my arm as I crossed the threshold. "Watch yourself," she whispered, eyes wide. It wasn't a threat. It was a warning.

The four of us ran through the dark kitchen. A guttural scream came from behind a closed door. I swallowed the lump in my throat, hoping to slow my thumping heart.

I ran into River's back as he stopped short where tile became carpet. There was a man standing outside the second door to the right, where the squeaking of a mattress could be heard. His fingers were laced together, sitting right above his navel. His beard was graying, well-kept, as was his chin-length hair.

"I might allow you to explain," he said. His voice was low, smooth, but it rumbled in my chest.

"I have to save her." The voice that came from River's mouth was so unlike his own that it made my head snap up to make sure that, yes, it really was still River standing beside me.

"You have such little faith in our Heavenly Father," he sighed.

River shook his head. "He helps those who helps themselves."

The man looked at me with deep disgust. Bile filled my every cell. A tidal wave of hatred bubbled up like vomit, hanging at the tip of my tongue. Danger bells, which had been so quiet, were banging together and echoing in my ears.

"And how will they help our Sparrow?" The old man slowly brought his eyes to greet Rivers.

"One of their own was possessed a few days ago." Another scream, a scream from the bottom of her stomach, pierced the house. River cringed. "I prayed for guidance and this is where I was pointed. I'm beggin' you."

He crossed the living room and got on his knees before the man. I exhaled and smoke poured out of my nostrils. I sucked it back, looking around to see if anyone had noticed. The man put his hand on top of River's head, which was bowed to look at the ground.

"For we have not a high priest which cannot be touched with the feelings of our infirmaries. But was in all points tempted like as we are, but without sin." River nodded. "Son, you'll be disenchanted, I'm afraid. Sooner rather than later. And you will hurt Sparrow further with this interjection in His works. But you have humbled yourself for another before me. I forgive you."

"Thank you." River stood up and turned back to us. I couldn't meet his eyes. The older man opened the door.

I took one look at Sparrow and the room swayed. Her cheeks were hollow, her lips ripped to bloody shreds by her fangs. Black veins stood up under her eyes, along her neck, up her arms. The mattress was creaking under the force with which she yanked herself off of it. She didn't get far against the restraints which tied her wrists and ankles to the bed frame.

But it was her eyes, rolled back so only the whites showed, that got me.

Bernardo put his hand on my back. Hold it together.

There were tall candles on every surface. The faces of Jesus, Mary, and others stared at us, casting flickers and shadows on the walls. There was a shuffle to our right and then a woman was there in the dimness. I could make out a sharp cheekbone and then a set of green eyes.

Bernardo gripped my arm because the only thought in my head was to run.

The Elders.

These were the Elders.

"You must've lost your ever-lovin' mind," the woman said to River.

"Papa let them in, we have to let 'em try."

"They're not touchin' her." This man's voice was reedy. "The Heavenly Father's got a plan."

Sparrow screamed again, a warped noise which pierced my soul. I couldn't take it anymore. I grabbed my mother's hand, then Bernardo's, and I lit myself on fire.

River's mom jumped back and pulled River with her. We three walked to Sparrow's bed and I cooled down as I knelt by her. Ofelia wiped tears from Sparrow's cheeks.

"The flies," she sobbed. "The flies are in my brain."

My heart stopped. "Oh my God," I whispered.

Ofelia untied one of Sparrow's hands and held it between her own. Sparrow howled deep in her chest and thrashed her legs. It was déjà vu.

"Fina, hands over the heart." I put my hands on Sparrow's skin. Flames erupted the second I touched her. She shrieked, a much more human noise. I blew it away. Ofelia handed me the sancti verba and pushed me out of the way. "Bernardo."

Bernardo stepped in front of me, one knee on the bed, and leaned over Sparrow to press his hands to her chest. She stared up at him and went still.

"Raven," she whispered.

Then she yanked her leg up to knee Bernardo, but instead we heard a pop as her ankle came out of socket. Her chest heaved under Bernardo's hands as she sobbed. Bernardo swung his other leg over and straddled her thighs.

"Shh," he murmured. She squirmed under him. He spread his body over her torso and tried to press her to the bed.

"Hands on the solar plexus," Ofelia told him. He nodded and winced as Sparrow bared her fangs at him and hissed. "Salt, in the bag." I reached inside and grabbed the canister. "Open it." I took the lid off. "Open the sancti verba." I set it on the floor and opened the cover.

I held my hands over the book like a planchette. "I call upon the whitest light to surround me here on the hour of my incantation. I call upon my guardian and the Blessed Mother to invoke the magic within my veins. I call forth the incantations hidden here. Videor."

Ink poured like blood onto the pages as they fluttered, moved by a wind I could not feel.

"We come here to banish this evil which has tried to overcome this soul," I read. Ofelia's hands glowed white. "We make this body strong so its soul might fight the darkness within. We expel the vermin taking residence in this soul."

Sparrow groaned. "They talk beneath the blood-rimmed moon." Sparrow's head rolled from side to side. I looked up at Bernardo. He was shaking his head.

Can't hear her.

"Blessed Mother we implore you to work in this child," I continued. "To touch where our spells cannot, to expel this evil to the salt of the Earth." Sparrow tried to yank her hand from Ofelia but the light had bound them together.

"Dragon girl!" Sparrow screamed.

I froze.

"Keep going," Ofelia commanded.

In the center of Sparrow's chest rose a red-hot, raised form from inside. It was a cross, double-stricken, with an infinity sign at the bottom.

The sancti verba pages fluttered to a stop on the same symbol.

The Leviathan cross, alchemical symbol of sulfur, long believed to be the mark of the Devil.

"Little dragon girl," Sparrow chuckled in that electric fan voice. "I told you to come home. We're waiting for you."

"Fina, keep going!" Ofelia shouted. I couldn't move. Sparrow looked over at me, her blood-covered teeth gleaming in the light from the candles.

"Raven, owl, vulture, underneath a blood-rimmed moon," she said again. "Ravens ate his heart because it was yours." She closed her eyes.

"Mom," I whimpered. I covered my mouth with my shaking hands so I didn't scream.

"Now!" she told Bernardo.

"Debellavi!" Bernardo commanded.

Her chest rose off the bed and then thudded back. All at once, she was silent and still, a small line of blood dripping from her mouth.

"Come back." Bernardo shook her shoulders slightly.

She coughed once and fumes like sulfur hit my nose. A black mass dripped over her chin. The flies rose from her mouth, buzzing and swarming in their hive.

Behind me, I heard someone dry-heaving.

"Consido," I said. The bugs froze in mid air. I balled the swarm up until it fit in my palm, a stiff hunk of crushed flies, and smashed it into the salt. Smoke rose up from under my hand and I could hear sizzling coming from the pile.

Bernardo got up and stood at the edge of the bed. He wiped the gore from her chin with his thumb. The tenderness in it made my heart ache. Ofelia stood and helped me up, taking the sancti verba from me, Bernardo taking the salt.

"Well done," she said, squeezing his arm gently.

"Well done yourself," he half-smiled back at her. I could hear them, but it was like a phone call in a tunnel, my eyes trained on Sparrow, her words echoing loudly in my head. "We suggest placing Apache's Tears on her windowsill. She'll be susceptible to negative energy for a few days." Bernardo dug in his pocket and set the smooth, black stones on the bed beside Sparrow. We started towards the bedroom door.

The lights were switched on and I had to squeeze my eyes shut to get the blinding flickers to go away.

"Glory be," the older man said, as casually as if we'd stopped a leaking pipe.

"Glory be." He was echoed by four stunned voices in stereo.

"It has begun," he continued as he came to the center of the room. "The Great Battle begins when the raven, vulture, and owl talk beneath a blood-rimmed moon." His eyes, those same green-grey eyes, locked on mine. "The time has come to draw our lines in the sand."

I still couldn't feel my body, still worried the terror would tear me from reality at any moment. I glanced at the leaders of the group hell-bent on destroying my family since the beginning of time.

And a tiny part of me roared back to the surface.

"First of all, these are a fire hazard." I pursed my lips and blew, every candle flickering out at once. I glanced at Sparrow's motionless body. "Second of all, you're wel-come."

I slammed the door behind us.

11. RIVER.

I sat on the edge of the bed and worked her wrist out of the rope.

"You scared me," I talked to her unconscious body. "This was a crummy prank." The bed shook with the force of my laughter. I was losing it. I was sure the only way she would ever be still again is when she was dead.

Nova appeared in the doorway, wringing her hands. Anxiety rolled over me.

I jumped up. "What's wrong?"

She rocked back and forth, heel to toe. "I need to confess something to my Elders Council." Papa held out his hands. Mom shrugged off the desk and stood to Papa's right. Abel pulled himself off the wall and came to Papa's left.

"Please," Papa murmured.

"I ask my Elders to consider getting protection from the witches."

Mom pinched the bridge of her nose. "Nova, I appreciate you tryin' to lighten the mood but honey, we're tired as can be. It's not the time."

"I'm not jokin', momma. They've clearly got blessed objects they -"

"Blessed?" Papa repeated, his voice growing with anger. I cringed. "You believe sorceresses hold objects from our Heavenly Father?"

"Not blessed, maybe, the word is… powerful?"

"Even if we wanted their help, they're not gonna be willing," Abel said.

"They were willing to help Sparrow," I said quietly, my eyes on her limp body.

Nova's hand rested on her belly. "I don't want my daughter to need their help."

"If it's time for the Great Battle then it's time to go where He is leading us," I said. "He led me to the Manor's door and he saved my best friend using the witches. That's good enough for me."

"Are you implying because I don't want to hold court with the heirs of Rhiannon that I go against Him?" Papa asked.

"The enemy of our enemy is our friend," Nova recited.

"Many false prophets are gone out into the world," Papa replied. I got a weird chill across my shoulders. "You heard the Devil use Sparrow to tell that little witch to come home. She is the enemy. She is more than willing to keep her hands in the pot and masquerade as a helping hand if she can turn us against one another."

"She came here because I begged them to because you were gonna let Sparrow die!" I exploded.

Nova grabbed my arm, but I yanked away. Papa closed the space between us and clapped my shoulders. We were nose to nose.

"When you take my place as the Prophet, then you will understand the ways of our Heavenly Father." He spoke so softly I could barely hear him. "But today you are not the Prophet, son. I am. I am the ultimate authority in this congregation. And I am telling you, this congregation will never prostitute ourselves to mediums and necromancers out of desperation." He let me go and looked between Nova and I. "Take your sister home. She needs to rest."

"Yes, sir," I said through gritted teeth.

Nova and Noah lived three houses up the street. I stormed out of my house with her close behind.

"What are we gonna do?" she asked.

"You're not doin' nothin'," I snapped. "You're goin' home."

"I might be pregnant, but I will still beat you up. Now what are we gonna do?" she demanded. She met my stride, even with half a watermelon strapped to her front.

"Go over there," I sighed. "Ask, beg, for their help. For anything we can get to protect us all. I really don't know."

"Let's go, then."

"If we do this, there's no tellin' what's gonna happen when we come back."

"There's not gonna be anywhere to come back to if we all end up like Sparrow. If you trust 'em, so do I."

We reached the gate shack. Nova knocked on the frame and Noah popped his head out.

"Hey, you didn't die!" he chuckled as he pushed the button. "Where y'all goin'?"

"Town, be right back," Nova leaned in to peck his cheek.

As soon as the gate shut behind us we started to run. Dust kicked up into our faces and mouths, the metallic taste of dirt hanging on my tongue. I balled my hands to start pumping my arms, and my fingers stuck together. I still had Sparrow's blood all over me.

I almost laughed. A bloody man in flip-flops running down a dirt road, with a pregnant woman right behind him in a knee-length denim skirt. Running away from the only home we'd ever known to the prison we'd built for the Devil.

To protect ourselves from the Devil.

The turn in to the gate was right ahead. I could feel the static wall, the invisible hum around the Manor. A few more steps and we'd be able to see the roof of the house. I reached behind me and grabbed Nova's hand, willing her to keep up.

My nose was the first thing to connect with solid nothingness. The smell of roses engulfed us as I hit my knees, inches away from the gate. I clutched my face and groaned.

"Good night," Nova hissed. I looked up at her through watery eyes. She held her wrist.

"That didn't happen before."

"Before?" she demanded. I shrugged, heat flooding to my cheeks.

She pulled me up with her good arm and brushed my hands away from my face. "No blood."

I put my hand on her belly. She patted it.

"What do we do now?" I asked nasally.

Nova picked up a rock from the road. "Maybe if we break it…" I jumped out of the way as she wound up her arm. She tossed the rock and ducked just in time to avoid becoming my nose twin.

"It's impenetrable." Bernardo stood before the opening gates. When he looked at us through the nothingness, it was like looking down an asphalt road in the middle of July - everything coated in a shimmering haze.

"What is it?" I reached out to poke it, half expecting to be shocked this time.

"A barrier. Usually we practice an open-door policy, but desperate times…" He shrugged. "We weren't looking forward to a house call from your grandfather for our interference."

"The Elders don't leave Barton," Nova said. "Ever."

Bernardo raised his eyebrows at me. "Desperate times."

"Why do you think we're here?" Nova put her hands over her belly. "I've never been so desperate, okay?"

Bernardo thought a moment, looking from Nova to myself, not expression unreadable. But finally he sighed, putting his hand up as he spoke. "On my word, take five steps forward. No more, no less. Ready?" I took Nova's hand and nodded. "Now. Retextus." He snapped his fingers.

"One, two, three, four, five," I counted aloud. Warm rain drifted over us as we took the fifth step. I turned around to look at Shell Court. It was hazy now, a TV station only reachable with antennas. I reached out and touched cool, solid nothingness.

"Amazing," Nova whispered. "Could y'all do that to Barton?"

"It would have no effect," he replied. We started up to the house. "Your sovereign shielding from the heirs of the enemy prevents our spells from touching you."

"How do you know all this?" I asked.

"I'm... perceptive."

I had another shiver of familiarity.

"And because I'm perceptive, I'm going to venture you're here for some help?" he continued. I nodded. "You've come in the nick of time."

We went up the stairs of the front porch. Bernardo opened the door. "Both of you please come in."

The smell of the house was practically unbearable. I heard Nova catch her breath beside me. The kitchen was off to the right. I could see piles of herbs, bottles and vials, some empty and some full. Candle wax had hardened around the sink handle. Through the narrow doorway into the dining room, I could see a table covered in open books bound in red leather, stones of all colors, knives and fruits and candles. There was yelling, chanting, in another language. Maybe more than one.

Bernardo pointed to the high stools in front of the counter. "Have a seat."

Nova gripped my hand tight as Bernardo went into the dining room. A thin door slid from the wall and cut us off from the family.

"How can you stand it in here?" she whispered, the desperation plain through her eyes.

"It's never this strong, they must be doin' something real big in there." I looked around the room.

The door opened and Fina slipped out. She looked like she'd seen a ghost. Her hair was wild around her face and she had a red smear across her face.

"Hey," she sighed.

"Is this a bad time?" I asked.

"Actually, I'm glad you're here." She twined her fingers together, her eyes falling to her feet. "Sort of. I need you to do something for me. For us."

"Of course." I would jump off of a cliff for her.

"You don't know what it is," she chuckled.

"Is it gonna help the people I love?"

"I sure hope so." She bit her bottom lip.

"Then let's do it."

The dining room door opened again and two, three, five more witches filled the kitchen. A foot of marble countertop stood between us and them. Nova's shoulders were up to her ears, her eyes wild, and her knuckles turned white at her side. I squeezed her hand.

Fina's mom clasped her hands together and put them over her heart. "How is Sparrow?"

"Sleeping." The image of Sparrow hanging from a ceiling fan stained the back of my eyelids. "I never thought I would see her sleep again. I don't know how to thank you."

"We have a way," Fina sighed.

"Okay," I said, nodding.

"We know Aradia wants Fina, although why is not clear. But it seems she's unwilling to take Fina directly, or perhaps she can't?" Fina's mom shook her head. "At any rate, we've bottled a preventative." She held up a brown, sharp-edged bottle. "And we believe we know who will be next."

"Me," I breathed. "It's me, isn't it? Because I…" I stopped.

Fina looked at me, eyes glassy with tears.

"Because you what?" Her voice cracked. Everything around us blurred for a second, turning to static.

"Because he's gotten close to you," Nova sighed. "So now he's gotta drink whatever that is."

"Exactly," Fina's mom responded.

"Okay, so I drink it. What then?" I asked.

"Then you're safe," Fina said.

"What about everyone else?"

"We're working on it," she snapped. "Look, she's escalating, okay? The gap between Che and Dia was a lot bigger than the gap between Dia and Sparrow, and if she gets her hands on you -"

"Che?" I stopped her, my heart beating hard. "What do you mean, Che?"

Every witch's eyes went to the floor, and for an unbearable moment, there was no noise in the Manor.

"Che was possessed when he died," Bernardo finally said, his voice low.

Wave after tidal wave of grief crashed over me. I couldn't be sure if it was Nova, me, or a mixture of both. The wildness in his eyes the night at the game. How he was so unlike himself.

Sparrow had been so unlike herself at school today.

"Vultures got to him," Bernardo murmured. "Ravens got to Dia." He glanced behind him, at the straight-haired woman in the corner. "Sparrow got a bit of all three, it seems."

"Not even mortals are safe?" Nova asked. I took her hand and she gripped my fingers like she might fall off the edge of the earth.

"No one near me is safe," Fina said, so quietly I almost missed it.

"Stop that," the bearded man hissed. "We're getting there. We are getting there," he insisted, placing a calming hand on Fina's shoulder. "But with the escalation, we need to ensure we head off the next possession. We need you to protect yourself."

I looked at Fina, at that glinting blue in her eye, not lightning now but shimmering water. Warm and deep, bottomless like the rest of her.

"I need you to trust me," she whispered.

"I do," I promised. I held out my hand to her mom. "I'll do it."

"Right now?" Nova demanded in a low voice, digging her fingernails into my hand.

"We'd prefer that, yes, in case of side effects," the bearded man said. "Do you have any allergies?"

"Just garlic, unless there's cat hair in there, too." I tried to smile but my face felt frozen stiff.

"No garlic, no cat hair." Fina's mom reached across the counter and handed me the bottle. I popped the cork, taking a deep breath.

Nova slapped her hand over her face and stood up, the color draining from her cheeks, knocking over the stool she was sitting on. Saliva flooded my mouth as I inhaled. I thought I would pass out. I sucked at my teeth, praying harder than ever before for them to stay put.

"There's blood in that," Nova said, her voice muffled behind her hand. Her thumb and finger pinched her nose shut.

"I see that." I put the cork back on and exhaled. "I can't drink witch blood."

"Sparrow did," Bernardo replied under his breath.

"Sparrow did?" Nova repeated.

"Sparrow does lots of things she's not supposed to." Understatement of the century. "We don't drink from anyone who's not like us."

"My neck says otherwise," the big brother - the screamer - retorted.

"I just…" I looked at Fina. She had to understand. She reached her hand across the bar.

"Okay," she murmured, her eyes on the bottle, her shoulders drooped low.

"I'm really sorry," I whispered.

"I'm sorry," she told me, her voice tight. "I'm so sorry, River."

I took her hand off the counter and brought it to my lips. She closed her eyes, and a single tear ran down her cheek.

I looked over at Nova, tears in her own eyes, her hands laced over her belly. She held it like Papa held his. She was brave, so much braver than me. If it was her, she would have chugged that potion in a second.

But it wasn't her. It was me.

I was the one who ran here begging for help, and I was the one refusing the only help they could give. I was the one admitting I loved Fina, loved her enough to be Aradia's next victim, but also admitting I didn't trust her. Admitting I'd rather lose my soul than take a chance on her. She'd taken so many chances on me.

The bottle popped when I yanked the cork off.

I tipped my head back and let the entire vial run down my throat, the sweet burn, the tang of dirt, the sensation of biting into the juiciest piece of fruit I'd ever had.

Warmth of Heaven but hotter, more like hellfire than sunlight. Angels singing louder than ever, practically screaming.

I felt hands slip under my elbows and was vaguely aware of being put on the floor, but I was already floating. I was swallowed in a cloud of softness.

When I woke up we were in the woods, Nova and Sparrow and me. The sun was setting. I was thirsty. Thirstier than I had ever been. Restriction had done a number on me this time. Sparrow was thirsty, too. Her wrists were black and purple from the ropes. Nova's belly was giant.

I told her to wait. I would bring her something, something really good. I could already smell blood, deep in the trees. I went towards it.

She was watching the vulture eat, shining golden light and golden hair and golden eyes. I'd never been so happy to see someone in my life. She hugged me tight and pointed at the ground.

"Look at them," she whispered to me. I couldn't stop smiling. The vulture's head twisted wildly and the stomach of a black bird, its body splayed before us, split open. Blood pooled around them, running over my feet, her feet.

"Beautiful," I said.

"Isn't it?" Her voice was like honey. "My little dragon girl is beautiful, too. Isn't she?"

"Beautiful dragon girl," I repeated. "I love her."

"I love her, too, darling. That's why you must bring her home to me." She started to laugh and so did I.

I looked down at the vulture and the raven once more.

But the raven was Fina, split open in the middle, bottomless eyes staring at nothing.

I couldn't stop the vulture. I couldn't close my eyes. I could only scream.

"She won't last another day. This." She pointed to the carnage, beauty turned horror, in front of us. "Is her destiny if she does not come home."

And I could taste it again, the hellfire, the juiciest orange, the sweet burn. No, I tried to say, but instead could not stop screaming. Her blood was filling my mouth, running into my throat. My stomach was engorged with her blood.

"All you know how to do is destroy," she told me.

"I'm sorry I'm so sorry I'll do anything I don't want to –" The blood was building up in my esophagus. I tried to spit it out but nothing would come.

"Bring her to me or drink until you explode," she said. "She belongs to me, the little dragon girl." I started to gag.

I reached up above Fina's body and grabbed the sharpest branch. I had to get it out. I was swelling with blood. It began to drip from my ears, my nose. My stomach was bigger than Nova's. Where was Nova?

I brought the branch down straight through my middle.

But I could still taste the blood. I was still drinking but I was shrinking. She was gone. Fina was gone. It was only me in the woods now. I started to cough up the blood of the girl I loved. I looked down at the branch sticking out of me, blood, hers and mine, dripping around it. Then things went black.

A little white something floated in front of my eyes. I reached out for it but couldn't touch it, my hand passing right through it. I watched it grow bigger.

Oh.

I had died.

This was the tunnel, and the white thing was the light everyone talked about. Walk towards the light.

It got bigger, faster, as I walked towards it. This was definitely the end of the tunnel.

Would I get to meet my niece here before she was born? I wasn't afraid, but I was sad to leave before she came.

I gagged again, and began to cough. The light got brighter. Was I coughing out my soul? The Bible didn't mention this part. The light was blinding now, so blinding I had to close my eyes. But my eyes were already closed. The light was shining through my closed eyelids and my back was against a wall but I'd been walking so long -

I opened my eyes.

"Oh, glory be." Nova's hair brushed over my arm as she rested her head on me. She was crying. I moved my left shoulder and it stung. The back of my head throbbed, too.

At first I could only see white, but it slowly came into focus. I was back in the kitchen.

"Fina?" I whispered. I put my hand on the back of Nova's head as she sobbed. "Fina," I repeated.

"Hey," she said softly, I turned my head towards her voice.

She was here. She was right in front of me, alive, whole, not even a little bloody. Smiling at me. Man that smile.

"I would never do it," I said. "Never, Fina, I love you, I would never hurt you, I swear -"

"Hush," she said. Her hand landed on my cheek. I pressed my lips to the inside of her wrist. "It's okay."

"I'm really sorry."

"I'm fine, River. It wasn't real. It was all in your head."

"I tasted you." I shook away from her touch, my eyes running over her, looking for holes in her precious flesh. Nova sat back as I started to get up. I was stiff as a board. "I know I did."

"In the potion," Nova told me. "The blood in the potion. That's all. You didn't move a bit."

I looked around, at the worried faces surrounding me.

When I caught Ofelia's eye, she smiled. "Side effects. Belladonna causes drowsiness and occasional lucid dreams. How are you feeling?"

"Fried," I muttered as I finally steadied on my feet. "Like a hair dryer that fell in the tub."

Nova chuckled. She looked over at Fina and laughed harder. Fina started laughing, too, and then I couldn't stop myself, either. It was the hysteria of relief. I hadn't hurt anyone. It was all a terrible, terrible dream.

Even if I could feel the blood between my toes. Even if I could still taste fresh, thick roses in the back of my throat. A dream.

"We should get goin' before they know we're gone," Nova said to me.

"They know," Bernardo said. His fingers dug at the dried flecks of paint on his jeans.

"How do you figure?" Nova asked.

A car horn blared outside, long and angry, until it rang in my ears. My truck's horn.

Nova and I looked at one another. I wished for the light back, the tunnel, even the vulture.

"Because they're outside," Bernardo said.

11. JOSEFINA.

Half terror, half rage.

River's hand shook as I gripped it with my own. He stared at the floor, eyes unseeing.

"Let's go, Nova," he murmured, his voice flat. She nodded robotically. Both of their eyes had gone dark. I didn't let go of his hand as they headed to the front door. Ofelia and Elian were right behind us.

"You shouldn't come," Nova said to me. "They'll eat you alive."

"Doubt it," I muttered.

It shocked me how dark it was outside. The porch light was off. The white truck sitting at the open gates had no headlights on. Once we were down the stairs and on the bricks, River let go of my hand.

He and Nova both started to drag their feet, their long strides becoming smaller and smaller. I couldn't see until we were practically on top of them - the three Elders standing just
on the other side of the barrier. Even knowing they were there ahead of time, even knowing they couldn't touch me, it didn't matter. Nothing could prepare me.

The streetlights on Shell Court gave enough light for me to see River's mother. There was almost no resemblance - she was lily-white, with straight, auburn hair - but those eyes didn't lie. Hers bore into me now, green-grey glaciers. I could feel her freezing my insides, filling me with frost.

She looked at River, and only then did I exhale.

"Home. Now. Both of you." Her voice sounded exactly like Nova's. I wished I'd had a mother to see myself in.

River reached out and pressed a trembling hand to the barrier. "We can't, momma."

Her head snapped towards me. My breath caught in my throat. "Put it down." Her tone didn't change, but her words came from between her teeth. I raised my hand but River swatted it
away.

"Momma, please," he said. "We need help."

"Are you apostatizing?" the older man asked. His beard shifted as his jaw moved. Dread like concrete poured into my chest, how similar he and River were. I glanced up at River, at his slack jaw, his wounded eyes. He looked so childlike.

He shook his head. "Of course not," he said in that little voice.

"Disobedience of this caliber usually results in desertion. I'm just sorry you dragged your sister into it." The man looked at Nova's belly. "Who knows what could have happened to the baby, being here."

"What?" Nova squeaked. Her breathing got heavy. "You - you think something h-h-happened?" She wrapped her arms around her middle. "What happened to her? What happened, Papa, tell me, please, what did I do? Please, pl -" She caught her breath and sobbed. River put his arm around her and pulled her into his chest.

My anger began to overwhelm my fear.

"Your baby is fine," I muttered. "We're not poisonous."

The older man - Papa, Nova said - smiled a soft, congenial smile at me. This was River's future, like their mother was Nova's future. All tightly woven together like a well-knitted blanket. Like the vines winding around the light post by our driveway.

"If you weren't poisonous, my successors wouldn't be groveling at your feet like dogs. I know all about your kind. More than you could imagine." He turned his attention to my parents. "What were you going to do for them? Some ten cent miracles? Were you going to soil our hallowed ground again to perform magic tricks on a sick child?"

"Nothing," Nova whispered. She sniffed and wiped her face. "Nothing. There was nothing they could do."

"I doubt that. Their ancestors were well-versed in meddling with innocent souls."

"Whose ancestors?" I demanded.

"The little dragon girl's ancestors," Papa replied. His face was a blank slate, but the slimy smirk right below the surface made me clench my fists. "Aradia and Rhiannon were quite close. Vengeful. It wouldn't surprise me one bit if they came together in the same body. Seduce and destroy." He shook his head. "Shameless."

The switch flipped. The source of it all was standing in front of me – every rumor, every threat, every reason I couldn't be with River.

I snapped my fingers. "Retextus." The barrier vanished. Elian's big hand gripped my shoulder, but the heat made him pull away in the same instant. I closed the space between Papa and me. His face didn't falter, the same stupid half-smile on his thin lips.

"There's no need for vengeance. I've already brought your grandson to his knees. No magic required." I matched his pathetic smile.

There was an explosion next to him as River's mom lunged towards me. The third man, Sparrow's father, held her back. I opened my mouth and let smoke pour out. It swirled around Papa. I could see smoke rising from my eyelashes.

Little dragon girl, indeed.

"He is the earth but I am the sun," I told Papa. "And you know it."

His face faltered, only for a second, only enough to fill me with satisfaction.

"Go home, River," I said. I really meant goodbye.

I watched them pile into River's truck and peel off towards Barton Heights. The smell of diesel and mud filled the air. The gates closed in front of me.

I turned around.

The look on Ofelia's face threatened to crush my heart into dust. It was a look I knew all too well, a look she tried to hide from me time after time. Each time we had to leave town because of my temper. Each time I damaged property. Each time I hurt one of my siblings. The look of a woman who bought a kitten and got a cheetah.

Frightened disappointment.

I took a deep breath. "Plan B," I said. I started back up to the house.

"Plan B?" Elian demanded. "Plan B. Do you have any clue as to what you've done, Fina?"

"The question is why doesn't she possess me directly if she wants me? Why use the people around me?" I continued as I went up the porch stairs, ignoring his anger.

"Fina!" Elian bellowed. I stopped halfway through the den. The door slammed. My siblings stood between the den and the kitchen, watching.

"Where did they go?" Dia asked as she stirred a large bowl.

"Home," I replied.

"What's the plan from here?" Carmen interjected.

"Oh, the plan," Elian said. "Yes, there is no plan now. There won't be any assisting the people of Barton Heights at all. In fact, I'll be shocked if we aren't run out of this state with torches and pitchforks."

I swallowed hard. The high of destroying Papa's smugness was fading, and in its place was crippling remorse.

"What happened?" Dia asked.

"Oh, Fina, tell them what happened," Elian snapped. "Please, regale them with your tales of quippy arrogance while people die around us!" I bit down on my bottom lip and tried not to blink.

"Elian," Ofelia warned. She turned to my siblings. "The Elders of Barton Heights have asked that we don't interfere."

"Do they understand it's life and death?" Bernardo replied.

Ofelia nodded. "There is nothing more we can do. We cannot convince everyone to save themselves."

"They're probably better off." I didn't mean to say it out loud. The tears were building on the rims of my eyes. I was going to blink soon and then it would be useless to pretend.

"Don't tell me you're going to believe a single word that man said," Ofelia murmured.

"It wasn't what he said." I met Ofelia's eyes. "Why didn't you tell us about Aradia before?"

Ofelia looked over at Elian. "We didn't see the point. The other species have always kept to themselves."

"Until now," I said. "Until we… I," I sighed. "Until I started mixing with another species. Suddenly Aradia comes to town in pretty much the same second. Starts this Great Battle, kills Che, hurts my sister, all for what? For me, right? So, Barton's probably better off without me. Everyone would probably be better off without me."

I stared at my feet as the dam broke. Little drops fell from the tip of my chin onto my shirt. The only sound in the house was me trying not to make sound as I cried. Everyone stared at me, not sure what to say. I bit down on my tongue to stay quiet.

"I'm sure she wants you to believe that," Bernardo said softly. "Fortunately, no one else does." I looked up at him. He smiled.

"We've never been ones to go quietly," Dia added. "The Blessed Mother didn't, and neither do we."

"Rhiannon lost the throne to none but herself," I murmured, years of recitation bubbling to the surface.

Dia nodded. "It was her choice, to the bitter end. She chose to die rather than lose her light, rather than succumb to chaos and darkness. She died to bring us to life. She died to give the light a second chance. And you're going to succumb so easily to darkness?" She shook her head. "I think not."

"What if it's too late?" I asked him. I met the eyes of every member of my family. "What if it's too late?" I demanded again. "What then?"

"It isn't too late until Aradia has your soul in her hands," Ofelia replied. "Until then, you fight. We all fight. Do you understand?" She took my face in her hands. I looked into her dark eyes. My mother's eyes. The first eyes I saw when I came back. "Prophecies and possessions and prayers," she chuckled. "All just different arenas of battle in the same war. The war is only starting, and it is ours to win."

"How?" I whispered.

Ofelia smiled. "We follow in the Blessed Mother's footsteps. We fight until the bitter end."

I nodded and smiled, as much as I could smile.

"I love you," I told her.

"I love you," she murmured as she hugged me. "Go get some sleep. It's very nearly three." She pulled away. "In fact, we could all use some rest. It does no good to work in delirium."

I went up the stairs and closed my bedroom door, locked it, and sat against it.

"What do I do?" I wasn't sure who I was asking. Rhiannon. Aradia. Myself. It didn't matter because no one was answering. I stared at my burning, trembling fingers.

Unmarred by flames or fangs.

I always thought it was just poetic language.

I rested my throbbing head against the door and let my heavy eyelids close. A small voice in the back of my brain told me not to sleep. It told me she'd come for me in my dreams.

But it was the draught not the dreams. She hadn't come for me yet.

I woke up from a buzzing sound. I lifted my neck off the door and wiped drool from my chin. The buzzing continued. I jumped to my feet. Flies. Where were the flies?

The noise stopped. I sighed and shook myself. I leaned over my dresser and got right up to the mirror, staring into my own dilated pupils. I was cracking up. I rubbed my dried spit off my face and cleaned the mascara from under my eyes.

It was just my dark circles.

Sleep, Fina, for the love of God. No wonder you're hearing -

The buzzing started again. I jumped and covered my mouth with my hands so I didn't scream. I fell to my knees and tried to breathe. It got louder. It was coming from my nightstand.

I crawled across the floor and the light caught my eye.

"It's your phone," I chuckled. "You idiot. It's your phone." I laughed as I wiped away my tears, painfully aware of how close to a breakdown I really was.

I picked up the phone as the buzzing stopped. Three missed calls.

From River.

I hit 'call back'.

"Sorry, were you sleeping?" he asked.

"Are you okay?"

He chuckled. "I know it's late but, do you wanna run away with me?"

"What?" I sat on my bed.

"I'm never gonna see you again if I stay in Barton. And Aradia's gunnin' for you, she knows you're here. Maybe if we leave, things'll …" He trailed off.

"I don't think it works that way," I whispered.

"I gotta leave, Fina. I can't stay in Barton. I want you to come with me. I love you."

My chest began to ache. My brain started working, synapses firing too fast for me to keep up with. We could be together. No looking over our shoulders, no worrying about Elders. Together. Safe. Everyone would be safe, far away from me.

We could be together.

I chewed on my thumbnail. I could hear the motor of his truck running in the background.

"Can you give me like, ten minutes?" I asked.

"Really?" I could hear his smile. "Serious?" I stood and opened my closet.

"Yeah I need like, ten minutes, I have to pack and -"

"Yeah, yeah, yeah fine! Meet me at the school in ten minutes." I pulled my duffle bag from one of the shelves.

"The school?" I repeated.

"I gotta leave my truck," he told me. "It's in their name. It'll give them a reason to come after me."

"Right." I opened the dresser drawers and started tossing random things into my duffle bag. "Okay, ten minutes."

"Okay," he chuckled.

"I love you," I whispered.

The line went dead.

12. RIVER.

I didn't dare look behind me. I watched two owls dance around each other in the streetlights as Nova and I rattled around the bed of the truck.

My ears were ringing, a piano string was stretched too tight across my skull and someone was plucking it. I was clenching my teeth but if I stopped my head would blow up.

Pieces of Fina in my pocket, the taste of her in the back of my throat, the feeling of her fingers between mine. I held on to them, tight as I could.

Noah opened the gate for us.

They felt like evidence I should purge, like proof of my crimes, proof of her damning words. I couldn't let them go - let her go. I was never going to see her again.

Abel drove the truck to the Pike house and we parked. I jumped down and opened the bed for Nova. I helped her to the ground.

She looked at me and I screamed with my eyes, straining against the haze of guilt and shame. She heard me. I knew she did because her tired eyes went glassy.

Abel put his hand on her shoulder. "Head on inside, Nova Grace. Get some rest." Abel looked at me and inclined his head to the truck. "Let's go."

I closed the bed as we took off again.

Of all the ways I thought Fina would kill me, I never thought she'd throw me to my own wolves. She exposed me, my obsession with her, my sacrilegious worship. Every word was true.

I knew exactly where we were going. The truck stopped a foot from Church. I got out and dragged my leaden body, Papa leading the way, mom and Abel behind me.

The doors slammed and echoed in the barren sanctuary. I faced down the crucifix behind the altar, higher and larger than anyone could reach. Jesus looked down at us all, his face contorted in pain. I was next. I pinched myself for thinking it.

We went behind the altar to the black wooden door. Papa took the ring of keys off his belt loop, the keys to everywhere in Barton, and unlocked the vestry.

I remembered the first time I set foot in there. I was six years old, Sparrow was seven, Nova was almost thirteen. Papa brought us back after late Sunday service. We touched the marble table, taller than every one of us then. We were sweating in minutes, but we couldn't stay away from the pokers and the fireplace.

"You three will not only be Chosen," Papa had said. "But I believe you will be the most Chosen of any child in this congregation. Our Heavenly Father's light shines on you all, to succeed the Elders when we are no longer able to lead. As the Shepherd leads the Flock."

I remember, even at six, understanding this room, this table; they were something of legend. This was a place where people were made and broken.

Now, the Elders took their seats behind this table, and I stood in front of them with so much shame I could hardly look up from my feet.

"River Silas Matthews," Papa said. I glanced up. "Who do you kneel for?"

I closed my eyes. "Our Heavenly Father and his Prophet."

"Do so." I got on my knees. "Confess before the Gathering the extent of your sin with that thing."

"Papa," I pleaded.

"You can do it with dignity or you can do it with Barton Law."

I swallowed the lump in my throat. "I've kissed her. More than once."

"And?" Papa said.

"And…" I stared at the woodgrain of the floor. "I love her."

I heard my mother start to cry.

"Has it performed its craft on you in any way?" Papa asked. It. The word pierced me.

"She's burned me."

"Did it give you any of its craft tonight?"

"Nova told you there was nothing they –"

"Did it give you any of its craft tonight?" Papa raised his voice.

Papa never raised his voice.

My chin shook. I kept my face towards the floor.

"No, Papa," I said.

"God as your witness?"

I'd never lied, God as my witness, in my life.

"God as my witness," I whispered.

Papa closed the space between us and grabbed my arm, pulling me to my feet. He led me to the fireplace. I dug my heels in but they slid along the concrete floor.

"This is what you have to look forward to," he said through clenched teeth. He shoved me to my knees in front of the crackling flames. "This is what you risk, your soul in this fire forever."

He grabbed the back of my neck, hard, pushing my face toward the heat.

"Exodus 22:18," he said. But fear had paralyzed me, and I couldn't answer. His fingernails dug into my skin as he pushed me closer. A scream was rising in my throat. "Exodus 22:18," he repeated.

"Thou shalt not suffer a witch to live," I choked, a bead of sweat forming on my brow.

"Engrave it on the back of your eyelids, River. Because if you ever speak to that thing again, she will not live to say another word." He let go of me. I scrambled away from him, from the fire. "God as my witness," he spat.

"Yes sir," I whispered.

"Stand up, son." Papa held out his hand to me, helping me to my feet. I watched him return to his seat, my legs trembling. "I'm sure this Gathering agrees, the successors should not return to mainstream."

"We do," Abel replied.

"You'll stay within the gates until I say otherwise, do you understand?"

"Yes, sir." The bones in my chest were being crushed, one by one.

"This will be the final test of faith I can afford you. I will not put Barton Law on you."

"Please," I whispered. "I'm weak."

"Your true heart has to guide you. We will see if He still has your heart," Papa said.

"I'm so sorry I let you down." I swallowed the lump in my throat. I would not cry in front of the Elders.

"No son, I ask that you forgive us for allowing you to be led so astray." Papa put his hand on my shoulder.

"I forgive you," I said.

"I pray you'll allow us to celebrate a prodigal son's return, and not make us mourn the pruning of another bad fruit." I winced. "We'll take you home now, son."

"Is Sparrow still there?" I whispered. Papa helped me to my feet. "Is she awake?"

"She's fine," Papa said. "Awake, but shaken. You need to feed her."

I nodded. "I will."

"And while you're at it, you can explain why she isn't allowed to go mainstream anymore."

I stared at Papa's Adam's apple. I could not face his eyes. "Yes, sir."

We stepped out into the humid night. My legs didn't feel like my own. I wanted to sink into the ground. I climbed into the bed of the truck and we started to the house.

I wanted to collapse in on myself, for all my bones and organs and skin to fold over like a decomposing body.

I wanted to fall apart.

We parked in the driveway. I was always smart, level-headed. I was always the one other people asked for help.

Not anymore.

I opened my bedroom door.

Sparrow sat cross-legged in my desk chair, spinning herself slowly.

"In retrospect," she said. "I would have slipped off this chair before I ever got the belt around the fan blade."

I rushed at her and picked her up. I crushed her body to mine and then it came, hot and horrible, I was crying into her bruised neck.

"I'm so sorry," I told her as I caught my breath. "Sparrow…" I set her down and looked at her, at her smudged makeup over her eyes, at her bloody bottom lip. She wiped at my face with her red-stained hand.

"Yeah," she sighed. She took my hand and we sat on the edge of my bed.

"We can't go back to school," I whispered.

"Of course not."

"I can't ever talk to her again, or they'll kill her."

"I heard," she murmured. "You don't have to -"

"Yeah I do," I sighed. "If I don't I'll explode. I should never have thought I could have something like that."

"You regret it?" she demanded.

"Of course not."

"Would you take it back?"

"No," I insisted. And it was true. Even if it came to this, the little time I'd had with her was worth it.

"Exactly," Sparrow said.

"They're not gonna be able to help us if this happens again, and it's gonna happen again." I looked at her wrists, purple and red from the ropes. "You need to drink. You look sick." I held out my arm for her.

The familiar sting hit me below the elbow. After the thousandth time it was nothing to feel blood being pulled from my veins. Sparrow was way neater than I was. I watched her throat as she swallowed. She ran her tongue over the spot and pressed two fingers over the wounds.

"Thanks," she sighed. "I was really thirsty. Possession is a lot of work, believe it or not."

"I believe it," I muttered. "You drank a potion, huh?"

"I bit Bernardo, too." I looked up at her. "At home-coming. It was an accident."

"How do you accidentally bite someone?"

She smirked. "On accident. Anyways, maybe if no one else is around the witches, Aradia won't have a reason to come after us."

"I hope you're right," I sighed. "Because we're on our own."

The door opened. "Let's go, Sparrow," Abel said. Sparrow stood up. I didn't let go of her hand until I had to.

"I'm sorry," I told her again. She looked back at me and winked. Abel turned off the light as he shut the door.

I took off my shoes and got under my blanket. Maybe I would feel better in the morning.

I laughed at myself. It was unconvincing even to me.

I reached beneath my shirt and held my cross between my hands, so tight it almost burned.

Our Father, who art in Heaven, hallowed be thy name. I closed my eyes. Thy kingdom come, thy will be done on earth as it is in Heaven. I pulled the blanket up around my ears. Lead us not into temptation but deliver us from evil.

My dreams only mocked me. I was in Possum Lake, at my Tree, in the pouring rain. I smelled oranges all around me.

"Fina!" I heard her laughing. "Fina, where are you?" I demanded into the darkness.

There was a splash below me. I looked over the edge of the rock. Black hair floated right at the surface. I reached down and pulled, trying to bring her out of the water. It was seaweed.

"Fina," I sighed. "I know you're out here."

I turned around and there she was, sitting cross-legged in her red bathing suit, mud coating her legs. She smiled up at me.

"Are you okay?" I asked her. She put her finger to her lips. I sat down beside her. She laced her fingers into mine and just like that, my heart was full. Every ounce of sadness was gone.

I'd been looking for her my entire life.

I watched her stare up at the storm, with more light than last time. No lightning. Only the full, uncovered moon. A rain without clouds. A moon bigger than I'd ever seen. Darker than I'd ever seen. A black, fathomless eye in the sky.

"They said it was a blood-rimmed moon," she said, but her mouth didn't move.

"What?"

"The Great Battle. Under a blood-rimmed moon or whatever. Not a black moon." She looked at me. "Looks like an eye." Her mouth still didn't move.

"That's what I thought, too," I chuckled. "An owl's eye. A raven's eye. A vulture's eye."

"Barn owl," she said. She wrapped a finger around her honey-blonde hair. "The owls see all. They have universes in their eyes."

"Is it watching us?" I asked her. She squeezed my hand.

"We are the universe," she told me. I smiled. She pressed her lips to my neck. The heat electrified my veins. "We're the fissure in the fabric of the universe." Her voice echoed in my ears. I bit my lip. "We could destroy it all. It could be so beautiful."

"How?" I breathed as I knotted my fingers in her smooth hair. Her teeth caught on my earlobe.

"Follow the owls," she whispered.

I shot straight up. My blanket fell to the floor. The light from the porch shone through my open window.

My window was open.

My hair was wet.

12. JOSEFINA.

I threw my duffel bag onto the roof of the porch. It slid to the gutter and stopped. I climbed out behind it and stuck a pillow on the sill to keep it from slamming shut. I was a pro at escaping quietly after many years of being stuck as a teenager. I crawled to the edge and threw the bag to the ground.

There was enough rain and moisture to make me worry I would slip off the roof. I hung onto the gutter and let my feet find the banister of the porch. I jumped from the banister, backwards, onto the grass. I only slipped a little.

I picked up my bag and ran around the garage to the front of the house. Bernardo had parked behind me in the driveway. I balled my fists and silently screamed, kicking at the ground as I frantically tried to figure out what to do. I went between our two cars.

I had just enough room to back up and swing around in the yard without destroying his front bumper. I had maybe twenty seconds to get out of the yard before the sound of the motor would wake people up.

I opened the passenger door and threw the bag in, then ran around the front and jumped in. I started the car and closed the door at the same time to minimize noise. I was grinning like an idiot.

I was running away. Stupid, dumb teenager. Running away with a boy. I shook my head.

Idiot.

I backed up with no lights on until I could almost taste the paint of Bernardo's fender. I swung it hard to the left, and clipped one of Ofelia's rose bushes. I cringed. I touched my bracelet and the gates opened. I hit the gas and my tires screeched.

I winced thinking of the tracks in Elian's meticulous grass.

"Retextus." I snapped my fingers right as I passed through the open gates. The haze disappeared before me. Hopefully they'd realize it was down once they realized I was gone.

When I turned off Shell Court the sadness set in. You won't be gone forever. Just for a little while. You deserve to be happy.

Remington became the 33. I turned on my lights. I was the only car in any direction, and on a road this flat, that meant for miles.

I started to get cold feet after five minutes. Should I call Ofelia? Should I have told someone where I went? In case the Elders got to River before I did? They'd kill me for sure.

Or I'd kill them.

I looked at myself in the rearview and shook my head at my own smile.

I was only evil where it mattered.

First Street led to Thistlewolf High's parking lot. It was in half a mile. I still didn't see a soul on the roads. Was River already there? I hoped he meant this school. It was the only school I knew about in Dunnaway County.

I turned onto First Street and really started to get nervous. I looked down at my phone. I unlocked it and then locked it again. I unlocked it, went to River's name in my recent calls, and then locked it again.

When I pulled into the parking lot, I could breathe again. His truck was near the gym, towards the front of the parking lot. I parked a few spots away. I couldn't see River in the truck. I got out and grabbed my phone.

River's phone went right to voicemail. I closed the door and walked around the truck. The smell of sprinkler water filled my nose, all rotten eggs and copper. I didn't see River.

I started to get a sinking feeling in my stomach.

A metal door slammed a few yards ahead. I gasped and flinched. As I moved, the light from the parking lot glinted off something in the gravel.

I bent down and picked up River's keys.

He'd gotten caught.

The door slammed again - not slammed, it didn't even open in the first place. Something was hitting it from inside. I ran up to the building, through the wet grass and smelly water, and waited for it.

Another hard, metal thud. I yanked on it with all my might and I fell back as it came open easily. I got to my feet and ran into the building. As the door shut, the light went from minimal to nonexistent. I turned on my phone's flashlight and shined it into the lunchroom. Leg after metal leg of a stack of chairs shined back at me. I put my ear against the auditorium door.

The slamming sound echoed through the building.

Not the doors. The bleachers.

I ran down the hallway to the gym, my phone's light bouncing off the walls. Another slamming sound, like someone being tossed into the bleachers, over and over.

I pushed open the gym doors, guns blazing.

There was only one person inside. The high windows let enough light in for me to watch River pace around the center circle, his bag in his hand.

"Hi baby," he murmured.

"What the hell are you doing?" I demanded as I started his way. I went to shine the flashlight on him but it was off. I pressed every button on my phone. It was dead.

"What do you mean?" he asked. He swung his bag over his shoulder and slung it to the floor. He dragged it and slung it again.

Water dripped warm onto my cheek. I wiped it away and looked up as I took a few steps towards River.

"I thought you got caught, you dropped your keys out there." I held up my hand and swung his key ring around my finger.

"Oh," he muttered. He slung his bag down, hard. More water, this time on my arm. I wiped it on my shorts and moved up yet again.

"What are you doing?" I chuckled. "We have to go, remember? We're running away."

I slid a little on a puddle near the center circle. I steadied myself and looked down.

The water was way too dirty to have come from the pipes above us. I followed its trail, a circle of dirty, dark water with River in the middle. He swung his bag over his head.

Water sprayed across my face. I caught some in the mouth, all copper and sulfur and filth. I gagged and spit.

"Sorry," he murmured. I wiped my mouth with the back of my hand.

The light from the windows illuminated the blood smeared across my skin.

The world tilted around me, my feet rooted to the floor as the floor became the ceiling.

River tossed the bag - the body, the dead deer's body - into the bleachers. It landed with a hollow, echoing thud.

He looked at me, his eyes and teeth shining against the blood covering his face. His chest was heaving as he grinned.

"Okay, all done," he gasped. I nodded slowly as I took a step back.

"Wow," I murmured. "That's pretty cool. Are you ready to leave?" I took another step. If I can make it far enough away I can get to the hallway and back to my car -

"There's no leaving," he chuckled. "You told me what to do and I'm doing it, baby. You said follow the owl so I'm following the owl!" he laughed. He started towards me. "And everything's gonna be okay now because I know what to do, and no one has to get hurt anymore."

I nodded as I kept backing up. "Oh, really? That's awesome, River, you figured it out. I'm really glad. Let's go outside so we can talk -"

"You have to stay, dragon girl."

I froze. "We…" My heart shattered, so completely that its fragments filled my throat, making it hard to speak. "The potion," I whispered.

"You said you loved me, too." There was no more space between us. "Do you want us to be together?" he asked.

Get him to your mom, Fina. Before it's too late.

"Of course, that's why we have to go! We have to get out of here before we get caught!" I grabbed his hand.

Flames ignited between us. River jumped back.

"Oh," I breathed. I doubled over, my stomach churning and tightening. I put my hands on my knees and tried to catch my breath.

"That hurt," he whispered.

"I'm sorry," I gasped. I straightened up and held out my left hand. "Debellavi."

There was an explosion in my chest. I fell to the ground, sliding towards the doors. The burn of hardwood on my bare skin tore through my back.

He was over me in seconds, his hands on either side of my face. My totem hung from his neck, almost grazing my shirt, taunting me. I stared into lifeless, white eyes. There was no air, only the putrid smell of ashes and sulfur and blood. I wiggled my arm out from under me and reached for the totem.

He pinned my hand to the ground, flames spreading all the way up his arm. He screamed, high and clear, his eyes squeezed tight in agony. The skin on his arms began to blister and sag.

"Okay, okay, let go, I won't move, I swear I won't move! Please!" I sobbed. River sat up on his knees and let me go. He cradled his bad arm and shook his head.

"I really tried to be nice," he muttered. The voice was all distortion, through the fan. "You can do this the easy way or he can fry for all I care."

I jumped to my feet and sprinted towards the bleachers. Get to the window, bust the window, and go get help, get to the window -

I felt the bleachers shake as he ran up after me. I reached the top and grabbed the concrete sill.

My ankle slipped out from under me and my face connected with the wooden bench. Blood poured from my nose, my eyes watering immediately. I scrambled backwards as I made out his dark shape coming towards me on the top row. I let my whole body explode in flames as I ran down to the middle and sprinted the length of the bleachers. I jumped off and ran to the visitor's bleachers.

"Fina!" River screamed.

River's voice.

I paused halfway up and turned around.

River stared at me from across the gym, his unseeing eyes shining from behind a wall of fire. I looked down at the floor.

The circle was more of a ragged oval, drawn with the blood of that deer. In the middle was the cross I saw on Sparrow's chest, the mockery of the crucifix.

A loud thud brought me back to the present. A blackened River was crossing the floor of the gym, coming towards me, careful not to step in the circle.

I bolted up the bleachers and climbed up to the windowsill. I started banging on the glass with my fist. The bleachers squeaked and groaned as River came barreling my way. I smashed both hands against the glass. I heard a crack. I couldn't tell if it was my wrist or the window.

River snatched the back of my shirt and I was flying to the ground, every second a new sharp agony in a new place as I bounced down the bleachers. I was a heap at the bottom when I realized the entire structure was quickly being engulfed. Blood was pouring out of my right arm. I could feel the warmth pooling underneath me. I could taste it, too.

I tried to stand but there was no use. He was there again, burnt all over. He grabbed my hair and dragged me towards the circle.

"Please, please, please," I whispered, like a broken record.

I reached up and took his hands, letting fire swallow the left side of his body. I could hear him crying.

"He can live if you behave," he rasped. I let go immediately. I dug my heels into the ground and made myself dead weight. With a searing rip, his handful of my hair came loose. I crawled towards the doors.

His feet landed between me and the door.

"He burns, dragon girl. You do your part or he goes down with this place." He looked up and I followed his stare. Flames licked the roof of the gym. Both sets of bleachers were towering infernos.

"Blood of an innocent," he heaved as he came towards me. "Just drip a little. And this can all be done."

"Make me. Come into me, leave him out of it."

"Can't. Have to keep that soul pure."

"Why? What do you want from me?" I demanded. Keep him talking, Fina. Get the totem and keep him talking.

"You are grey like her," he said. "You'll win the battle." He put his foot on my chest and pushed until I was flat on my back. He stepped on my chest until I thought I would crack in half. I grabbed his ankle and held tight as he tried to get me off, screaming and flinging his limbs wildly.

His other foot connected with my temple, and I lost vision as I was thrown backwards. I was the one who screamed that time.

Then I was in the air, his hand around my throat. I clawed at his grip, flames enveloping his already charred arm. He probably couldn't feel it at all.

I looked at him through pinholes. I kicked my legs with my last ounce of strength. One connected with some part of him, some part sensitive enough for him to drop me and double over.

The roof started to groan, and a chunk of debris fell between me and the doors. Another piece fell, flaming, beside me.

This building was coming down. No one was going to find us until we were dead and buried in burning rubble.

I tried to stand up. River was crawling towards me on just his arms, his lower body dragging behind him.

He grabbed my hair and pulled me towards him. He licked the side of my face. His tongue turned black and started to flake. There were tears in his eyes, bright green against the burst blood vessels.

Green.

I glanced down at the totem, dangling between us.

"River," I whispered. "Can you hear me?"

"You can have him if you come quietly," he breathed against my ear. "What's left of him."

I ripped the totem off of him, but before the words could leave my mouth he tackled me, his knee in my chest. Fire erupted around us.

He screamed a human scream. But he didn't flinch.

"I'm sorry," I sobbed. "River, I'm sorry, I'm so sorry."

Every nerve in my body ran to my neck, where his teeth tore my skin open. I kicked as hard as I could, but it was like trying to kick a hole in the cement wall. The smell of sulfur, of death, had my head swimming. Burning flesh, sweet like pork, joined the mixture. I tasted vomit. I was going to die choking on my own puke. I looked up at the destruction, at everything going down in flames.

Beautiful.

Everything was beautiful when it burned.

"River," I pleaded. My voice was nonexistent. "Back to the salt." I wanted to let go, to fade into the flames. I belonged in the flames.

I could just let her have me. I could be in the flames forever.

"Fine," I sighed. "Fine."

Have me, but not him.

I put my hand on River's chest. "Debellavi."

He was on fire on top of me, all weight, no grip. I pushed at him but he didn't move.

"River?"

I pulled his hair to lift up his head and wide, glazed eyes stared back at me.

I knew I was screaming but it sounded like the fabric of the universe was ripping. There was no way I could still make noise. I rolled him onto his side and blew, putting out the flames. I had to get him out. If there was any chance he could live, it would be destroyed from smoke inhalation. He exhaled once, and a whirling mass of little black flies came out of his charred mouth.

"Consido!" I wheezed. The swarm froze. I smashed it between my hands. "If you want me, you come get me!" I screamed into nothingness. "You hear me?! You show your face!"

"Fina."

I froze.

The bones in River's hands were visible. Most of him was black, ashes, the rest was blistering and cracking open. Blood - my blood - covered his face and chest.

"River." I crawled toward him on my trembling limbs.

"Kill me." I looked at his tarred face, the whites of his eyes bright again, even brighter against the blackness.

"No River, it's going to be okay. Stay with me, okay?" I lay down beside him, our noses almost touching. The sulfur smell was long gone. Now it was worse, more gag-inducing. Now he smelled like cooked meat. "Stay with me, just a little while."

"Kill me," he sighed.

Another piece of the roof fell to the ground, this time in the center of the circle.

I got on my knees, blinking away my tears.

"Okay, I'm getting us out of here. You are not going out like this, River, you are not dying in here." Blood from my forehead dripped into my eye and mixed with my tears. I pulled myself up. My knees knocked together. I gritted my teeth and grabbed River under his arms.

I cringed as he shrieked. "I know, I know," I murmured. I dragged him towards the doors. The roof sagged in the middle. More debris started to rain on us. "We're almost there." I couldn't feel my bloody arm.

"Fina, Fina," River sobbed. "Just stop. Stop." I dropped him and crumpled to the ground.

"I can get us out," I whispered. I curled up next to his head. "I'm sorry."

"Shh," he murmured. "Stay with me."

"Okay." I closed my eyes.

13. RIVER.

Back through the vacuum I came, rushing like water to one point, one solitary atom through to the light.

My nerves electrified. My throat was raw, the taste of angels heavy in my mouth. I heard someone screaming.

The light got brighter. I was being touched. More hands, more light, electricity.

Cold fell over me through the blurriness, rain and light, shooting aches through my lightning nerves.

"River."

I opened my eyes.

Shadows leered over me. My eyes refused to focus.

"I'm right here, River. You're okay," the shadow said.

I looked around but saw only shapes.

"I'm okay," I repeated. Of course I was, except I couldn't see.

Someone squeezed my hand.

Sparrow. Her eyes wide as saucers, her hair sticking out at every angle.

I smiled at her. "Hi, space cadet."

"Crummy prank," she chuckled.

"Huh?" I looked around more, hoping shadows would become people.

And they did. But no one I knew. Horrified people staring down at me. An older man, a rail-thin, messy-haired boy. All staring at me, waiting.

I shifted my body and felt the dirt beneath me, the ratty towel on my naked body.

"Why am I naked?" I asked Sparrow.

A hand touched my cheek. "It's going to be okay, River."

I looked up at the girl touching me. Her eyes were red-rimmed. She was covered in blood. She ran her fingers over my chin, my lips, my nose. It felt nice.

"You're bleeding," I told her.

"Not anymore."

"Why am I naked?" I asked.

"You were in a fire," Sparrow said. "Your clothes burned. But you're fine." She pointed behind me. I craned my neck and saw smoke billowing up towards the sky, the smell finally registering in my nose.

"Oh, no," I murmured. The girl who touched me started to laugh.

"Yeah," she chuckled.

"You're warm," I told her. She wiped at her eyes with the back of her hand. "Why're you cryin'?"

"Because you scared me."

"I did?" She nodded. "Sorry," I mumbled. "Do I gotta keep lying in the dirt?"

Sparrow laughed. "No, no if you can move, we can go home."

"I mean I think I can move." I wiggled my fingers. "Yeah I'm fine."

"I can drive you guys," the girl said. "Bernardo can follow in my car."

"Y'all can't come into Barton," Sparrow said.

"We did before," the girl replied.

"Not after this."

"We'll get you to the gates, then," the boy said. He and the girl must have been twins.

"And your parents can come get him."

The girl took my free hand, and she and Sparrow pulled me into a sitting position.

I came face to face with fire. Every instinct in me failed, my chest seized, and I scrambled backwards, pulling the girl down beside me.

"I…" I squeezed my eyes shut but the heat still touched my face, softly, like a woman's hand. The dry, thick drowning of smoke. I coughed once.

"It's okay." The girl sat up on her knees and held my face in her hands. I stared at her, at those bottomless eyes, shining with tears. A sliver of blue shown through the brown, and the blood on her forehead almost made it see-through. She searched my face with that sliver.

"I don't like the fire," I whispered. I looked down at my bare legs. How did it take my clothes and not my skin?

"I know," she sighed. Her thumb stroked the skin beneath my ear. She leaned in, the heat of her body enveloping me, unbearable heat coming from her bloodied mouth. I pulled away, taking her hand off my face.

"Um, I… thank you so much, for helping me. But I have a girlfriend."

"What?" she laughed. I looked over at Sparrow.

"I think we can get home, I really feel fine."

"You clearly have some sort of head trauma," the older man told me. He pulled something out of his pocket. "Can you look into the light for me?" A bright light shone in my eyes. I blinked a few times.

"Are you a doctor?" I asked as I followed the light with my eyes.

"For all intents and purposes I am, yes. Now move your eyes only, not your head."

"I don't do doctors," I told him.

"Nothing to be done," he said. "You seem to be conscious, coherent. Can you stand?"

"He's not coherent, he doesn't recognize me," the girl retorted, her voice tight. Sparrow grabbed my arm as the older man helped me to my feet. I kept a grip on the towel, the only thing giving me even a little dignity.

"Okay, then, there we are," the older man said. "Let's get you to your car, shall we?"

"Dad!" The girl shouted.

"Fina." He released me slowly, letting my weight ease into Sparrow. He put his hands on the girl's shoulders. "Let it come back on its own. You've both been through great trauma. At the moment you're the one worse for the wear. Please go home." She shook her head, her mouth tightening into a thin line as she started to cry again. "Fina," he murmured. "Please. Get some rest. Please." He was almost whispering.

Her twin took her arm. "Come on, Fi."

The girl - Fina - looked at me, then at Sparrow.

"Bye," Sparrow murmured, her voice thick.

Fina let her twin lead her away, their backs to us, their four feet moving as two.

The older man turned to us and sighed. "Okay, then. Home waits." He smiled gently at us.

"Sparrow, did you find the keys?" Sparrow handed him my key ring.

"I'm really fine, I can get us home," I said.

The older man shook his head, smiling all the time. "I'd prefer not to take the chance, if you'll allow me to get you home safely."

I didn't argue. I let them guide me to the truck, my legs like radio static. I was sore all over. But I didn't feel the stinging stickiness of a burn, like when I touched a seatbelt buckle in July and my hand blistered up.

The gears in my head began to turn.

The man got me into the passenger seat, with Sparrow tucked between us. I held her hand tight, tethering myself to the only thing I knew.

The engine roared beneath us, and we started out of the parking lot. The headlights illuminated parking spots, painted red, black, and white.

"We're at the high school," I murmured. "The high school's on fire, huh?" Sparrow nodded. "What happened to that girl?"

"What girl?" Sparrow asked.

"Fina? She's all bloody. Why is she bloody if there's a fire?" Sparrow twitched but didn't respond. "Tell me. I know you know. Why do I not have burns if I was in a fire?"

"You were lucky," the man responded. "The story of what happened is long. You'll remember when you wake up in the morning. It doesn't matter tonight. All that matters is both of you -" he looked at Sparrow. "All of you, getting some rest."

"They're waitin' for us at the gates," Sparrow told him.

"Wonderful," he replied.

I stared at the foggy window, my mind a jumbled wreck. There were pieces of blackness, sometimes chunks and sometimes slivers, of tonight. Longer than tonight.

"Is Nova pregnant?" I asked.

Sparrow nodded. "Yep."

I grinned. "She is?"

"Yeah," Sparrow chuckled.

"See, I remembered that."

"Do you remember me?" Sparrow asked.

"Of course I do." I squeezed her hand. "You're half of me. How could I forget you?"

She rolled her eyes. "Cheeseball."

The man chuckled. I looked at him and felt my joy, my happiness of remembering, fizzle.

"And I know you," I said to him. "You and that girl, too. Don't I?"

"Yes," he replied.

"That's why you're helpin' me."

"It's why we knew where you were."

I sighed and clenched my free hand against my leg. "I'm really sorry, sir, I just… I don't know who you are. None of y'all." My jaw tightened as a wave of sadness washed over me. I knew them enough to feel sad that I didn't anymore.

We turned down a dirt road, where the tops of trees touched over top, creating a canopy of shade and darkness.

"Shell Court," I murmured. "Shell Court. Home." Sparrow nodded. "I remember this, too."

"I suppose we won't be seeing as much of each other now," the man said quietly. Sparrow shook her head. "You have the whole world at your feet. Please don't forget it." Sparrow sniffed but didn't respond. A warm drop fell on our intertwined hands.

"Are you cryin'?" I whispered. She popped me in the chest with the back of her hand.

"Hush," she hissed.

The truck stopped in front of the chain link fence to home.

"Home," I said. I was a toddler again, just naming things I saw or recognized. The gate opened but we didn't move.

"Home," I said to Sparrow.

"Yeah, home," she chuckled. "Just hang tight."

"I'll leave you to it," the man said as he opened the door. "Goodbye."

"Bye," Sparrow whispered. "Thanks."

"Yeah, thank you so much," I told him.

He nodded and closed the door behind him. I watched him in the rear view, walking on the shoulder.

"He's gonna walk all the way home? That's not right," I murmured.

"He doesn't live far."

Noah left the gate shack and knocked on the driver's window. Sparrow reached over and let him in.

"Glory be," he said. He hugged Sparrow and looked over her shoulder at me, eyes shining. "It's a miracle y'all are alive."

"He doesn't know what happened," Sparrow interjected. "Trauma or somethin'. We're hoping it comes back once he sleeps."

"I hope it doesn't," Noah sighed as he put the truck in drive.

"Nova's pregnant, huh?"

Noah shot me a funny look. "Yeah man, any day now."

"Any day now?" I repeated. The air in my lungs went out in those three words. "Any day now," I whispered.

"River," Sparrow murmured. "It's okay." She rubbed my arm. "It's okay. You just need some rest."

"I need some rest." I nodded.

Abel's blue pickup sat in my driveway. Noah helped me get out and keep my dignity. Abel was waiting on the front porch. He grabbed my other arm and they helped me hobble inside.

Everyone sat in our living room: Mom, Papa, Willow, Nova with a huge belly. No one looked surprised. Mom even smiled as she got up. She put her hand on my cheek. Only then did I realize how disgusting and dirty I was.

"Momma," I sighed. Tears welled up in my eyes. "I'm really sorry, momma."

I didn't know why. I just knew I was.

"Hush," she whispered as she began to cry. "My poor baby."

"Let's get him cleaned up, dressed," Abel said to Noah. The two of them hauled me off to the bathroom.

"Please let me do this part myself," I said to Abel. "I'm embarrassed enough." Noah opened the door.

"We'll be right outside," Abel said as he shut me in.

I turned the shower on, not hot. I didn't want to feel anything hot again. I sat down, resting my forehead on the soap ledge. I let the water pelt my back. Salt and dirt and something sweet ran over my mouth, across my chest and my legs. I squeezed Willow's shampoo bottle over my head. The smell of oranges filled the bathroom. I scrubbed at my hair until my arms burned from the strain of holding them up. I used the lather, now grey, to clean my face. Then I looked up into the stream and let the water do the rest.

When I got out, a pair of my sweatpants were sitting on the sink. I pulled them on and looked at myself in the mirror.

Yep. Still me. Still looked like me. A little skinnier, maybe. My eyes were tired. I looked at my teeth. All there.

I knew who I was. But I didn't know what I didn't know.

I made it to my bedroom without help from Abel or Noah. My sisters were waiting for me, Nova in my desk chair, Willow on my bed. She got up so I could lie down, and then perched beside me on the edge.

"You scared us," she murmured. I lifted my sandbag arm and poked her in the ribs. She squirmed and slapped my bare stomach. "Hey! I'm tryna be nice to you!"

"I know, it's weird, quit it," I chuckled. She stuck her tongue at me. I looked around her to Nova. "What are you havin'?"

"Huh?" she said.

"The baby. Last I remember you had just found out, now you're bout to pop. Boy or girl?"

"You don't remember at all?" she asked, her brows furrowing.

I sighed. "No. They say I will once I sleep. I guess I got knocked around or somethin' but my brain is like scrambled eggs."

"Well, get some rest. We'll all be out here if you need us. Come on, Will."

"Nova!" I called. She turned around in the doorway. "Please."

She smiled. "Girl. Savannah Faith."

"I love that name," I whispered.

"I know, you picked it." She closed the door behind her, but not all the way. I could hear everyone in the living room. I dozed off to the sound of their voices, all blending into one. Eventually, they seeped into my dreams.

"It was bound to happen. He was way too close to the source."

"Hey, he held his own with her though, 'bout killed her from what I understand."

"Gym burned to the ground, Sparrow said. He laid her out good."

There was laughter.

"There ain't a Matthews on this planet that will go down without swingin'."

"I know that's right!" More laughing.

"Now he's been baptized in the fire, and he'll never have to worry 'bout that girl again."

"She's still alive, Papa."

"For now."

"Eye for an eye."

"Amen."

13. JOSEFINA.

I dug my fingernails into the arms of the green leather chair and exhaled through my nose.

"I don't know what you want me to say," I said to her back.

"That building was hardly five years old." Principal Gellar continued staring out the window of her office as she spoke.

"Principal Sawyer," Ofelia interjected. "We have already expressed our regret as to what happened. I'm not sure what else needs to be discussed here."

Principal Gellar turned and smoothed the front of her skirt before looking down at Ofelia.

"Mrs. Camejo, you and I are aware of what really happened in that gym. I cannot in good conscience allow your daughter to remain in this school knowing what she's capable of."

"May I remind you there was more than one student in the gym when this occurred?" Ofelia replied.

"And one was there to be sacrificed." She stared at me.

"You'd be hard pressed to find a body in there," Ofelia said. "Or any evidence to suggest my daughter had something to do with the fire."

"There are children in this school who know the truth," Mrs. Gellar snapped. She put her hand over the back of her desk chair and gripped it tight. As if she was hanging on to keep from jumping over the desk. "If someone makes a child in this school feel unsafe, that person has to be dealt with accordingly."

"Excuse me?" I sat up. "Since the second I walked in here, I've felt unsafe. Don't give me that." I crossed my arms.

"You never came to me about that, Josefina," Principal Gellar said behind a flat smile. "I can promise you it would have been handled had I been notified."

"I never came to you because your daughter was one of the main ones bullying me!"

Ofelia put her hand on my shoulder. I deflated back into the chair.

"If you want to expel my daughter for committing a crime I suggest you have evidence first. Or a police department that would believe a 17 year old girl with magical powers killed a possessed boy in the school gym." Ofelia stood. I followed her lead. "I think we're finished here."

"Josefina," Principal Gellar replied. "Clean out your locker, and do not come back."

"Mrs. Gellar," I replied. "Make me."

"If you interfere with my daughter's education in any way, I will sue you, and the entire school board," Ofelia interjected.

"Is that a threat?" Principal Gellar demanded.

Ofelia leaned over the desk. "You have yet to see a threat, Lindsey."

13. JOSEFINA.

Principal Gellar's eyes bugged out of her head. She inhaled sharply and pointed to her office door.

Ofelia grabbed my hand and we walked out into the hall.

"Am I going to class today?" I asked her.

"Of course not," she replied. She pushed open the doors and we rushed towards the parking lot.

"Am I leaving the school?" I tried to keep my voice even. I wasn't sure what I wanted. School could only get worse after this. But River. But maybe he wouldn't come back after what happened.

But maybe he would.

"Of course not," she repeated. She clicked her key fob and the lights blinked on the Chrysler. "She isn't going to push us out." She looked at me. "Push you out." She let go of me and opened the driver's side door.

I had hardly closed the door before we were speeding off. Ofelia's knuckles were white as she gripped the steering wheel.

"Are you okay?" I asked her.

"I am," she replied, her voice calm. She glanced at me, and then looked back at the road. "You will finish school this time, Fina."

"Why does it matter now? Why does any of this mortal stuff matter now?"

Ofelia's lips tightened over her teeth. "Because for now, you have the luxury of mortal stuff. I don't know how long that will last."

My breath caught in my throat. "But you said I was safe."

"I know what I said."

"Then why are you going back on it?" I demanded. My voice bounced off the inside of the car and rang in my ears. A line appeared across Ofelia's forehead. I couldn't breathe.

"I meant what I said when I said you are safe. We've bound the town, we will consecrate you. We will protect you from anything to do with Aradia."

"So, then what? What do we do when it stops working? How do we know when it stops?"

She put her hand over mine and squeezed it.

"Do you have faith?" she asked me. I blinked the tears away and took a deep breath.

"Yes," I whispered.

"Faith in the Covenant?" I nodded. "Faith in Rhiannon?" I sniffed and nodded again. She smiled. "Then we will find a way."

We turned down Shell Court. The gates of Barton Heights glinted in the sunlight. My hand twitched under Ofelia's.

"What if I'm not strong enough?" I asked her.

"You don't have to be. You have us." I smiled at her.

We pulled in through the open gates and the dirt turned to brick. Elian was standing in front of the garage, stoking a roaring fire inside a metal trash can. Thick, acrid smoke rose from the flames. I could smell it before we got out.

"The belladonna," I whispered.

"We salted the earth where it grew," Ofelia said. "It was foolish of us not to realize it sooner. The sleeping draughts, the potion we gave that poor boy. It was all swimming with her plant. Never again."

We got out of the car and Ofelia came around the front. She hugged me. I breathed in the smell of her hair, jasmine and rose.

We did smell like roses. I'd never noticed before.

I followed Ofelia up the steps and into the house. She went towards the kitchen but I cut through to the back porch and closed the door behind me.

I hoped I'd convinced Ofelia that I had faith. Because I wasn't sure I did. We'd dragged River straight to Aradia. We ignored the signs - the birds, the flies, the smell.

I had ignored them.

It all happened around me.

Why?

I was the least powerful, with a talent she already possessed. I was the hardest soul to take. I was the most protected, then and now.

But she'd still moved mountains to get to me. Aradia was as old as Rhiannon. She knew the things only Rhiannon - and Silas - could know. What did she know that made her want me on her side?

I climbed into the hammock.

A consecration ritual, a boundary spell. None of it would keep the truth at bay for long.

I looked up at the cross towering over the tree line. The truth. Everyone thought their truth was the only truth.

I pushed myself off the wall and swung in the breeze.

My truth was I had killed a boy I loved before he could kill me.

With River, I think that would have been my truth no matter what.

CPSIA information can be obtained
at www.ICGtesting.com
Printed in the USA
LVHW011923071118
596100LV00018B/510